FUTURE

FLOTUS?

To my favorite "trouble maker" Anna Marie!
All my love,
Amy Denson

Amy Denson

Published by AMDP

ISBN-13: 978-0-692-97718-7

Cover design by Ashleigh Denson and ELV Shorr

White House Celebrates a Successful Festival of Innovation

By: Adam Herald

President Jackson Cashe hosted a celebration in Washington, DC to conclude the inaugural Festival of Innovation. Thirty-one days ago, festivals and exhibits were launched all over the country to showcase America's advances in technology, science, music, arts, and humanities. Director of Communication, Rich Miller bragged, "Since the Separation of States, the new government has flourished. The Festival highlighted the American spirit that overcomes and rises at every obstacle!" Entrepreneurs, artists, musicians, and scientists were featured throughout all twenty-four states.

In the first year of his term, the youngest president in America's history took us to new heights. In a show of goodwill, President Cashe opened up the application process to former citizens of the United States. Out of 1,200 participants, eighteen citizens from the Allied States of America showcased their talents along with the best and brightest Americans.

The White House State Dinner boasted of every opulence available. Several Grammy winning artists performed throughout the evening. World renowned chefs worked together to create the feast of all feasts. Celebrities not in attendance, hosted their own extravagant parties in every city. The country's finest vineyards and distilleries shipped in crates and barrels for the banquet.

Wine was served to guests in goblets of gold, each one a unique design. Liquor was served in heavy crystal old-fashionends. Every VIP guest left with an enviable swag bag.

President Cashe's strategy to preserve the country's reputation and establish a strong presence, was successful. Make sure to pick up a copy of our special edition Festival of Innovation issue. The issue will include a list of innovators grouped by category along with the top presenters. Also included will be the *Scene Stealer* section highlighting how our favorite celebrities participated, including an exclusive interview from President Cashe's ex-fiancé. The special edition hits newsstands Monday morning while the online edition will be available at midnight.

MOST READ STORIES THIS MONTH:

1.   The search is on for a new Secretary of Education. Maggie Barton resigns under pressure of new reform talk.

2.   Learn more about the Department of Innovation.

3.   Hollywood celebrates its biggest night. See fashion highs and lows

4.   President Cashe's fiancé, Vanessa walks the red carpet with her costar Vladmir Rosenkoff.

Chapter 1

~Haddie~

Haddie hears the screeching alarm beckoning her to start a new day. Groaning, she pulls the pillow over her face trying to block out the sound. She hits the off button and finally sits up in bed. The darkness still envelopes the sky and the cold temperature in her room has her shivering to her bones. Climbing out of bed will be the hardest thing she does today. She misses the warm sunshine of South Carolina. She would give anything to smell the salty air and sand of her favorite beach today. Unfortunately, she is living in what feels like Siberia, otherwise known as the northeast during winter.

She slowly pulls off the covers and kicks her legs over the side of the bed. She sits, staring out into the darkness. The only light comes from the hallway nightlight that her roommate, and favorite cousin, Maryssa insists on keeping lit every night. Haddie chuckles remembering the time Maryssa broke her toe last year when she kicked the toilet in the middle of the night. From that moment until forevermore, there would be a nightlight in Maryssa's life. It is only funny now that Haddie doesn't have to care for Maryssa, the drama queen, and her broken digit any longer. The laughter and promise of coffee makes it easier to stand and turn on the light. A few stretches and a sun salutation later and she shuffles down the hall to the bathroom.

Haddie's mind races through her finals schedule as the hot water warms her to her core. The scent of lavender and mint soothes and energizes her at the same time. As a thirty-one-year-old retired ballet dancer, Haddie is the oldest in her college classes. This is her last year before beginning medical school and only one final and few online classes next semester stand in her way. Haddie's anxiety mounts as she remembers the French II test she has this morning. Foreign language is not her strongest subject and never will be, but it is another requirement she must meet in order to fulfill her dream. Why she needs to know French, or any other foreign language to be a doctor is beyond her. Haddie likes numbers and science. Cold hard facts she can process and manipulate. That's what she understands. Steps. Stretches. Counting and breathing while hitting her mark on stage. Haddie likes structure.

Conjugating verbs and memorizing French nouns is not going to help her diagnose a rare flu strain or a case of lupus. Maybe she can use French during her acceptance speech for the Nobel Peace Prize when she finds the cure for Ovarian Cancer. Ovarian Cancer. The sadness creeps in as she thinks about the ravaging illness while pangs of longing fill her body. The disease eats away at its victims and their families. Haddie shakes her head and tries to refocus. She can't go there now. French. She focuses on French.

As soon as she turns off the water, Haddie hears singing. *Maryssa must be awake.* Maryssa and Haddie have been best friends since the day they were born. Their mothers were sisters and gave birth the same week. They spent every waking hour together since they were born. Haddie and Maryssa began ballet classes at the age of three. Both women love the beauty and strength of the dance. They grew up on the same street and were in the same grade. They even both had their hearts broken by the same crush in middle school. Darn that Billy Blane.

Maryssa's family moved from South Carolina to Washington, DC their sophomore year in high school. Uncle Malik, Maryssa's dad, is the head chef at the White House. When they left, Haddie went with them so she and Maryssa could attend the prestigious Capital City Performing Arts School, together. Haddie's parents hated to let her go, but didn't want her to miss out on such an incredible opportunity.

After graduation, both Haddie and Maryssa auditioned for the National Ballet Ensemble. Other than Maryssa's six month internship in Paris, the two were able to dance together for nine years until Haddie injured her knee. Retirement comes early for ballet dancers.

Maryssa danced for another three years before retiring herself to begin culinary school. She finished her finals yesterday but has work today. She will be long gone by the time Haddie is ready. Maryssa works as a dish washer and back-up server in the White House with her father. It's a long way from the streets of Paris, but Maryssa is able to learn from top chefs while paying for culinary school. She was cleared by security with her dad and they eat lunch together on most days. Maryssa and Uncle Malik keep trying to get Haddie to work at the White House too, but she loves working at the university library. The quiet and the books make Haddie feel grounded and safe.

Haddie dresses quickly and pulls her thick chestnut hair back and wraps the curls into a tight bun. She picks her trusty purple headband to wear. She wore it the day she auditioned for the Ensemble. Hopefully, it will bring her luck on this test. Her favorite gray sweatshirt is a must for today. The softness and smell of lavender fabric softener comfort her as she pulls it over her tiny frame.

Haddie grabs a granola protein bar and her water bottle as she runs out the door to catch the Metro. The cold air hits her smack in the face as she opens the door. Winter break can't come at a better time. After killing herself this semester with eighteen hours plus clinical work, she is ready for a break. She flies out tonight to spend Christmas with her family in Charleston.

The warm South Carolina weather and sunshine call her name. One more final and she will head home. All Haddie thinks about is her parents and niece Chloe. The four-year old's brown ringlets will get Haddie through the day. She can already smell her Mom's gingerbread man cookies and her Dad's famous chili simmering on the stove. A few more hours and she will be home. She can almost taste it.

~Jackson~

Jackson wakes to a raging headache. He drags the pillow over his face as he tries to recall the source of his pain. Remembrance fills his mind as he groans and calls for his personal aide, Marcus. A tall, smart looking man in his mid-forties scurries to the side of Jackson's bed. Jackson's head throbs so loudly that he doesn't even try to flirt with the attractive nurse trailing behind Marcus with an IV bag.

"Sir, I've taken the liberty of acquiring a bag of fluids to be administered this morning. Your unusual state last night beckoned me to be prepared." Marcus pauses at Jackson's bedside.

Jackson nods in acceptance, the movement making his head throb more. The nurse quickly begins her work while Marcus runs through Jackson's schedule for the day. A groan escapes his lips as the light starts to creep in through the curtains which weren't closed last night. "Marcus, does it look like I'm in any condition to start my day?"

"Sir, as instructed last night: 'Marcus, do not let my hangover stop me in the morning! I have important things to do!'." The sound of Marcus's voice begins again and the pillow goes back over Jackson's head.

"Mr. Barnes, Mr. Miller, and Ms. Lyn are waiting outside. Should I let them in now or shall I wait until your IV finishes and you've showered?" The condescending tone in Marcus's voice as he speaks the last word tells Jackson he looks as bad as he feels this morning.

"No, let them in now. I doubt they can make my headache throb any more than it already does."

"Truer words were never spoken." Marcus mumbles and heads for the door. He ushers out the nurse and in the trio of trusted advisors.

As Jackson props himself up in bed, his three loyal advisors shuffle into his room and begin pulling out their tablets and phones. Another day to tackle and succeed. Hayman Barnes is a longtime family friend. He went to school with Jackson's father. Rich Miller, Director of Communication, is Jackson's fraternity brother and the greatest spin master in Washington. Madison Lyn lived in the same dorm as Rich and Jackson. Her no fail attitude was ingrained in her since birth by her Chinese father. She is the smartest person he knows and has saved his ass too many times to count. That is why she is his deputy chief of staff.

Hayman is double fisting coffee and already talking before he sits down on the couch across the room. "I'd offer you some, but I should probably wait until your IV starts working." Hayman's blond hair is perfectly styled and held into place with some type of product. He looks like a medium built Ken doll in his sixties. He dresses to the nines and is always polished. Hayman Barnes is the perfect chief of staff. No detail is ever overlooked with him. "You look awful, by the way."

Rich chimes in, "The only other time I've seen you like this was after senior sendoff at Mario's. That was some night." Rich looks off into space as he remembers. Jackson shoots daggers at his friend and Madison shakes her head.

9

Are they smirking? Why are they smirking? Don't they work for me? Shouldn't they at least pretend to feel bad? I am in pain over here and they are cracking jokes. I need coffee!

"Marcus!"

"Your coffee and breakfast are being sent up as we speak." Marcus sits on the blue bench at the edge of Jackson's bed. The bench completes the square of seating around a large circular coffee table. The room, decorated in rich blues and greys, has a masculine and classy feel. The lamps provide just the right amount of light to work but aren't so bright to make Jackson's headache any worse. The room is large enough to have a seating area for work parties such as this. The three loveseats coordinate perfectly with the color scheme and are sufficiently comfortable for people to work without making them want to stay a while and chat. Each member of his team has picked their own couch to spread out on as they begin covering highlights for the day.

Madison launches into her morning briefing. "The final numbers from the Festival are through the roof. The State Dinner was an enormous success and highlights from your speech are trending all over social media. We have both sides of the aisle wanting to help with the environmental bill focusing on solar power, but the education reform talk has set up a few red flags. We need to appoint a new Secretary of Education asap to push through the agenda quickly. You need to look at the names today and make a final decision......."

Jackson hears Madison talking but can't stop looking at the coffee table in front of her. The strong, dark cherry table reminds him of the desk in his father's study. He would sit opposite his father on the weekends at that desk. Jackson lived for the weekends with his parents. His weeks were spent with tutors and lessons, but the weekends were strictly family time for him. He would read the comics and the sports page while his father took calls and conducted business in his office. Jackson Cashe II taught him everything he knew about politics and making deals at that desk. Marilyn, his mother, would bring them both peanut butter cookies and milk. They would all sit around the desk and eat cookies. He hasn't seen the same smile from his father since his mother passed. The ache fills his chest.

Jackson's thoughts shift from his father's desk back to the coffee table where Marcus places the tray carried in by a butler. Jackson smells the black coffee and his mouth is watering. He gulps down the entire glass of water sitting next to his bed on the nightstand then saunters over to sit with his team. His blue striped, silk pajamas are wrinkled from a hard night's sleep. The IV stand trails behind him as he sits beside Hayman on the most comfortable of the couches.

The scrambled eggs are just the way he likes them. The bacon is crispy and fills the air with a heavenly smell. Jackson begins eating while trying to pay attention to Madison more closely. *Referendum, speech, ratings, I'm back on track.*

Hayman picks up when Madison stops and begins talking about the weekend. Vague memories are starting to come back to Jackson. A week of activity, the dinner, the speech, the VIP party after the speech, the alcohol. He rubs his head. *The governors of Massachusetts and New York really like their bourbon.* Jackson's head starts thumping again, but the IV is finally working. Jackson focuses on the highlights from the week and Hayman's account of everything.

"The governors were very pleased with the events, but we'll need to do some follow up with them on the outreach programs. We successfully presented to the world that we are as strong as ever and oozing with power and magnificence. Overall it was even better than we expected. It was ingenious of you to invite state leaders from the Allied States. The few who attended had

11

meaningful conversations with our team about reunification. Rich's 'after party' plan played an integral role in negotiations." Hayman pauses as Rich bows his head in mock humility. He quickly continues, "Even the Vanessa situation seems to poll well. Everyone was stunned, but apparently, no one really liked her. Bonus, we think we may have an idea on how to spin the split in your favor."

The fork full of eggs stops midair. Jackson shakes his head. "Wait, what?" Realization starts to settle on Jackson and memories of the fight come rushing back to him.

Silence fills the room as his most trusted advisors stare at him expectantly. Finally, Rich chimes in, "Surely you remember the scene she caused by not coming to the after party? You had no choice. She is a hot mess. Total diva." All eyes were glaring at Rich. "I'm sorry, but we all know it's true. Don't let the door hit you, if you know what I mean."

"What Rich is tryyyiiing to say is that there was no major fall out over you breaking the engagement with Vanessa. As it turns out, she was not very popular with your constituents." Madison attempts to refocus Jackson while she stares icily at Rich.

"Where is my phone? Has she tried to contact me?" Jackson looks for Marcus who is already bringing over Jackson's phone.

Hayman's booming voice startles Jackson. "No. You did the right thing last night. She embarrassed you and we can't let that type of behavior set a precedent or succeed. She is harmful for our branding. Our sources report she caught the first flight she could to Greece and is staying on a yacht with a male model friend of hers. You need to let it go Jackson and use this to our advantage."

Jackson scrolls through his phone. *Nothing. No calls. No texts. Nothing. She is long gone. I know there were problems, but man, she just bolted. Shouldn't I be more upset?*

Hayman breaks into his thoughts, "Jackson we have an idea that could sky rocket your already high approval ratings. Please listen to the plan before you shut us down completely. We really think this could draw attention to the country and bring back tourism. Foreigners are still concerned about the stability after the Separation. The riots have died down in both countries, but the chasm is palpable. This idea will show other countries that we have a strong economy and are back to business. We've already put the wheels in motion so you'll be hard pressed to say no. Rich, please share the strategy, while keeping your personal opinions to yourself."

Rich's dimples become more defined as a smile breaks across his face. He excitedly moves to the edge of his seat and launches both hands into the air while he starts speaking. "So, you've heard of The Bachelor, right?"

"No. No. No!" Jackson shakes his head vehemently.

This is not happening!

~Finals~

The sun burns away the cold from the morning as Haddie inhales the unusually warm December air in deeply. The day has really shaped up to be a top ten DC day. She aced her French final. The sun peeks its lovely head out of the clouds and warms her up enough that she stuffs her heavy coat in her backpack. Her sweatshirt allows for the perfect mixture of warmth and chill as she begins her walk home.

She grabs a mocha iced coffee and a gift for Maryssa from the coffee shop in front of the library. She heads off campus and down the main street of town. The bells from the Salvation Army ring loudly as she walks along the storefronts. Every window displays festive Christmas decorations and wrapped gifts. Her favorite department store boasts a family drinking cocoa in front of a mock fireplace while warmly showing off their designer sweaters.

Surrounded by Christmas gives Haddie another pick me up in her step. Her bags are packed with T-shirts, jeans, her favorite kicks, and a few novels she's been dying to read. Her plane is scheduled to leave at 6 pm and she can't get home fast enough. She will even have time before Christmas to go shopping with her mom and maybe even catch up with old friends. Yes, today is a wonderful day.

Haddie's apartment is three blocks from campus on a tree lined street. Just a few weeks ago, the now barren branches were filled with gorgeous reds, oranges, and yellows. Haddie loves the walk home from class. Thank God, she's been accepted to the medical school so she can continue living here with Maryssa.

Music is always playing when Maryssa is home. Haddie opens the door to sounds of deep bass resonating off the walls. Once again, she is grateful for well insulated walls and kind neighbors.

"Hey, était votre test français?" Maryssa asks as Haddie drops her keys on the table by the door.

"Bonjour! I did well, if I do say so myself! I even answered the bonus question about the Eiffel Tower." Haddie hands Maryssa a large green tea and a magazine. "Your favorite drink and tabloid trash, for my favorite tutor!"

"I had to make sure you could speak the language so we can visit together one day. The gifts are much appreciated!" Maryssa's whole face smiles as she takes a long drink of tea. She tosses the magazine on the table. The front cover has a headshot of President Cashe's ex fiancé with the word "NEXT!" across her face. "Ooh, this is a good issue. I'm dying to know the deets of what happened with them. Now, what time do we need to leave to get you to the airport?"

"I'm ready whenever, so it's up to you. I'd like to get there soon. I might be able to catch an earlier flight on standby." Haddie plops down on their soft, grey suede couch. They picked it out together and made sure they found the perfect blend of comfort and style. They lucked out and found a couch that must be what clouds feel like. It was plush and cushy in all the right places. "Are you sure you don't want to spend Christmas with us? I'm sure Uncle Malik can get a couple days off from work."

"While I would give anything for one of Aunt E's gingerbread men, my dad isn't ready yet and I can't leave him." The sadness in Maryssa's voice fills the room with silence and thoughts of Aunt Ruth flood both women.

Haddie's Aunt Ruth died of ovarian cancer three Christmases ago. Her death came one month after Haddie's sister Lizzie's death of the same disease. The family was utterly beseeched with grief but fought to celebrate the lives and faith of both women. Haddie felt so helpless watching these two giants in her life fight such a horrible illness. She vowed to destroy the disease that tried to destroy her family.

The family hangs on to Christmas memories more than ever now, but it also makes the season equally meaningful and filled with longing. Uncle Malik says that it is too hard to go back to their old street. He just isn't ready yet. These days, he fills his time with work, his only daughter, and favorite niece.

Maryssa shakes the sadness from her head and continues flipping the pages of the magazine on her lap. She breaks the silence with the four words that always fill Haddie with anxiety, "So, my dear cousin, I have an idea."

The exaggerated groan is meant to elicit an eye roll from her "dear cousin" Maryssa, and it did just that.

"Haddie, trust me this time. Listen to the whole idea before you say no. It's really an amazing opportunity. It's been all over the news this morning. You love skiing and have time on your hands next semester. It's the perfect plan for you to relax, enjoy a luxury resort, and make some money!"

"What are you talking about? Are you sending me on a vacation?" Haddie laughs at her cousin.

Maryssa pauses and takes a breath before the next words rush out of her mouth, "You know how much I love The Bachelor, right?"

"No. No. No!" Haddie pulls a blanket over her head while trying to block out the next words out of Maryssa's mouth.

~Alone in the White House~

Jackson wanders the hallowed halls of the White House. He can feel the history and immense responsibility on his shoulders as he strides past rooms in the residence. The weight of the world literally sits on his shoulders. The pressure is terrifying and exhilarating at the same time. He is the youngest president in history, turning 35 on July 4th, Inauguration Day. He is also the one tasked with healing the country after the Separation.

It has been 18 months and per the polls and the experts, the country is stronger than ever, but it doesn't seem that way. He

16

refuses to watch the news channels, but does ask for briefings from Rich every day on how things are being reported. The last few months have been eerily peaceful. A peaceful transition of power. No blood shed and not one weapon raised. Yet it felt so wrong.

The Separation feels like a sad divorce between two people who love each other but just couldn't live together any more. The United States of America divided by state boarders into the Allied States of America and the United States of America. Riots leading up to the Separation only showed how divided the county had become over the years. Fundamental differences that could no longer be negotiated nor tolerated by the either side destroyed a nation founded on free thinking. It is extraordinarily difficult to work with the opposing party after years of painting them as monsters. Cooperation takes on the appearance of caving or backsliding. Violence and outrage stole the opportunity for respectful discourse and compromise.

Both governments spent months working together to divide assets and infrastructure. Untangling military and transportation systems was the hardest, but they managed to find a way to work together. There was no way to divide equally, so they negotiated a deal to co-manage a joint military system with a governing body similar to NATO. There is an exit strategy so that both nations will have an equal and separate military system, but it will take years to finalize. Until then, the goal is to protect both nations from attack during this vulnerable time. If either nation wants to use military personnel for peace keeping in other countries, they must supply the operational funds. The thought of it all gives Jackson headaches. He snivels at the irony that both countries were able to negotiate separation terms, but couldn't work together on policy.

The country had been so divided for years. There was no reconciliation and no compromise. One great nation had split in two. The lines drawn like lines of an electoral college map. Families were torn apart and friends lost forever. The sadness overtook Jackson. He ran for president with a deep passion to strengthen what was left after the Separation and possibly bring some states back to the Union. If he could just show them how this new system worked and allowed everyone to have equal and unalienable rights, surely the states could reunite. His goal is to rebuild a structured government who provides services for every citizen. He knows he can unite the country under an umbrella of equality. It had happened before in our history. History, this house reminded him that it always repeated itself. Those who didn't learn from it were doomed to repeat it.

Jackson stops in front of his favorite portrait. A painting of the White House with the sun shining down on the grounds and illuminating this beacon of freedom. Jackson loves this building. He believes in what he's doing and what he can accomplish. He will make this nation great again.

The White House is quiet this morning. Most of the staff is home celebrating Christmas with their families. Jackson could have spent the holidays with his father and step-mother, but a romantic ski trip to Lake Tahoe didn't scream 'family' to him. Especially since his step-mother was his age and her only topic of conversation was herself. No, that did not appeal to him.

The growling of his stomach reminds Jackson that it is after lunch and he has missed it. He walks towards his security detail. "Travis, would it be too much trouble if I just ate in the White House Mess today? I hear the Navy chefs got a hold of Malik's famous lasagna recipe. It seems to be sparse around the building and I would kill for some of Malik's lasagna. It is his wife's recipe; did you know that? She was from West Virginia. They met while he was working at the Greenbrier Resort. Apparently, there is a huge Italian population in the state. Many Italian immigrants found work in the coal mines during the unionization and strikes. They sent for their families when they found work, but they were the subject of brutal discrimination. A bomb was exploded in one mine camp and killed hundreds of Italian men. The stories he tells are unbelievable. Sorry, I got on a tangent. Back to Malik. He traveled to a festival there one weekend and met his wife working at her family's vineyard booth. They hit it off and started writing letters. They fell in love writing letters and got married six months later. Can you imagine? Anyway, they moved to South Carolina after he finished his apprenticeship. He mixed his love of southern cooking with her family recipes and the two of them made magic together. Which brings me back to my original question, would it be too much trouble to eat Malik's magical lasagna?"

Jackson pauses waiting for a response from his burly secret service agent. *Who am I kidding, he can't say no, I'm the president.*

"Sir, just give me a minute and I'll make it happen." Travis starts talking into his wrist and directs Jackson towards the nearest stairwell. Jackson continues sharing his knowledge of the coal mine wars as they walk to the White House Mess.

~After the Holidays~

Haddie heads for baggage claim once she's off the plane and starts looking for Maryssa. She is carrying a container full of gingerbread men and peanut butter cup cookies. She can't wait to tell Maryssa all about the kitchen set Chloe got for Christmas and show her videos of the mini diva singing and dancing. It was so hard to leave them this morning. It made it easier knowing that she would be having dinner with Maryssa and Uncle Malik tonight.

Maryssa has already grabbed Haddie's bright purple suitcase and is holding a sign that reads, "Queen Haddie."

19

Haddie shakes her head and walks toward her favorite cousin. "What, no balloons and a band?"

"Haha, don't tempt me or next time it will happen." Maryssa laughs and grabs the container full of cookies. "Oh, how I love Aunt E! She is so good to me."

"You know you have to share those with your Dad too, right."

Maryssa offers Haddie a side hug with her free hand. "I have missed you!"

As the women head for the car, Haddie feels like they are being followed. She keeps turning around to look over her shoulder. She brushes it off as travel wariness and climbs in after throwing her bags in the back seat.

Haddie catches Maryssa up on all the home town gossip and family updates. When they make it back to their apartment, Haddie pulls out her phone and begins the slideshow of Chloe's Christmas.

"She loved the purse full of headbands and hair clips by the way. That was one of her favorite gifts. She wanted me to tell you and *Unca Mayik* thank you from the princess." Haddie shows pictures of Chloe's hair pulled up with three headbands and a butterfly clip. "However, Chloe wasn't the only one who was graced with the hair products. As you can see I had an appointment at her salon as well. I think this is my best look yet." Haddie laughs and flashes the screen towards Maryssa showing her ten butterfly clips holding up her long, thick, brown curly hair complete with a lopsided ponytail.

Maryssa grabs the phone and texts herself the picture. "Now this is going to be the new wallpaper on my home screen!" She laughs hysterically.

"Don't you dare show that to anyone!" Haddie takes back her phone from her cousin and joins in the laughter.

Maryssa sinks farther back into the couch and gets quiet. "I miss being with family so much at Christmas. I'm not sure what would have been harder, being alone, or being reminded of Mama at every turn." Maryssa's eyes glisten. "Daddy and I had a great holiday. We went ice skating and tried some new recipes together. You must taste our Bourbon Caramel Cake! It's to die for, but there was definitely something missing."

"I know what you mean. Watching Chloe on Christmas morning put an ache in my heart so deep I couldn't breathe. My sister should have been there watching her daughter opening presents. It's hard to believe that a few years ago, we had a house full of family celebrating Christmas. Everything has changed. We missed you both so much."

Sensing the profound need to change the subject, Haddie puts away her phone and pulls out her new laptop. Her parents gave her a loaded laptop as a Christmas and early graduation present. "Enough sadness, Aunt Ruth and Lizzie would kick our rears if they saw us wallowing. What time are we supposed to be at your dad's house for dinner? Do we have time to look up some exotic destinations?" Haddie had spent some time researching travel sites over break. Maryssa and Haddie had always planned to have one big hurrah trip the summer after graduation.

Maryssa sits up on the soft couch and leans toward the computer. "Ooohh, I just saw something about Greece on the Travel channel. Let's add that to our list of possibilities."

~Uncle Malik~

The aroma of sweet and spicy barbecue sauce fills the air. Classical music drifts from the kitchen. Maryssa and Haddie take off their layers of coats, gloves, and hats inside the red, heavy front door. They head for the kitchen. Haddie stops to look at the picture wall by the front door. She misses her Auth Ruth so badly. Aunt Ruth could make an entire room light up when she entered. Maryssa is the same way.

Haddie smiles as she touches the glass on a picture of her cousin's family on a camping trip. Aunt Ruth wanted to *connect with nature* but ended up connecting with poison ivy instead. Haddie loves hearing Uncle Malik retell the story. The memory makes Haddie smile down to her heart as she turns the corner into the Tuscan inspired, open kitchen. Her Uncle Malik is hard at work at the stove.

Malik Lavalier loves food. He loves the texture, the smell, the history of it. Food is his art. Every dish is a masterpiece waiting to be created and the ingredients, his paint. He hears the girls open the door and can't wait to see their beautiful faces. Those two girls brighten every aspect of his day. He understands their need for freedom and their own apartment, but he misses their nightly family dinners. Now, they only came on Sundays, which is better than nothing.

Before moving from South Carolina, the entire family would meet at his restaurant three to four times a week for family dinners. He learned soon after he began dating Ruth that the immediate Italian family unit consists of aunts, uncles, and cousins too. It is nothing for Ruth's mother, Mary, to cook a feast for thirty at a moment's notice. He learned more in Mary's kitchen than in most of his classes in culinary school combined. She was the greatest master chef and an even fiercer lover of her family. They named Maryssa after his beloved mother-in-law.

It took Mary a while to forgive Malik when Ruth announced they would be leaving West Virginia for South Carolina. Malik was given an amazing opportunity to start his own restaurant from a mentor of his. The only catch was that it had to be in Charleston, South Carolina. He went on to open other restaurants all over the south, but stayed in Charleston with his first and most beloved creation, Maria's Ristorante. Mary was proud of Malik, but hated that her daughters would be so far from her. Ruth's sister Esther, E as they call her, moved to South Carolina with Ruth. Yet another Italian custom, they stayed in packs, much like Maryssa and Haddie still do today.

"Ciao, Papa!"

"Ah, my favorite girls! I hope you brought your appetites and hard work ethic." Malik wraps both Haddie and Maryssa in a giant bear hug. "I made ribs and cottage fries. I figured Haddie would be marinara'd out after being home for two weeks. Poor E is a wonderful baker but she only knows how to cook pasta."

"Uncle Malik, I've missed you so much, and you're right about my mother. I've had enough pasta this month!" Laughter erupts from all three as they begin moving around the kitchen as a seamless unit. Haddie pulls out the plates, silverware, and napkins while Maryssa fills the glasses with sweet iced tea and lemons.

"After dinner, we're making Nunnie Mary's famous galette cookies. I can't help but crave them every Christmas." Uncle Malik points to the stained and well used recipe card sitting atop the galette iron. "You know, I'm the only person Nunnie Mary shared her real recipe with over the years. She is a very giving woman, but that recipe always manages to leave out an ingredient or two when she copies it down for someone who asks. I think that makes me her favorite." Laughter, again fills the room as they converge on the table.

After the blessing, the food is passed and stories are shared. Malik asks questions until he feels satisfied that he knows how everyone is doing back home. He feels better after he hears that Chloe and Beau are getting into a new routine since Lizzie's death. He has a special place in his heart for Beau. Losing the love of your life is a tough club to join. Memories of Ruth float in his mind. He is so grateful for the time he had with her and the gift of Maryssa. Malik shakes his head and relishes the moment he is having with the girls.

"Who is ready for baking?" Maryssa breaks into his thoughts as she starts clearing the table.

"So, Uncle Malik are you going to share the galette recipe with us or are we going to have missing ingredients?" Haddie grabs the recipe card and waves it in the air.

"Of course, it's your family heritage. However, I will not let you write it down until I'm confident that you've mastered it. A chef without a gift can destroy any recipe." Malik begins pulling out ingredients. "I'm proud to say that you two inherited Nunnie Mary's gift. Although, to be honest I am surprised that you two are still talking."

"Why would you say that Uncle Malik? We couldn't stop talking if we tried."

Maryssa starts coughing uncontrollably and shaking her head.

"I see. Well, based on Maryssa's panic stricken reaction and Haddie's oblivious response, I'm assuming we'll need some coffee to talk through Maryssa's confession."

Haddie's glare accompanies a very slow and threatening, "Maryssa Marie Lavalier, what did you do?"

"You can't *Marie* me when you have the same middle name, Haddie Marie Robinson. It loses its meaning. Now, just stay calm. One day we're going to laugh about this with our kids. Think of it as a scholarship program and long vacation rolled into one."

"Spit it out, Maryssa." Haddie snarls.

Maryssa puts distance between herself and Haddie by walking to the other side of the kitchen island, just to be safe. "So, I submitted a video application for a new reality TV show called *Future FLOTUS?*. Get it? It's a dating show for President Cashe." Maryssa pauses to gauge Haddie, then picks up again before Haddie has a chance to protest. "It starts filming this month and only lasts for three weeks then you have one week of silence while the show airs. The first portion is at a posh ski resort in Colorado so you can ski and relax before your online classes start. Plus, you get a $25,000 stipend for just being on the show."

Haddie speaks slow and deliberately. "Why, no, better yet, *how* did you submit a video application for me, without me?"

"Oh, that was easy. I used clips from our ballet days and family albums. I just did a voice over narration to tell the story of your life, which I obviously know well, because it's mine too." Maryssa grins. "They loved it, because you were chosen as one of the fifteen women. They called me about your background check last week." Maryssa is so proud of herself.

"Did you mention, in the video that I don't even like President, spoiled brat, Cashe? Also, I failed to hear the part where you also applied for this show?"

"I couldn't since I work at the White House. Besides, you need to lighten up and have some fun. You're so uptight these days."

Haddie shoots daggers at her cousin then covers her face with both hands in frustration.

Malik tries to deescalate the situation. "Let's sit down and talk it all through together."

"I can't believe you're mad at me for this. I signed you up for a luxurious vacation and you get paid! You should be thanking me." Maryssa leans against the counter and crosses her arms.

Haddie's glare returns.

Malik purposefully stands between the two girls as a buffer. "Who wants creamer in their coffee?"

~Suck it Up Buttercup~

The traditional office is decorated with expensive artwork and antique decorative lamps. The furniture is French provincial and reminds Jackson of a museum. Hayman's wife, Janice, decorated his office in the same style as their home, pretentious. His father favored a similar decorating style, but Jackson's mother managed to always add homey touches. His mother would roll her eyes at Hayman's office. Jackson is pulled from his thoughts by Hayman's admonishing voice.

"Jackson, you really must prepare for Colorado." Hayman is packing files into his leather laptop bag. Jackson likes sneaking into Hayman's office when he needs to relieve some of the pressure that weighs him down by sitting in the Oval Office. Just walking across the threshold removes fifty pounds of weight from his shoulders.

"Madison has all of the reports you'll need, but make sure Marcus includes the ones from your desk. We have meetings scheduled with the governors of Colorado and New Mexico. The

26

governor of California is also trying to fly over for a meeting if his schedule allows. There are two California women in the group so he would like a photo op with them. I'll keep you posted on his schedule changes. This is tremendous outreach and PR for those western states. They loved this idea when we pitched it to them. Especially Colorado. We will work on the flight over and should arrive in time for dinner with the executive producer. Have you spoken with Marcus about what to pack?"

"Remind me again, why I'm doing this? I still don't understand the rationale behind this fiasco. I'm supposed to be running the country not starring in a reality TV show with a bunch of nut jobs wanting fame and fortune."

Hayman shakes his head. "Nut jobs? Seriously, Jackson? You are overreacting a bit. Don't you trust me?"

Just then, Madison walks in and hands Jackson a large manila envelope. She hands a second one to Hayman. She directs her attention to Jackson, "Start packing or I'll do it for you and you'll be wearing Hawaiian shirts for two weeks."

Jackson opens the envelope and pulls out a stack of fifteen bios printed on the backside of headshots. He shakes his head as he quickly flips through the stack like a deck of cards he's dealing. "This is a bad idea. How did I let you three talk me into this?"

"We have surveillance photos too, if you'd like to see the contestants in their natural habitat." Madison walks out of Hayman's office and yells over her shoulder. "Pack, Jackson."

"How did you let us talk you into what exactly? Being fawned over by fifteen gorgeous women? Do you not trust our judgement? Do you honestly believe we chose a group of 'nut jobs' as you called them? Thousands of women were vetted for

27

this opportunity. We conducted security checks and hired investigators. These women are well educated, well bred, and interesting. Bonus, they are also extremely attractive! You are welcome for that, by the way." Hayman stares at Jackson incredulously. "Think of it as a dating website but in person. We did all the work for you just as a computer system would have done. You just need to fall in love. How difficult is that?"

"It's the 'interesting' part that scares me. Knowing you and Rich for as long as I have, the extremely attractive part was a given."

"Well Jackson, it is in motion now. There is no turning back so buck up cowboy. Rich is already in Colorado working with the production crew and our flight is in a few hours. Rich and Madison will oversee the filming and crew and I will have final say with production. You just enjoy two weeks at a luxury ski resort in Colorado with a group of gorgeous women."

"Again, I ask, who is running the country?"

"You are! Relax. Instead of bowling or playing pool during your down time, you will be skiing the slopes or ice skating. If you are that upset, I'm sure we can find you a bowling alley in Colorado. It's only two weeks. The second part of the show takes place in DC. You will still be working hard. Plus, this will bolster your already high PR numbers. The people love you. Let them feel special by giving them a glimpse into your love life. It is the least you can do after parading around with that vapid woman you were engaged to. Now stop worrying and go pack."

Granted, Vanessa was a mistake. She seemed so normal at first. She does want to be an actress. She should win an Oscar for her relationship with me. "Fine, I'm going."

Jackson storms out of Hayman's office and heads towards the residence. He swings open the door to his room, "MARCUS!"

"I've already started packing sir. Also, there is a lovely lady in the bathroom waiting to give you a spray tan when you are ready."

"Who? A what?"

"I believe Mr. Miller ordered it sir. We don't want you to look pale on the ski slopes, now do we? She is very attractive. Maybe you can just marry her and we can avoid this whole trip, sir."

Is that a smirk? This is a nightmare!

"I would expect nothing less from Rich and Hayman."

A spray tan? For Colorado in the winter? I need to check my blood pressure. This is exactly why people think I'm superficial. A suntan in January. Good grief!

Chapter 2

~The Arrival~

Twenty-five thousand dollars.   Three weeks. Twenty-five thousand dollars. Three weeks. I just need to get through three weeks. Focus on the positives. Three weeks of skiing and laying by the indoor pool with a book. That's not bad. Twenty-five thousand dollars to spend time skiing at a posh resort. I've totally got this. Three weeks in luxury.....with a man I think is utterly disgusting. Ugh, why am I doing this? Twenty-five thousand dollars. Three weeks skiing at a luxury resort. Okay, I can do this. Breathe, Haddie. Keep breathing.

Haddie Robinson & Annabelle Dubious

The man holding the sign looks much more polished and snazzy than Maryssa did last week at the airport. She would rather have the balloons and band that Maryssa threatened than her reality. The serious look on the man's face reminds Haddie that she will be surrounded by security and secret service agents all week. She takes a deep breath and walks in the direction of the serious, sign holding man.

A gorgeous, leggy blond stands next to him gazing into her compact. She looks as if she stepped right out of the pages of a fashion magazine. She looks every bit the type who would attract President Jackson Cashe.

Great. I get to spend three weeks caged up with a group of self-absorbed, blond airheads. She's probably just like his fiancé that everyone talks about for her mean streak. I'm probably the token brunette for the show. Good, maybe he won't even look at me.

"Hi there, I'm Haddie Robinson. I take it you're my ride?" Haddie grins at the man, who never breaks his stoic vibe. "And, according to the sign, you must be Annabelle?" Haddie holds out her hand to the beautiful bombshell.

"Yes! It's so nice to meet you. Can you believe this? It's so surreal. Please, call me Annie. Annabelle is reserved for my mother and grandmother. I love your scarf. The aquamarine really brings out the color in your eyes. I'm sorry. I'm talking too much. I'm just so excited."

"Thank you so much. I hope you haven't been waiting long."

"Ma'am, the schedules were planned to minimize waiting. Shall we head to the car? Your bags are being loaded as we speak." The smart looking man leads the way to the doors.

The night air is cold and crisp. Haddie can see her breath in the air. Outside, a bright and shiny limousine awaits the two women. As the driver opens the door, the women climb inside and are offered champagne in crystal stemware.

Oy vey! This is so pretentious. This is going to be a long three weeks.

Both women settle into their seats as the limo pulls away from the curb. "So, Annie, what do you do when you are not a contestant on a reality show and being driven in limos?"

Annie laughs. "I know, this is crazy, right? I'm so not the reality TV show type, but I couldn't pass up this opportunity. I've had a crush on Jackson Cashe since he spoke at my college graduation when he was the Speaker of the House. He's so charismatic." Annie takes a long sip of her bubbly drink. "I've been studying him ever since. Oh, that sounded so bad. I'm not a stalker." She laughs and shakes her head. "I'm a political pollster.

I'm actually co-owner in a firm I started with my sorority sister. We track women's issues and advise politicians on how to make the most impact. We started in California but have expanded to other states. After the Separation, things became more interesting. We mostly work in the United States but continue to keep a close watch on the Allied States where we have a few clients. It's a fascinating time in history with such polarizing views. The issues are surprisingly the same which begs to question did we really need to separate or just communicate and compromise better? I'm so sorry, there I go again with the talking. I'm probably boring you. Or worse, alienating you with my views." Annie takes another sip.

Boy, did I judge her wrong. Maybe this won't be too horrific of an experience.

"For the record, you weren't boring me at all. I am very interested. I would love to hear some of your insights. It sounds like you are passionate about your work and have an extensive knowledge in your field."

"Let's hope we're roommates then, because I tend to rub people the wrong way when I get on a roll." Annie ignores her phone as it starts vibrating and continues talking. "So Haddie, what is it that you do when you're not a reality TV celebrity?" Annie mirrors Haddie's original conversation starter.

Haddie smiles at Annie and starts to relax for the first time since Maryssa announced that Haddie was a finalist for the show *Future FLOTUS?*. It has been very tense around the apartment for the last five days. As always, Maryssa's heart was in the right place, but this definitely pushes the limits of their relationship. Maryssa knows Haddie can use the money to pay for school, and who wouldn't want a free luxury vacation?

"I'm a retired ballerina. I danced for nine years with the National Ballet Ensemble. After I tore my ACL from a bad landing, I began taking college courses. I'm currently in my last semester with a pre-med degree."

"Wow, you must be so busy. Are your professors okay with you taking off three weeks from classes? I can't imagine doing this with your schedule."

"It's weird, it all fell into place so I'm not missing any classes. I scheduled some general elective classes online this semester. My plan is to increase my work hours to help pay for books and supplies this fall when I start medical school. I'm able to get my reading finished early and then I can jump right into the assignments when I get home."

"Are you a Grey's fan? Do you want to be a surgeon? I totally did, until I remembered how much I hate needles." Annie chuckles.

"That would make surgery difficult, good choice on your part." Haddie laughs with Annie. "I'm not set on a track yet, but I'm leaning towards Oncology or cancer research. My sister and my aunt both passed away from ovarian cancer. It's something I'm obviously passionate about, but I'm also intrigued with helping athletes heal from injury so Ortho is on my list too."

"That's so cool. You would love the new study we just conducted on how women are educated on the different types of cancer. We specifically researched how to educate women on ovarian and thyroid cancers at the same level as they are about breast cancer without saturating the market. I would love to hear your opinion"

"We definitely need to be roommates!"

~Missing Mother~

Jackson Cashe grew up in Vermont. He learned to ski as soon as he could walk. His grandfather on his mother's side was a ski instructor on the mountain. When his mother was alive, they practically spent the entire winter at their vacation home in Killington. He started every day on a slope. Jackson grew up with a private tutor so missing school wasn't an issue. His father insisted on nannies and boarding school, but Jackson's mother refused. She grew up with working class parents, attended public schools, and had a mother who was a teacher. They compromised and hired the top tutor they could find instead of boarding school. Jackson never understood how his parents ever fell in love. They were so different, yet complimented each other perfectly. They were each other's balance. His father was decimated after his mother's death. Both men missed her so much.

The cold spray of snow on his face breaks him out of his somber mood. The whirring of the wind as he speeds down the hill covered in fresh powder is exhilarating. The smell of pine trees and cold mix to give him a euphoric feeling. This is where everything makes sense to him. He is reminded of his smallness surrounded by the trees and mountains.

What would Mother think of this? A dating contest. She would be appalled.

Jackson cuts left as he nears the lodge. He slows then stops right as Madison waves for him to come inside the building. They have rented out an entire lodge for two weeks. They need enough rooms for his staff, secret service, the women, and the crew. The security measures alone were ready to drive him crazy. This is completely unnecessary and irresponsible. He still wonders how he let Hayman and the team talk him into this mess. Jackson feels badly for the family vacationers who were displaced because of this *brilliant* idea.

Jackson makes it inside as Hayman and Rich are in a serious conversation with the producer and her assistant. Madison comes up behind him with a mug of hot chocolate and a fresh peanut butter cookie. She starts her usual run down of the day.

"You don't have anything scheduled, production wise, until the introduction cocktail hour and dinner tonight. The women are settling into their rooms now. Sandra has them housed on the same floor to keep them contained. They are in pairs to *create drama*, or so she hopes it will. Some arrived last night, but most are arriving today. They will be in meetings all day explaining the rules and expectations. They will also be signing confidentiality agreements and contracts. Remember, we start with fifteen women. You'll release a woman every night until day thirteen. Tonight, is just a get to know each other round. After that, the remaining three women will be transported back to DC for the second phase."

Jackson rolls his eyes.

"It will probably help you to woo the women if you don't look so miserable about being here with them. There are worse things in life than being trapped in a five-star ski resort with fifteen beautiful, successful women for two weeks." Madison was nothing if not honest, some would say blunt.

"Doesn't this just seem trivial to you? The country is in turmoil. The old one is literally divided into two equal yet separate parts. Both trying to divide and survive. I have bigger fish to fry than worrying about my dating status." Jackson shakes his head as he waits for some words of wisdom from his longtime friend.

"What you fail to understand is that the country also needs to see you at peace. If you are settled and confident, they will be too. The People need to see you enjoying the new way of life so

35

that they can start enjoying it. You are the one everyone looks to, so look alive instead of stressed and tense all the time. Give the country something happy to celebrate instead of the constant reminder of what has happened."

Jackson takes a bite of the cookie. It is soft and chewy. It reminds him of his mother. He can't stop thinking about her today. He remembers how happy his father was when his mom was around making him "sit and smell the roses" as she would tell him. After she died, his father was never the same. The roses were all destroyed. "Maybe you're right. It couldn't hurt to be open minded about this. Hopefully, Rich and Hayman haven't booked a wedding venue yet. It wouldn't surprise me if they've already picked the winner." He shakes his head. "Occasionally, you make sense Madsi." He uses her nickname and it's her turn to shake her head. "Don't let that go to your head!" He smiles as he takes another bite of the cookie.

"Yes, I am the only voice of reason in this madness we live in, so don't forget it. Now, go get cleaned up so we can introduce you to your future bride." Madison winks and walks towards Hayman, Rich, and the executive producer Sandra.

Sandra is talking animatedly. She points to where staging for hair and make-up will be during filming and where the sound technicians will distribute mics before tapings. Her assistant Lisa scurries around the vast ballroom making sure each department head is in the right place and has everything they need.

Rich has created a board with the headshots and bios of all fifteen women. They will review the board every night after taping to discuss strategy and initial feedback from a discreet panel of viewers. The panel will allow them to have raw data on each woman and the show in general. The hope is that it will speed up post production cuts and marketing. Hayman plans on encouraging Jackson to pick the favorite and most popular, whereas Madison hopes he finally finds the right partner. Rich is just hoping for Jackson's happiness and a "hot chick" for his buddy.

The ballroom is busy with activity. Madison will work closely with Lisa so she watches her movements as the woman directs the chaos. Every sentence Sandra speaks, adds to Lisa's responsibilities, which perpetuates Hayman adding to Madison's as well. She fervently takes notes on her tablet as she listens to the three of them create Jackson's dating reality for the next two weeks. She makes mental notes for how to handle Jackson this week and get Rich to see clearly instead of through the lens of cameras. Madison can't help but relate to Lisa, the one who actually does all the work while the others run their mouths.

Jackson owes me big time.

~The Competition~

The floor is a hub of activity. Beautiful women are running into each other's rooms and standing in the hallway chatting. Their day of boring meetings and contract signing had been a huge buzz kill for the women, but the excitement of getting to meet President Cashe tonight is bubbling over now.

Haddie has watched the women all day long trying to figure out everyone. She is determined to use this as a study in behavior. Maybe she can incorporate it into some of her psychology courses. Surely these women have major issues if they are willing to present themselves in front of a man like a piece of property. The vanity surrounding her is overwhelming.

This whole event is starting to remind her of the Bible story her mother was named after, Esther. The king had taken a group of women into the palace to choose a wife after getting rid of his.

The women were the most beautiful in the land and were at his beckon call. They all tried to entice him and win his favor.

Great, I'm helping to set feminism back millenniums!

Haddie hears Uncle Malik telling her to stop looking for splinters in the eyes of others when she has a two by four sticking out of hers. Uncle Malik's advice has gotten her far in life, she's not going to stop listening to him now. Haddie takes a deep breath and tries to see the other women with open eyes.

Since Haddie and Annie arrived together last night, they managed to snag one of the larger suites to share. Annie knew another contestant from her graduate program and went to visit her room. Macey, the other woman graduated magna cum laude from Stanford and would surely be made partner in her brokerage firm within the year.

Annie opens the door and pulls Haddie's attention back to the present. "You have to meet Laura, you'll love her. I met her at the ice machine. She works on Wall Street and has a great read on the *blondie twins* at the end of the hall. Word on the street is that they're both underwear models and vicious when garnering attention. I also saw a friend of mine from California, Sophia. She's an environmental lawyer. We did some poll work for a non-profit she manages. This is starting to feel like a weird reunion to me. I didn't realize this show would end up being such a small world, and competitive. I'm starting to get nervous."

Okay, so maybe I could be wrong about these women. I apparently have an issue with stereotypes. I'll just blame it on my bad attitude. I need to snap out of this bad attitude. Haddie looks down and tries to refocus.

"Oh, I adore your heels! Those are so adorable!" Annie stops to admire Haddie while reapplying lip glaze.

"Thanks. I have an addiction to purple. They're a little taller than I usually wear, but my cousin Maryssa found them and knew they would be perfect with this dress."

"Well, you look fabulous. Good thing you're not into winning over Jackson or else I'd have to sabotage you." Annie pauses, "Wait, you know I'm being sarcastic, right? I'm not a sabotage kind of person, I intentionally wanted it to sound like a canned reality show sound bite." Annie smiles.

"No worries, I totally get your sarcasm. In fact, I think it's why we were such fast friends. And you don't have to worry about Jackson, I'm for sure not here to steal him away from you or the others. I'm rooting for you all the way! I can be your wing woman." Haddie laughs as she finishes fastening the clasp on her strappy heels.

Haddie takes one last look in the mirror and follows Annie towards the door of the suite. The women make their way to the small ballroom where the first event will take place. Tonight, will be a meet and greet with each other and Jackson. According to the producer's assistant, the goal of tonight is to get to know the competition and the prize. Lisa is their main contact person. Haddie feels badly for the woman. She's been running around all day working hard to make sure everything runs without any hitches.

Haddie quickly scans the room and realizes that indeed, she is the only brunette chosen as a contestant. She is surrounded by blonds and red heads. Those were the types of women Jackson had been seen with over the years so she isn't surprised.

Good, maybe he won't even look at me.

The executive producer claps her hands loudly and speaks forcefully from the corner of the room and reminds everyone to act normal. The women were instructed earlier in the day to stand in small groups and hold their own conversations. Jackson will make his way around to each group.

Annie introduces Haddie to Macey and her roommate Lyla. Lyla is a first grade teacher from New York. Her students made her a giant good luck card that is hanging in her room. Haddie tells Lyla all about Chloe and they share little girl stories. Sophia enters the ballroom last and joins their group. The five women hit it off immediately and begin making predictions on who will last the first week. They are laughing and smiling together.

There is another large group of women standing in the middle of the room chatting. Annie points out Laura from the ice machine and someone else recognizes a news anchor named Callie from Chicago. Sophia tells them about Suzanne, who is her roommate. They were paired together because they are both attorneys, but Sophia pointed out that there is a reason they both arrived separately to the ballroom. Sophia warned the others to watch out for her. Everyone recognizes the last women in the group. Shelby Winters has her own home decorators show. Haddie loves her use of shiplap.

Haddie can hear the three women behind her talking about physical therapy and sports injuries. She turns, trying not to be nosey, so she can remember to talk to them later. She recognizes one of the women as the professional cheerleader, but doesn't know the other two. They must be the nurse and the physical therapist she heard about earlier.

The final group of women stands off to the side, purposefully positioning themselves by the doors and away from the others. Every one of them looks as if they're walking a red carpet later. The blondie twins are there along with the runway model. Haddie tries not to make judgements about them, but they definitely are not trying to meet and mingle with the others.

A commotion by the door catches their attention. The cameras all point in that direction. The doors open and all eyes focus. President Jackson Cashe walks into the room and fourteen women race over to meet the prize.

So much for acting normal. He is just a man, ladies!

~Burning the Home Fires~

The White House is bustling with activity even though the President's senior staff are all in Colorado. Malik comes in early to work on a new recipe for beef and cheddar stew. Jackson mentioned he used to eat it when he was a child. Malik will combine a recipe from his culinary school days with one created by a chef he knows in Vermont. Catching up with his old friend was a bonus while recipe hunting. Malik loves merging and creating new recipes.

He has a full day of meetings with members of his staff. Sadly, most of the day will be spent behind his desk organizing, planning, and ordering. His team will be in shortly. They need to menu and staff plan for the next month.

Malik's office is tucked into a back corner of the kitchen. The top portion of two walls are glass so he can see everything going on in his domain. One wall holds a large white board calendar for all the staff to see. He has a petite desk, just large enough for his laptop that fits neatly into a corner. The room houses a small rectangular table with chairs for meetings and to use as a workspace to spread out his menus. Malik spends most of the morning at his computer studying the list of events over the next month and making notes.

Malik has worked as a White House chef for fifteen years. The same mentor who helped him start his first restaurant, pushed for Malik to replace him as head chef. A patriot at heart, Malik

41

couldn't resist the honor of serving his country. The Separation made things awkward. He would be a citizen of the Allied States had he still been living in South Caroline during the split, but with Ruth sick and receiving treatments in DC, they decided to stay. Once he was ready to leave, President Cashe was elected. After speaking personally with the man, Malik decided to stay on as head chef until he was ready to move back home to South Carolina.

President Cashe decided to downsize the White House employees to stretch the budget. Malik was tasked with restructuring the entire kitchen staff and protocols. His greatest struggle is balancing Jackson's desire for simplicity against Hayman's demands for a show of opulence. Malik has grown fond of Jackson Cashe. He has seen him truly grow as a leader and more importantly as a human since he took the oath of office. Hayman Barnes, on the other hand, has Malik feeling more uneasy.

The next order of business today is to meet with the new pastry chef, Martin. The last pastry chef was killed in a car accident last month. Malik has been pulling double duty crafting desserts while waiting on security clearance for his new hire. The process has been sped up since Martin is the cousin of Malik's main sous chef, Oscar. Oscar assures Malik that his cousin has a gift for pastries, specifically cobblers. The tasting interview impressed Malik.

Malik stands to write on the kitchen wall calendar. The white board spans every culinary event hosted at the White House from meals in the residence to State Dinners. Every chef, wait staff, and support staff are listed for each event as well as who is responsible for every possible portion of the meal and which kitchen will be used.

Malik begins filling in Jackson's personal preferences first, then he will start on the catered affairs. He finishes the next two weeks then stops and chuckles to himself. *Maybe Jackson's new girlfriend will make an impact on the personal menu.*

Oscar saunters into Malik's office with Martin on his heels, "Hey boss man! What is the first order of business today?"

Malik smiles at Oscar as he reaches for the man's hand then for Martin's. "Oscar. Martin." Malik gestures for the men to sit at the table facing the white board. Malik already has papers and lists scattered across the solid oak table top.

"Perfect timing, I just finished the main courses for the residence. Martin, how is your first day? I hope Oscar is showing you the ropes and not hazing you." Malik winks at his young and humorous sous chef. Oscar responds with an ornery shrug and smile.

"Yes, I'm learning everything I need to know, thank you." Martin replies deadpan.

Malik appraises the man for a moment before moving on to Oscar. "I have a head start on the rest of the month, but I can't plan much beyond next week for the President, as I don't know how his schedule will change with filming the TV show. Madison suggested that he might bring the three women here on private dates or he may choose to dine out with them. I have some suggestions, but nothing air tight until he returns." Malik catches a slight eye roll from Martin, but chooses not to put the man on the spot his first day. He makes a mental note to speak with Oscar later about his cousin's individual opinions.

"Martin, do you have any suggestions for desserts that will complement the menu? Keep in mind that President Cashe could possibly be wooing a new girlfriend so he may want some creativity from us."

Martin studies the calendar while rubbing his chin. "Well, I would suggest a peach cobbler if he has any southern women as a dinner guest. I just so happen to know where I can get my hands on candied Georgia peaches during the winter. A nice apple strudel will pair well with the pork loin you have planned for next Thursday. As you can tell, my specialty is fruit. Hard to get during the winter months, but I have a phenomenal source with an organic green house for year-round produce."

"I like the way you think." Malik adds Martin's suggestions to the board. "Obviously, we'll have to get your source vetted through security, but if you have used them before, that will help speed the process. I'm looking forward to the cobbler. I haven't had good cobbler since I left South Carolina."

"You say that about everything, Chef. I need to visit you in South Carolina. Apparently, everything tastes better." Oscar jokes.

"Guilty. I'm a sucker for my homeland. I would love to return soon." Malik pats Oscar on the shoulder. Martin sits stonily watching them.

Malik sits at the table and passes out a White House events calendar. He has highlighted areas they need to discuss. "Let's get started men, we have a lot of work to do today."

~Breathing~

The sun shines down on the mountain. Last night brought a fresh layer of snow which is sparkling like diamonds under the rays of light. An early morning run is exactly what Jackson needs to clear his head.

He jumps off the ski lift chair and glides to the bottom of the ramp. He pulls down his Oxley ski goggles and grips the poles tightly. Jackson breathes in the fresh air deeply. The cold burns his lungs and refreshes his senses. While the premise of his visit is still mind boggling to him, Jackson loves starting his day skiing. He thinks clearly on a snow covered mountain and everything falls into place.

Jackson jumps off his perch and flies through the air. The wind and cold powder spray his face. Trees are flying past him. He cuts right then left. He jumps off small packs of snow to get a little lift. He sees a secondary slope merging with his from the left. There must be a double diamond slope above this one that isn't on the map. As he veers right to avoid the tree line, a flash of back and purple cuts in front of him.

Wow! That's one skilled skier.

Secret Service cleared the mountain before they would let Jackson ski so he wonders who is besting him this morning.

Jackson kicks it into gear and tries to keep up with the phantom skier. He weaves in and out of the snow squall left in the wake ahead of him. Jackson swishes and swerves. He bends his knees deeper and leads with his head to increase his speed. The rush is exhilarating. He really needs this today. It's been a long week of speed dating and politicking. This takes him out of his head and gives him a clear mind. Everything is simple here and honest. Man verses nature. Simple.

The bottom of the slope is coming quick. He watches as the skier makes a hard-left cut and slows to a stop.

Man, this guy is good! Is that an agent sweeping the mountain?

Jackson releases the deep bend and starts to slow as he approaches the lodge. He watches as the skier pops the locks on the skis and carries them to the rental ski rack. The skier pulls off their gloves and goggles. As they pull off their knit cap, a curly, brown pony tail falls to her shoulders. She stretches her arms over her head and heads to the lodge doors.

Jackson follows her with his eyes as she passes by the wall of glass windows. She heads towards the elevator bank. As she steps into the elevator and turns towards the windows, Jackson freezes.

Wait, do I know her? No way. Is she a contestant?

~Learning the Lay of the Land~

"I know you don't want to win the president's heart, but I can't believe you went skiing on your first group date day." Annie shakes her head as she lectures Haddie. "You realize that the other four women have been in the salon all morning. They're getting primped and styled and you just got back from after skiing yoga. You have a lunch date in an hour and you just now finish your shower. You know you have to be down there early to get mic'd up and prepped for filming, right?"

Haddie laughs as she heads to the bathroom. She hears Annie mumbling her incredulous thoughts as Haddie turns on her hair dryer. The hot air swirls around her, mimicking her thoughts about the entire situation. It has been a surreal four days in Colorado. It seems like a lot of dating to cram into two weeks. Sandra has every date scheduled and planned meticulously. It is a well-oiled machine.

On day one, the fifteen women were divided into three groups. The plan was for Jackson to go on three five-person group dates on consecutive days. However, on day one during their meet and greet, the first woman was released after getting toasted, falling

46

down and breaking her nose. The entire cast and crew were shocked that Lauren went out like that. Although her departure has the production team scrambling to make the group dates fair, Haddie is sure the TV ratings on that event will make them happy.

Days two through four consisted of group date days. Annie's group went bowling and then ate pizza. The second group had cookies and cocoa after ice skating. Today, Haddie's day, the group date will be a cooking lesson with the head chef followed by lunch. According to Annie, President Cashe will make his way around to each contestant for individual conversations with every woman on the date. Haddie is glad they are cooking. Maybe they will be too busy concentrating for any real one-on-one time with him.

Whole group dinners are held each night with women rotating who sits next to President Cashe. Haddie enjoys watching the women maneuver and scam their way next to his chair. At the end of each day, one woman from the group date is released from the show with a bouquet of yellow "veto" roses delivered to her room. So far, Lauren, Sophia, and Lyla own the first vetoes.

Round two consists of four-person group dates similar to round one. Once those three women are vetoed, the remaining eight women will be divided into pairs for the next elimination round. Round three, will be four sets of head to head dating with two women in the morning and two in the afternoon. The final day in Colorado, round four, will allow President Cashe and the remaining four women to go on individual dates. At the end of round four, three women remain for the final round which takes place back in Washington DC. While the activities seem fun and exciting to Haddie, she desperately hopes she is vetoed today.

So far, Haddie has successfully managed to keep her distance from President Cashe. She assumes she'll be released after the date today. She has no intentions of flirting with him and prolonging the inevitable. Surely, he will see her as boring and uninterested. Unless one of the other contestants sabotages herself like day one, Haddie will ride out the rest of the week skiing and relaxing by the indoor pool without the voyeuristic cameras following her.

Haddie finishes drying her hair and applies some product to enhance her natural curls. Normally she would apply a thin layer of make-up, but they were instructed to have it professionally applied for their dates. This worries her. She typically sticks with foundation, lip gloss, and sometimes a dab of mascara. She is not much for wearing too much make-up beyond the stage and she has no plans to start now for the cameras. One last look and Haddie heads back into the room to dress.

Annie is laying out her clothes for dinner.

Haddie shakes her head and laughs. "You think I don't take long enough to get ready and I think you're crazy getting ready for dinner five hours early."

"Hey, Jackson is meeting the formidable Haddie Robinson today, I have to up my game for dinner tonight." Annie smiles at Haddie. "What are you wearing for your group date? Oversized overalls and a baggy hoodie?"

"That's a much better idea than the flannel nightgown and fluffy cat slippers I have laid out to wear."

"At least they'll let us remain roommates after your dismissal. You know, you might beat out the news anchor from Chicago. She wears so much perfume that it almost acts as a repellent. You may not like him, but at least you won't give him a headache when he is near you. You could actually make it through the first elimination round without even trying. Next thing you know, you are flying under the radar and end up at the White House for a week. Now that will be hilariously ironic."

Haddie's face lights up with laughter as she pulls on a purple sweater over her long, grey tank top. Her tall black riding boots slip on easily over her black skinny jeans. She fluffs her hair and spritzes just a tiny bit of vanilla body spray.

"Maybe I should stand next to Miss Chicago and our mixed scents will earn us the first double elimination." Haddie jokes. "Here goes nothing!

"Shall I wish you good luck or bad luck? I'd tell you to break a leg, but you might do it on purpose to get out of filming."

Haddie flashes a smile at Annie before she closes the door behind her and walks down the long hallway to the elevators.

Chapter 3

~First Impressions~

The kitchen is relatively quiet with only the master chef and a sous chef on hand. Haddie has been in many a bustling kitchen and was raised in her Uncle Malik's restaurant. She appreciates the prep time before organized chaos erupts. Haddie knows that this is a precious time for a chef. She introduces herself to Chef Maxwell and passes on greetings from her Uncle Malik back in DC.

"Oh! How is my dear friend Malik? He was my fiercest competitor in culinary school."

"He is wonderful, thank you for asking. I bet he is bored silly with most of the White House staff in Colorado for two weeks, but I'm sure he's keeping busy creating new masterpieces. Speaking of which, I'm so excited to learn from you today. My cousin Maryssa is so jealous."

"Ah, that's right, Malik's daughter is following in his footsteps. You tell her she is welcome in my kitchen any time!"

"She will be elated to hear."

Chef Maxwell leans closer and speaks in a quieter tone. "I was so heartbroken to hear of Ruth's passing. I sent him pears after the funeral. I know those were her favorite. She was an enchanting woman. She had a way of lighting up a room. You know, I never knew what she saw in a no talent hack like him." Chef Maxwell winks at Haddie and follows it with a hearty laugh.

"Thank you for your kind words Chef. We all miss her terribly. I will pass along your condolences to my uncle and cousin."

"While you are at it, tell him I have an opening for a line cook if he needs work. Surely after so many years at the White House, they have realized he can't cook." More laughter and smiles pass between the two.

"I will surely tell him, Chef." Haddie smiles her infectious smile.

"Ah, I see that you have your Aunt Ruth's smile. It lights up your entire face."

She blushes. "I appreciate the compliment, more that you know." Haddie pauses in thought before reality hits her like a brick. "Well, I better report to the production staff or they might track me down and show the world all my warts."

"Surely that will be the briefest set of material they record." Chef Maxwell tenderly grins at Haddie. "Good luck young Ruth, I look forward to watching you create your own masterpiece today."

Haddie smiles and waves as she makes her way from the kitchen into the large dining room. The production staff has taken over a majority of the room with their tables and electronics. People are moving quickly about doing their jobs. It strikes Haddie that they are moving as seamlessly as a ballet ensemble. Everyone with their own part, but working as a until to create a master performance. She watches and contemplates this new theory.

A production assistant pulls her from her imagery and directs her to a table. There, a sound technician quickly wraps an elastic band around her waist and snakes a wire up under her sweater. He finishes by clipping a microphone on her V-neck sweater.

Haddie is grateful that she thought about wearing the grey tank top under her sweater. She is a modesty expert after years of dressing quickly in front of others in between dances and performances. While she understands that she needs to wear a microphone, there is no need for everyone on set to see her sweater pulled and stretched about her.

After she is wired for sound, the assistant directs Haddie towards a tall table with lights.

"You are the first contestant I have seen today." A bubbly, tiny girl with bright red hair helps Haddie into the director style chair. "Most of the women brought their own glam squad to get them ready. Hi, I'm Sadie, by the way."

"I'm Haddie, and I guess that makes you my glam squad."

"Well, I've been admiring your cheek bones all week, so I'm gladly at your service. Now tell me about your make-up style."

Haddie blushes again for the second time today and chuckles. "You are looking at my make-up style. Foundation, lip gloss, and mascara. That's about it for me. When I danced, I was heavy on the lipstick and mascara, but still very minimalist. I only wore what the costume called for and nothing more."

Sadie concentrates on Haddie's face and falls silently into deep thought.

"I'm afraid, I'll be too boring for you. You may wish that another contestant sat in your chair today." Haddie looks down at her hands gracefully folded in her lap.

Sadie pulls Haddie's face up with her hands and stares a minute longer as she turns the chin right then left.

"As a dancer, I would think you see beyond the surface to the beauty of the basics. It's not always about more, it's about the stroke of the brush. The layers create the drama, not the flash." Sadie picks up a small black container and a long make-up brush and begins working on Haddie's face.

Haddie sits in the chair contemplating Sadie's insight. It seems she has been making assumptions all week. Haddie shakes the unwelcome realization from her mind and attempts to change the subject.

"How are all of these women bringing glam squads? I thought the resort was closed except for limited hotel staff and those directly involved with the President and production."

"You are so cute. You're not a reality TV junkie are you?" Sadie stops her hands and looks pathetically at Haddie.

Haddie can only shake her head no.

Sadie rolls her eyes and starts working again before launching into Haddie's educational portion of the day.

"Haven't you wondered where the other contestants are during the day?"

"Not really, I've been staying busy skiing and reading. I just assume they were doing the same. My roommate makes trips to the salon at the resort, but no posse has shown up in our room."

"Bless your naïve little heart. Well, most of these women have teams staying at nearby hotels. They leave here in the morning and get worked on all day. They have stylists along with hair and make-up artists planning for each day. Other than the school teacher and the drunk girl from day one, you are the only contestant I've seen all week."

53

Haddie stares into the mirror and considers what Sadie has just told her. *That makes sense based on how intently these women have their eyes on the prize. This is yet another reason I should not be here. Thanks, Maryssa!*

"I think I heard a few women hired a team of women from the resort. Maybe that's why your roommate makes so many trips to the resort salon."

Sadie stands back and looks. One more swipe of the brush and a rub of a tissue.

"There, you are perfection."

Haddie turns in her chair to face the lighted mirror. She gasps at herself and stares.

Oh, my goodness.

"Wow!" she whispers. "Those women are wasting their time and money. You truly are an artist. I can't believe what you've done to me. I don't look like I'm even wearing make-up and yet everything is defined and flawless. I'm in awe." Haddie turns her neck to see every angle of her face.

Sadie crosses her arms, leans into the table, and smiles. "Thanks. That means a lot."

"Don't take this the wrong way, but you don't seem very into this whole process. You're either clueless or don't care if you win. Not that I care, I'm just curious."

Haddie waits, considering her answer. She wants to be truthful without insulting her new friend.

"I guess you are right on both counts. My cousin signed me up for the show without my knowledge. I blew this off as a joke meant for super models and I was the just token smart girl. Honestly, I completely misjudged the other women. I quickly learned that just because it's not my cup of tea, doesn't mean it's not of value to others. We all have our own desires and dreams. This still isn't my cup of tea. I'm actually hoping I get released today, but I don't begrudge the premise any longer. If anything, I've been enlightened."

Sadie's gaze bores into Haddie. She finally breaks her hold and smiles. "Haddie, it was truly a pleasure to meet you. You seem like an insightful and honest person. I hope you are not released so I can get to know you better. I'll gladly be your glam squad."

Haddie rises from the chair and steals another look in the mirror. "No need to stay in the mix, I go skiing every morning and swimming in the afternoons, you can get to know me then." Haddie laughs and turns towards the producer who calls for the women to the assemble in the kitchen. "Thanks for the compliment and the magic, Sadie. I hope we talk again soon." She walks towards the kitchen.

"Hey Haddie." Sadie calls after her.

"Not to burst your bubble, but the news anchor is going next. Her perfume gives Jackson a headache." Sadie turns to clean her station as Haddie heads into the kitchen.

~Sunken Soufflés~

The large picture window in the penthouse conference room spans the ski lifts and the tubing slope. They are bare this afternoon since the resort is closed. Jackson imagines families filling up the snow with a rainbow of tubes. He stares out the

55

window trying to process the events that have transpired this week. Three women down, nine more to go before he can return to his own bed in Washington. Each date and large group dinner proves his original theory; this is pointless. So far, the women are the same he finds on his own, intrigued by the idea of dating President Jackson Cashe. He is supposed to be restoring and strengthening a country, not speed dating. While the women are beautiful and interesting, none has really held his attention. He enjoys his conversations with the pollster and the nurse, but just like the others, he can't get passed their infatuation for him.

Madison knocks on the open door of his makeshift office. "Jackson, it's time for the next group date."

Jackson turns in his chair and rolls his eyes at Madison. "Great, more time wasted realizing I should be focusing on the country instead of women." He sulks in his chair with his chin resting on his fist.

"I am not having this conversation again, Jackson. Suck it up buttercup. Besides, you'll love this date. You are having a cooking class with Chef Maxwell followed by a food tasting event. Here is a little bit of trivia for you, since you love useless trivia information, Chef Maxwell attended culinary school with Malik Lavalier. That should make you happy."

Jackson stops in his tracks and looks at Madison. "Seriously? What are the odds of that happening?" He thinks of a young Malik and chuckles in wonder. "That does make me happy. I didn't realize I would be so homesick for DC, but this should help."

Madison gives Jackson a quick overview of the women in this group date as they walk towards the kitchen. He stops to get his mic on then a quick swipe of Sadie's brush. Sadie tells him her latest joke. On the first day, they both shared corny jokes, now it's their thing. He winks at Sadie and follows Madison while she talks.

"A news anchor, don't I usually try to avoid the press? Wait, is she the perfume girl? "

"Jackson!" Madison quietly scolds him. "They are in the next room. Keep your comments to yourself, oy vey."

He mock zips his lips and holds up his hands. Madison continues.

A defense attorney. Hmm, hopefully I never need her services professionally. A retired ballerina, seriously? I'm sure she's not pretentious at all. This just keeps getting better. Maybe I can start double eliminations.

Jackson walks into the kitchen as the production assistant, Lisa, gives the women directions. "Please do not hog the camera or the President. Stay focused on your station so we don't have any kitchen fires. And please, for the love, do not use foul language. Sadly, we had to use the censors a record time yesterday. Let's try and keep it classy ladies."

He watches as the women fidget with their hair and check their reflections in the stainless-steel bowls in front of them. All but one. The women turn in unison as they hear Lisa call Jackson's name. *Same story, different day, or date.* All but the brunette at the end. Jackson notices that she also has her station spread out so that there is no room for a partner to sit. *Hmm, interesting. Wait, is that the skier? I'm pretty sure there is only one brunette. It has to be the skier. This could be fun after all. I wonder if she's the attorney.*

Jackson walks to the front of the kitchen and stands right beside Haddie's station. He extends his hand forward, "Chef

Maxwell, it is an honor to be in your kitchen. I am very excited to watch you work. I understand you know our very own Chef Lavalier? I have to admit, I'm a groupie of his." Jackson flashes his campaign smile.

"President Cashe, it is I who is honored." The men shake hands. "I'm so sorry about your luck having to endure Malik's food. Hopefully today you'll taste a real culinary masterpiece." Chef Maxwell winks conspiratorially at Jackson. "Malik seems to be the main topic of my kitchen today. His niece.....ah, daughter is also studying to be a chef."

Chef Maxwell stutters as he sees Haddie shaking her head behind Jackson.

"Let us get started, yes?"

Jackson looks back and forth quizzically between Chef Maxwell and the strange brunette who is now looking down to avoid eye contact. "Yes, please Chef."

"Do you mind if I share your station first?" Jackson tries to engage Haddie who insists on staring at her tools.

There goes that fake campaign smile again, ugh. This is going to be a long hour. Can't he read body language? Mine says, "Stay away buddy."

Finally, resigned to look up, she offers an insincere smile. "Are you sure? I think the others have more room at their stations. Mine seems to be crowded. Plus, I'm a real klutz, I wouldn't want to spill anything on you.'"

"Oh, I'm sure. You look like you know what you are doing. Plus, I'm a great assistant." Jackson mimics her then reaches out his hand to shake Haddie's. "I'm Jackson. Maybe I can help organize your tools. I can organize this station like I organized the budget."

What was that? I can't believe I just said that. She must think I'm the tool.

Haddie resists rolling her eyes and gives a fake laugh as she faces forward to hear Chef Maxwell. "We should really listen. I wouldn't want to miss a crucial step." Haddie scoots her chair as far to the edge of the table as possible as Jackson sits beside her.

Chef Maxwell demonstrates the art of making the perfect crepe, then moves on to omelets and quiche specialties. Once he finishes the exhibition portion, he models how to make the perfect quiche bites for his audience. The women are to make homemade mini crusts for cupcake molds then choose their own ingredients for the individual quiches. Haddie is excited. She can make crust in her sleep. She has been making quiche since she was small. Her plan is to knock this out and get rid of Jackson.

Haddie hands Jackson the basket full of eggs and a bowl. "Here, crack twelve of these while I start the crust."

Jackson takes the items and stares at Haddie.

What is her story? Have I offended her already? I'm very charming. Surely, there is a misunderstanding.

Haddie adds an ice cube to the small water pitcher. She quickly combines flour and salt then mixes both together with a fork. She then adds the ice water to a measuring cup filled with oil. She mixes those together first before adding the mixture to the flour and salt. Again, she uses the fork to mix everything together into a dough. Jackson watches Haddie intently as she placed the dough between two pieces of waxed paper and begins rolling it out into a flat crust.

59

"How did you know how to do that?" Jackson looks in awe at her. "I heard the same instructions you did, but I didn't hear anything about ice cubes or waxed paper." Jackson waits but Haddie only shrugs. "You obviously know what you're doing. Look at the others. They haven't even started cracking eggs."

Haddie pointedly looks at Jackson. "Neither have you. Do you need help? Apparently, eggs are more difficult than the budget." Haddie smirks.

"Ouch. All right, I'll start cracking Chef." Jackson cracks three eggs expertly and tries to make conversation with the intriguing brunette. "You know, I'm actually quite skilled at cracking eggs. My mother and I used to make desserts together all the time. She taught me everything I know."

Still more silence. Haddie continues cutting the crust to place it in the muffin cups.

"Who taught you how to cook? You clearly know your way around a kitchen."

Haddie pauses not wanting to lie but not wanting to share her personal life on reality TV. "My uncle and grandmother are both great cooks. I spent a lot of time in kitchens growing up with them." Haddie adds milk and seasonings to the egg bowl in front of Jackson. "We just need to whisk the eggs and add the other ingredients and we're finished. Maybe you should share your egg cracking skills with the others. I'm sure they would love the help."

Jackson sits staring at Haddie. Contemplating her disdain for him.

Yep, she must be the attorney. Very factual and focused. Or, maybe she's a republican. I thought they screened these women. Apparently, liking me wasn't a criterion.

Lisa walks up behind Jackson and says, "She's right. You really need to mingle with the other contestants. We'd like for you to spend ten minutes at each station. You'll have time for longer conversations during the food and wine tasting after the cooking portion."

Elizabeth urges Jackson to get up and move on from Haddie's station.

"Haddie, I look forward to a longer conversation with you later." Jackson flashes his best flirtatious smile at Haddie, knowing it would drive her crazy. *This is going to be fun. I'm going to figure her out this week. That will give me something entertaining to do.*

Haddie smiles an obligatory grin and continues adding ingredients to the egg mixture.

Jackson glances back over his shoulder as he walks to the next cooking station. The beautiful red head jumps to her feet, cocks her head to the side, and flashes a brilliant white smile.

"Jackson, just in time! I'm still cracking eggs."

"Suzanne, right?" Jackson smiles.

Red smiles.

"Let's get cracking." He laughs. "So, Suzanne are you a professional chef or do you have another line of work?"

"No, silly. I'm a defense attorney. Cooking is definitely not my thing, but I like challenges." Suzanne looks intently at Jackson before winking.

Hmm, now I'm really curious about the brunette ski wiz.

The contestants and Jackson are encouraged to make quick stops at Sadie's table after cooking and before heading to the dining room. Haddie is first to see Sadie and positions herself towards the back of the large room.

Chef Maxwell walks up behind Haddie while his staff brings out the contestants' quiches. He whispers, "I'm not sure why you didn't want the president to know about your uncle, but I think it would have endeared him to you. He really seems enamored with Malik. Although that does make me question his judgement." Chef Maxwell laughs.

Haddie whispers back, "That's exactly why. He's not my type." She shrugs and smiles warmly at the robust man with blue eyes.

"Ah, I see you are also ornery like your uncle." Chef Maxwell chuckles as he walks past Haddie towards the front of the room.

"We have prepared a feast of our famous brunch appetizers for you all in addition to your lovely quiches. I'm sure they are delectable." He winks and nods. "But I thought you all would enjoy some other items as well. The wine tables have an array of samples from our local wineries. They have been hand selected to pair perfectly with the food stations they flank. I also have signed copies of my cookbooks *Entertain like a Chef* and *Wine and Cheese Bon Appetit!* for you all to take home. It has been wonderful meeting you all today. Now, please enjoy!"

The other contestants all follow Jackson to the first station. Haddie heads in the opposite direction.

~Puzzle Pieces~

Jackson misses his ski run this morning in lieu of briefings from cabinet members via secure satellite link. He would rather these be in person, but he makes due with his lot for the next week. The conference room is bustling with activity. Hayman barks orders at everyone while Madison furiously takes notes. Marcus enters the room with Jackson's Burberry fleece hoodie after hearing him mention he is cold. Jackson smiles warmly at his aide as he takes the warm and soft sweatshirt.

Even with all of this going on around him, he can't get the brunette out of his mind. He wasn't able to talk to her during lunch because he was bombarded by the other contestants and the skier managed to stay on the opposite side of the room. By the time he'd made his way over to her, she was speaking with Chef Maxwell. Jackson attempted to participate in the conversation to learn more about her, but she succeeded at switching the focus back to him with each question. Jackson was beginning to think he needed her on his PR staff. She was highly skilled at evading answers. At least she was more polite with a witness present.

Dinner came and went with the bombshell twins monopolizing his conversation, again. Per usual, the brunette stayed only as long as necessary. She was either playing some kind of coy game, or genuinely did not want to spend time with him. The thought begged to question, why even apply for the contest if that is the case. Regardless, Jackson is fascinated and focused on solving this puzzle. Cracking her code will be a fun distraction this week. Jackson has yet to meet a challenge he hasn't solved, she will not be the first.

Hayman begins talking as Madison ushers junior staffers out of the conference room and closes the door. "Madison will create action plans for our team to conquer before the next cabinet meeting." He turns to Madison, "Let me see the list before it's distributed. I have a few items I'd like to add for the HUD and Education Secretaries. We must get those two working together instead of constantly battling. They both have plans that will benefit the same target subjects, but they fail to see the similar demographics in the other's plan." Hayman shakes his head and releases a huff of frustration.

He continues, "Rich, work with your team on press releases for the schedule next week. Obviously, it will include more updates of a personal nature since there will be dating events at the White House and around Washington. Find the balance of hyping the contest without making Jackson seem like a frivolous frat boy on spring break." Hayman levels his gaze at the president. "Don't start Jackson, we all know your thoughts on this. We have it covered. Speaking of which unless anyone else has business to cover, we need to bring in the producer for an update." Hayman pauses as he scans the faces at the large conference table. "Great, Rich let Sandra know we're ready for her."

Jackson directs his attention to Madison. He quietly speaks only to her, "I have a request but don't read anything into this at all."

Madison leans closer and concentrates on Jackson's face. "Well, this should be good. Lay it on me."

"The brunette, Haddie, right?"

Madison follows his sentence with Haddie's nickname from the crew, "The little star?"

Jackson stares at his friend, confused and curious.

"They call her the little star because she is so bright and shiny and sweet to everyone, but she avoids attention as much as possible. She's like a tiny star in the sky that shines bright even though she tries not to. Sandra should talk about her today. She is very popular with the sample audience. Why? I thought you didn't like her. You never talk to her at all. I just assumed you liked the high maintenance diva type after Vanessa."

Jackson scowls at his long time friend. "Ouch."

Madison retorts, "Seriously, Vanessa was a real peach, and the bombshell twins always seem to be at your side. It was a logical assumption. Sorry if I offended you, but you definitely have my attention now. I really like Haddie."

Jackson assesses Madison's words and demeanor before sharing his thoughts with her. "I haven't spent time with her because she seems to be avoiding me like the plague. I'm not sure if I've offended her or if she's painfully shy. I'm curious about her."

Now it's Madison's turn to study Jackson for a minute. "Haddie is definitely not shy. She is very outgoing and friendly. I have noticed her always on the outskirts. I just figured you didn't show interest so she's moving on gracefully."

"Interesting." He pauses. "It's not me. Yesterday, I gave her my best dating moves. She seems to have nothing but disdain for me. That dispels my painfully shy theory. My other theories are that she's playing some kind of hard-to-get game, but that would be opposite of the impression everyone else seems to have about her. That leaves me with the first theory that she doesn't care much for me, but then why would she want to be a contestant?"

"Didn't you read her bio? She's fascinating. I've been surprised you haven't latched on to her because of..."

"Stop!" Jackson cuts off Madison mid-sentence. "No, I didn't read any of the bios because I've been busy being the President, and because you all give me a quick overview before the dates. Now that I see her as a puzzle to solve, I feel like it would be cheating on a test if I read her bio. In fact, I don't want you to tell me anything about her at all. I'm going to learn everything the good old fashioned way, by talking to her."

Madison sits back in her chair, crosses her arms, raises her coal black eye brows, and smirks. "Well, well, well. Now I'm really interested in the outcome of this situation. What will Hayman and Rich think about this? I'm guessing you want my discretion about this conversation and you will have it; on one condition."

"I don't negotiate with terrorists, Madsi." Jackson stares into his friend's blue eyes. "If I did, what are your terms?"

Madison smiles confidently. "I want you to promise me that you'll start taking this seriously and actually try to make a connection with someone. I've known you for a long time. I believe in you and I will always have your back, but you need someone outside of the three of us to trust and talk to."

"You never cease to amaze me my friend. You have my word. I know you have my best interest at heart so I will trust you and this ridiculous, I mean, well intentioned contest."

"I will remove Haddie's bio from the pile in your bedroom and I will instruct everyone that you only want contestant information to come from me. No one needs to know about your 'puzzle' angle." Madison writes herself a note to retrieve the bio later.

Jackson reaches over and squeezes his friend's shoulder before resting back in his swivel chair.

Sandra breaks their conversation by passing out an agenda for the next three group dates. Jackson starts to sigh but looks at Madison and replaces his scowl with a fake, cheesy smile.

~Sightseeing~

Haddie is engrossed in a new novel she began reading last night. It is a romance novel that takes place during the Civil War about a general who is injured and has to stay at the house of a confederate family until he heals. The general ends up falling in love with the woman of the house whose abusive husband is thought dead in battle. The book tells of secret love, differing politics, and families ripped at the seams. The talk of a divided nation brings new feelings to mind than if she had read this book years ago, before the Separation. Today, it saddens Haddie's heart.

Her thoughts shatter by the sound of the door swinging open and Annie ringing out, "Grab your bag, gorgeous, we're going shopping!"

"What?" comes Haddie's startled response. I thought you would be down at the spa getting ready for dinner tonight." Haddie sits up in her bed and looks questioningly at her new friend.

"Do you ever read the daily call sheets?" Annie cocks her head to the side and smirks at Haddie. "This new round brings later group dinners. We have at least seven hours before we need to get ready." Annie pauses, "Well, in your case nine hours and fifty minutes." She laughs as she heads for the closet.

Haddie looks sarcastically affronted. "Hey! I spent almost thirty minutes getting ready for my first date."

Both women laugh and move around the room like seasoned roommates.

"Seriously, the village has some super quaint shops. Bonus, I heard the coffee shop has a French press with organic fresh beans. You can park yourself there with a good book if you don't want to shop. Regardless, we are getting out of here for a while."

"You had me at coffee." Haddie grabs her purse and follows Annie out the door.

"Suzanne is paired with one of the blondie twins today and Shelby, the host of *Decorating Addict*. When I first heard that the three of them lucked out with the three person date, I was frustrated. I hate that those three get the smaller date this round. They're so mean to everyone else. Not to mention cray cray. The more I thought about it, it became funny. They're going to play indoor mini golf." Annie chuckles. "Can you imagine the blondie twins playing any sport? Not to mention, those three are all so vicious, they may beat each other with putters. I heard Shelby woke up at four this morning and the twin left at five to meet their style teams. They're probably wearing stilettos and golf skirts."

Haddie and Annie laugh so hard they bump off of each other trying to get into the elevator which causes another round of laughter.

"I can't wait to hear Sophia's account of the date. Surely, Suzanne will return and tell her something. I still can't believe Sophia is already out of the running."

Haddie retells her experience with the blondie twins during the cooking class. "I was surprised to see them doubled up at a

68

cooking station, but even more amused watching them try to crack eggs. Allysia tapped on the egg shell and shook it while Allyson whispered something to it." Haddie bursts out laughing. "I've never seen an adult try to talk the shell into cracking."

The women laugh so hard they are doubled over holding their stomachs when the elevator doors open. Haddie and Annie quickly try to pull it together but the laughter still shines all over their faces.

Madison Lyn picks her head up from her tablet and stares at the two women in the elevator. She walks into the elevator and pushes a button. "I can only imagine what has you two laughing so hard that your faces are red, but I sure wish I had gotten on the elevator a floor earlier to hear it."

The doors open again and Madison exits the elevator without looking back. The doors close as Haddie and Annie resume laughing uncontrollably.

As they finally make it to the lobby, Macey is finding out from the concierge the best places for lunch. She turns and waves them over to the waiting group. Haddie is surprised to find the six other women not on the date as well as the four women already released, waiting on the hotel shuttle. Haddie has only spent time with Annie, Macey, and Sophia this week, but she has had brief conversations with the other contestants at dinner. While Haddie had close friends within her ballet companies, they rarely spent time together after hours. The competition during the day was too much to bring home at night. Going into this, she assumed this competition would deter the women from making friends.

Yet another misperception on my part.

Haddie boards the shuttle behind Annie and Macey. She sits by herself but joins in on conversations with the other women as they drive into the small town.

Priscilla is a NICU nurse from Miami and Rachelle works for a large physical therapy center for athletes in Atlanta. These were the women talking to the cheerleader on the first day.

Haddie picks their brains on hospital etiquette and the best teaching hospitals. The drive goes by so quickly as the women share stories and get to know one another.

The bus stops in front of a beautiful town square with a small garden and a statue of a girl with ice skates. The women make plans together of which stores they want to hit. The streets are lined with quaint shops and tall light posts. It looks like a postcard ski town that has been left alone from the tourist traps in other areas. Haddie takes in the small town feel as the women break off into shopping groups.

Karli, the professional cheerleader, and Jenna, the model, quickly get off the bus and walk arm in arm on their own down the street. They clearly have no intentions of bonding with the others today.

Well, maybe not all my perceptions were wrong.

Haddie and Rachelle head to the book store while the other three make their way towards a chic looking clothing boutique. They all plan to regroup at Coffee Haven in an hour. Haddie relaxes and enjoys the fresh air and scenery. As they walk to the bookstore, Rachelle asks Haddie about her therapy and physical training as a ballerina. They discuss exercises and stretches that help after knee surgery. Haddie is so glad she came on this outing. She will never admit it to Maryssa, but this is a great experience, minus the whole reality show part.

After a few hours in town, the women carry their bags and coffee cups back onto the shuttle. While Karli and Jenna huddle in the front flipping through the magazines, the other ten women show off their purchases and bond over the craziness of their situation. Just as before, the ride is over quickly and the women depart the shuttle. Lisa is standing in the lobby making sure they have all returned safe and sound. Haddie and Annie walk over and thank her for arranging the outing. Lisa smiles and reminds them they only have four hours to get ready for dinner. Haddie and Annie begin laughing all over again.

~The Pastry Chef~

Maryssa bounds into the kitchen and then to her father's office and lays a big kiss on his cheek. "Bonjour Papa!"

"My sweet girl. You are here early today, your shift doesn't start for another hour. I'm surprised you are this excited to scrub pots and pans." He studies his daughter. Every time he looks at her he sees her mother.

"I know, but I finished class early and I was hoping we had time for you to show me that trick with the pepper flowers again. I keep cutting too far down and the other veggies fall out over the sides. It looks more like a massacre than a beautiful creation." Maryssa smiles at her dad like only a daughter can.

Malik stands as he takes Maryssa's hand and leads her towards the kitchen. "It's all in the knife you use. The pepper has to like the knife or it won't cooperate."

Maryssa loves how her father talks about food like it's living and breathing. The two walk towards the chopping station as Malik grabs two peppers and two pairing knives.

71

"We don't have much time. I need to prepare dinner for a meeting Hayman has planned for tonight. He's flying in specifically for this and flying back out tomorrow morning. I'm not sure what the rush is, but he seemed very adamant that tonight's dinner be perfect." Malik rubs the back of his neck trying to figure out Hayman, knowing that it is useless.

"That guy gives me the creeps." Maryssa watches her father make the first slice into the pepper like a surgeon beginning an incision.

"You know I'm not a fan either, but we're supposed to love our enemies. Even the ones that drive us crazy." Malik says the last part for himself.

Maryssa replies, "I was actually talking about the new guy lurking over by the pantry door watching us, but I definitely don't like Hayman either."

Malik glances over at Martin then returns to his pepper lesson. "That is Martin, Oscar's cousin. He is quiet and focused. I'm sure he will come out of his shell. He has a cranberry and lemon scone recipe that will make you cry, it's so good. He's very quiet, but a hard worker. You should help at his station today before you need to serve. He is making caramel apple pie. He has a fruit preserver that uses magic, I believe. The apples are so sweet, there can be no other explanation." Malik quietly laughs at his own joke as he directs Maryssa's hand on the bright red pepper.

"Have you spoken with Haddie yet?" Malik attempts to change the subject. No father wants his daughter noticing a handsome man who can bake, and worse, one with an enticing Scottish accent.

This must be what Mary thought of me and my French. I need to call my mother-in-law and apologize.

72

"Only briefly. She called while I was on my way to class. We were cut off while I was riding the Metro and I couldn't reach her back. She was on her way skiing. I think she had to sneak in the call because she was whispering." Maryssa sighed. "I hope she has an open mind about this and enjoys herself. I don't want her to miss an opportunity just to prove me wrong. She is so stubborn, you know?"

Malik laughs as he continues shaping his vegetable canvas. "Ah, yes, I do know. She shares that particular trait with her cousin."

Malik nudges Maryssa's arm. "Well, I have my sources and I have been checking on our little one all week. She is having fun and relaxing as you encouraged. As for any romantic sparks, I believe she will need to let her guard down a little for that to happen. I trust in a plan that is higher than ours. We must watch how things unfold and bloom for her. Much like your pepper, which I believe is perfect, just like you."

Maryssa holds a perfect tulip shaped pepper basket in her hands. She beams at her father and relaxes her shoulders as the tension rolls off her back. He leans down and places a kiss on the tip of her nose.

"Thanks, Papa."

"Martin." Malik calls out down the hallway. "Do you have time to teach my daughter how you make that amazing caramel drizzle?"

Maryssa closes her eyes and rolls her head backwards. "Oy vey, Daddy."

~She's Special~

Sadie pulls out containers from her large black steel rimmed case. Brushes follow the small black canisters of make-up. She organizes everything in her little corner as Haddie walks into the large ballroom.

"I brought you an iced coffee, three squirts of caramel and whole milk." Haddie hands Sadie a tall plastic cup with a purple straw. "That's how you like it, right?"

"How did you remember that? We had one brief conversation at the coffee cart two days ago. Are you buttering me up for something?" Sadie gladly takes the coffee and waits expectantly at Haddie.

Haddie smiles back. "I grew up working in my family's restaurant. Combine my genetic food service abilities with my coffee obsession and I could be a world-renowned barista!" Haddie sips her iced mochaccino and sighs with happiness.

"As for buttering you up, I'm merely showing my gratitude for your work. Instead of throwing roses on stage, I come bearing gifts of caffeine. Which in my humble opinion, is more practical." Haddie sits in the tall chair. "I am clay in the hands of a master artisan. Do your magic Miss Sadie."

"I thought you didn't want to win. Why do you need my magic?" Sadie sardonically replies.

"Oh Sadie. I don't care about the date. I would wear a paper bag over my head if they allowed me to. My roommate forced me to take off my sweatpants and she's in the group date with me. That should speak volumes. You're lucky I changed out of my holey t-shirt. I'm just a lover of art and I am truly honored to be your canvas. Lay it on me."

Sadie sets down her drink and grabs her large foundation brush. "Haddie, you completely baffle me. I have worked with countless reality TV stars and have had my share of celebrity clients, but you are an anomaly to me."

"Why is that, oh wise one?"

"You have danced in front of thousands, toured the world, and are now in the hottest dating competition in history and yet, you have zero ego. You constantly put others first and genuinely seem to care more about those around you than yourself. You are either a Machiavellian mastermind, or you are a very rare bird."

Haddie chokes on her sip of coffee as she listens to Sadie. "That statement fills me with so many sentiments I can't decide where to begin in response. First, you are too kind. I am a hot mess in a pretty dress. Second, I'm a firm believer in the Golden Rule. In my experience, you reap what you sow. Lastly, what a sad world we live in that kindness is a rarity, but psychopathy is not." Haddie shakes her head in disbelief and continues. "I just treat others the way I want to be treated. I am from a big Italian family. We work as a team and there is no I in team. I think our world would be a much better place if we all did that." Haddie stares off in thought.

"Yep, you're an anomaly. A glitch in society and surely in the world of celebrity. Most people I work with, only reap enough to sow exactly what they want. Or they pay others to do the reaping and sowing."

Sadie picks up the eyeliner and starts on Haddie's eyes. "So, are you excited about bowling today?"

"The last time I bowled, I got a strike on my very first try." Haddie beamed. "Unfortunately, it was the next lane over from where I started." She winked at Sadie before laughing at the

75

memory. "I hope the resort has a good insurance policy. Now if we were playing a game of HORSE, I would be in my element. My cousin and I have been known to hustle a few games now and then. No one expects ballerinas to be ballers."

Sadie stops applying make-up and looks at Haddie. "Now that, I would pay to see!"

Both women laugh and are interrupted by Madison Lyn. "I'm starting to wonder if Miss Robinson should start a comedy tour. Every time I see her, people are laughing hysterically." Madison smiles and turns to Sadie. "President Cashe needs a little touch up when you get a minute. He got a little bit of windburn on the mountain this morning. Hopefully, he'll skip tomorrow and let it heal a bit. When you're finished with Haddie, let Sandra know and I'll send him to your station."

"Sure thing."

Madison turns to walk away and says over her shoulder, "Let me know if you take your act on the road, I could use a good laugh."

Sadie finishes Haddie's make-up and stands back to look for flaws. "Perfect." She puts the used brushes aside and turns Haddie to see the mirror better.

"I'm speechless. You are so gifted. Thank you, Sadie." Haddie says in awe of her new friend. "Well, at least I'll look good making bowling ball sized holes in the walls. I'm sure the secret service agents will keep the president far from me today. I could cause a national disaster otherwise." Haddie chuckles as she ponders if she could be so lucky.

Sadie walks over to a bag by the wall. She pulls out an aquamarine colored scarf and walks back to Haddie. Sadie wraps the scarf in a knot and squirts just a dab of perfume in Haddie's hair. "There, now you're a masterpiece."

Haddie kindly turns towards Sadie and gives her a hug. "Thank you so much. You know, you're pretty sweet yourself."

"Please don't let that get out! I would hate to ruin my evil witch image. Now get out of here so I can work on His Highness."

Haddie hurries out the door of the ballroom just as Madison comes back in to talk to Sandra. She walks towards Sadie to check on her timing and quizzes the spunky artist. "Is that your scarf? The one Jackson said he loved the other day?"

Sadie weighs her answer. She levels her gaze at Madison and says, "Maybe."

Madison conspiratorially looks at Sadie, winks, then walks away. "If you're ready, I'll get the president."

Chapter 4

~No Wall Flower~

Jackson is looking forward to his group date today. Not only does he love bowling, but he has another chance to crack the nut that is Haddie. He reviews everything he learned about her during the first date as he walks towards the bowling alley.

Her family loves to cook. She doesn't seem to like me much. She's not a defense attorney. Yep, I have a lot of ground to cover today. Maybe I'll start with my joke about diplomacy and the Pope.

Madison is walking beside Jackson as she reminds him about the backgrounds of the women on the date. Everyone but Haddie. "I'm not giving you any puzzle pieces, but would a little friendly advice be okay?" Madison pauses and glances at her friend.

He nods his approval, but stays silent.

"Her roommate is also on this date, Annie. They have become very good friends. Women trust the judgement of their friends. That's all I'm saying. Oh, and please don't tell any jokes. They're truly terrible. You could not be a comedian."

"I'm truly offended. My jokes always get big laughs." Jackson argues.

"You are the most powerful man in the world. People have to laugh at your jokes. Trust me, you have many great qualities, being a comedian is not one of them."

"I'll take your suggestions under advisement Miss Lyn, but I'm keeping my diplomacy joke ready just in case." Jackson mockingly scowls at Madison as he opens the door to the bowling alley. The smell of stale beer and pine floors wafts into his nostrils. He breathes deeply.

Ah, I love that smell. Pappy Joe would love this old alley.

He walks towards the women who are putting on their standard bowling shoes. They quickly finish as they see him enter the room. Karli is the first to greet him.

What is she wearing? Good grief, she'll never be able to bowl in that skirt! Has this woman ever been bowling?

"Karli, it's good to see you again." Karli reaches out and gives Jackson a hug. "Where are your shoes? Last time I checked, they didn't make high heels for bowling." He laughs at himself.

Karli places a hand on his arm. "You are so funny. No, Jackson, I don't bowl. I wouldn't even know how to begin. I'll just sit beside you and be your personal cheerleader." She flashes her million-dollar smile. "Unless you want to teach me. I could use some help with my backstroke."

"Thanks, but since we're not swimming or playing golf, I think you'll be fine. Plus, I wouldn't want to be unfair to the other ladies."

Karli pouts and bats her eyelashes. Neither of which influence Jackson. He continues his greetings.

He extends hugs to both Annie and Rachelle. He notices that Haddie continues tying her shoes as slowly as she can. She nods hello and smiles an obligatory greeting.

"Jackson," Rachelle beams, "Haddie was just telling us that she is a terrible bowler. Apparently last time she played, an ER visit was involved. I told her that I would be able to work any of us out later if we got hurt. I'm great at massaging aching muscles."

"I think she's more concerned about breaking the actual bowling alley." Annie laughs and tries to catch Jackson's attention. She centers herself in front of the other women and leans in towards Jackson.

"I don't usually talk business on dates, but I saw on the news today some coverage on the education reform. My partner and I worked with the governor of California on their reform plan last year. I would love to share the information we learned. We found some fascinating differences between female and male learning outcomes."

Annie links her arm in Jackson's as she directs him towards the rack for the house balls. Karli glares daggers at Annie while keeping a death grip on Jackson's other arm.

Haddie quietly comes up behind Rachelle. "Really? Work us out? Massages? I'm so disappointed in you." Haddie laughs as Rachelle drops her head into her hands.

"I know! I don't know why I said that. I get so nervous."

The women giggle as they head over to the ball return to start the game.

Haddie sits on the opposite side of the chairs from Annie, Jackson, and Karli. Rachelle sits in the computer chair next to Jackson. Haddie watches the triangle of women surrounding him. What a surreal experience watching these two women, whom Haddie has mad respect for, fawning over the same man. It is competition as its finest.

Haddie kicks off the game by lofting the ball. Her yank shot causes the heavy ball to bounce once before slowly rolling, eventually landing in the right gutter before it even hits the halfway mark on the alley. She raises her hands in the air and cheers. She turns and sees the others staring at her in confusion. "Last time I played, the ball went into the neighbor's lane." Haddie shrugs her shoulders. "This is a good shot for me."

Jackson laughs and heads to the ball return. "Here, let me get that for you."

Haddie jumps in front of him. "No thank you. I can get my own ball."

Jackson smirks at her. "In all honesty, I was concerned that you would get your scarf caught and keep your ER streak alive, but by all means..." Jackson waves his hand towards the ball which just came back to the rack. "Your scarf is beautiful by the way. That's a great color on you. It brings out the blue in your eyes."

Haddie looks unbelievingly at Jackson and grabs her ball a little too hard while forgetting it's weight. She loses her balance and falls right into Jackson's waiting arms behind her. She jumps back on her feet quickly and utters a contrite, "Thank you." He chuckles behind her as she heads back to the lane.

So much for not noticing me. I'm such a klutz. Ugh.

Jackson enjoys his best game ever while conversing with the women and watching Haddie. Thanks to Madison, he manages to learn a lot about Haddie's thoughtfulness and quirks from engaging Annie in conversation. There isn't a lull in conversation the entire game. He enjoys watching Haddie, Annie, and Rachelle interact. They seem like long lost friends.

After completing a five-bagger, he attempts to sit beside Haddie. Karli follows him and sits on the opposite side of Haddie, putting Haddie in the middle of the two.

"So Haddie, tell me about yourself. The only things I know about you are that you are a great cook and a terrible bowler. Oh, and according to Annie, you snore when you are congested." Jackson sits back sideways in his hard-plastic bench chair and places one arm on the chair back partly behind Haddie.

"There really isn't much to tell. I enjoy sweatpants, ice cream, and binge-watching TV shows when I'm not studying in the library."

Karli snickers and twirls her hair in her left hand. "She's right about that. Haddie here is our little wall flower. She just reads and skis. Very boring. Sticks to herself. I'm sure this is the first time she's been out of her home state."

I was right. She is the skier. Interesting.

Karli continues, "Good thing she's friends with Annie or she'd probably stay in her room all day alone, like an old hermit. That's what we can call you, Hermit Haddie." She amuses herself.

Annie gasps and Rachelle stares open mouthed at Karli. Karli bore her claws and the others were shocked, but not Haddie. Haddie has seen women like Karli many times before in her dancing career. Karli doesn't phase Haddie.

Jackson opens his mouth to come to Haddie's defense.

Haddie shushes him with the raising of her hand. She turns to face Karli. "You are correct Karli. I am very selective with whom I spend my time with and Annie and Rachelle are phenomenal women. Did you know that both are published and rising stars in their respective fields? They fascinate me. I have learned so much from them. As a ballerina, I've been blessed to travel all over the world. I love watching people. You can learn so much about a person based on how they treat others. I've learned to see beyond the surface to find the beauty in others. Unfortunately, I've also learned that with some people, beauty really is only skin deep. While you think I'm being a, wall flower? Is that what you called me? Yes, a wall flower. Did you even stop to think that maybe I'm a hermit around you for a reason? Mean girls come in all different shapes and sizes. I choose to see the beauty in others, but in some people, you need a magnifying glass."

Karli recoils from Haddie's words and rolls her eyes.

Haddie turns back to the group and sees three sets of wide eyes and open mouths. "Annie, I believe it is your turn. Go get 'em sister." Haddie stands up and goes to sit beside Rachelle.

In the background, behind the cameras, Madison leans in to Lisa, "I guess we know who is getting the veto roses tonight, rah rah team!" Both women chuckle.

~President Playboy~

The next morning, Haddie rises early and heads out to the slopes. She can't shake the feeling that she's being followed, but she has been uptight since her run in with Karli.

What a mean girl! I love how she verbally attacks me and then blames me for being vetoed. The nerve of her!

Haddie shakes her head. To make matters worse, somehow Uncle Malik heard about her outburst and sent a cryptic note to her via Chef Maxwell reminding her to represent herself, her family, and her faith well. She knew what that meant. It was time to refocus and be still this morning.

83

Haddie enjoys the view from the ski lift. The snow in the trees, the vast mountains. What a glorious morning. She is overwhelmed by the creation before her and the Creator of it all. The slopes are quiet this morning. She can't see anyone below her and no others are on the lift. She whispers a prayer of thanksgiving for the quiet. She needs some stillness to reflect on this entire situation. She closes her eyes and feels the cold on her face and in her lungs. She breathes deeply through her nose and out her mouth.

The lift slows as it reaches the top of the mountain. Haddie glides down the ramp and heads west. She passes the last slope marked for guests and ducks behind a few more trees. She finally makes it to her destination. She stands at the precipice of fresh snow and a long, adventurous trail. She takes in the view then jump starts her run enjoying the mixture of cold powder and warm sun hitting her face.

Halfway down the mountain, she feels the presence of someone else. She turns just in time to see another skier coming up on her right. The build indicates that it is a male skier, and a skilled one at that. She watches as he bends and carves his way down the mountain. She admires his form and wonders if it is the ski instructor she met last week who told her about this secret run.

As they edge closer to the bottom of the slope, the mystery man slows and cuts a hard left. He seems to be waiting for her. The lodge is visible from where they are, but in the distance. Haddie feels uncomfortable and tries to maintain her distance. She stops near the man, but closer to the lodge and the edge of the next trail.

The man pulls down his goggles and smiles. Haddie rolls her eyes and turns. She starts to skate ski to get away from Jackson quickly. She notices the secret service agents on skis standing off a bit. She hears him behind her which makes her skate even faster.

"Haddie, wait!" Jackson races to catch her. "You win. I give up. What is your problem with me?" He stills, then jokes, "Are you a republican?"

That stops her in her tracks. Haddie turns and icily responds to the President. "That. That glib, arrogant attitude about the state of the country right now. That is my problem. You should be working to unify, and yet you are.....here; flirting with models and cheerleaders." Haddie waves her arms then turns to continue her drive to get back to the lodge and away from him. Over her shoulder, she yells, "And stop following me!"

She hears him laugh and she purses her lips.

"Why are you here then? Why would you want the chance to date such a narcissistic playboy?"

She turns slowly to face him. "My cousin signed me up without my knowledge. By the time I found out, it was too late to get out of it without drawing unwanted attention. I thought I would get a relaxing vacation out of the deal, but you must not be good at reading nonverbals. Just veto me already, please."

"Is that really what you want?"

"Yes!" She raises her arms in frustration and her voice along with them to accentuate her point.

He pauses as he takes in her words and wishes. "You have me all wrong, you know. If you would take the time to get to know me, you might actually see that we have a lot in common. I thought I was the cliché, but you seem to be the critical one. I thought more of you, based on how highly everyone around here talks about you. I guess I was wrong about you. Oh well, your loss." Jackson swishes past Haddie with the agents swiftly on his tail leaving Haddie staring in disbelief.

Jackson releases the bindings and lifts his boots from his skis. He places the long skis on the rack and brushes off snow from his pants. He sees Haddie coming towards him at a swift pace so he purposefully takes his time.

Game. Set. Match. This should be fun.

"Mr. President, wait a minute." Haddie stops right in front of him and frantically tries to release her bindings so they are on even ground. "I am sorry. You are right. I judged you based on what I have heard about you. I have not given you a chance." She rambles, almost a mumble, "I don't know what has come over me. I still don't think we would make a match, but I should at least be polite and listen to you. Again, I am truly sorry, sir. You don't even have to send me flowers. I veto myself." Haddie lowers her head.

"No."

"Excuse me, sir?"

"No. you will not be vetoed. Your punishment is staying in this ridiculous competition and getting to know me. And please, stop calling me sir! My name is Jackson."

Jackson walks into the lodge as Haddie stares open-mouthed at him.

Dear Lord, why can't I ever keep my big mouth shut?

~Hayman Barnes~

Hayman makes his way home after his private dinner at the White House. His driver pulls into the circular driveway and stops in front of the red brick colonial. The outside of his stately home is lit with lampposts. The inside lights indicate they have a full house tonight. Hayman rubs his neck, sighs, and opens the door. He hears music blaring from his teenage daughter's room. He drops his keys on the oak entry table and fingers through the basket of mail. He hears talking in the kitchen as he heads towards the back of his house while loosening his necktie.

Chanel, his wife's white bichon frise, alerts everyone that Hayman is home. The irritating noise prompts Hayman's head to pound even more. He is exhausted from his day. This morning came at four am for him. He flew from Colorado after his breakfast briefing with Jackson. He arrived in DC at two in the afternoon. He managed to meet with a few support staff before his dinner. After much negotiation, he cajoled the nominated secretary of education, the presidents of two teachers' unions, and the leader for the association of charter schools to agree to dinner. He had planned it for weeks, unbeknownst to Jackson. He wanted to hammer out details while saving Jackson from the drama. Hayman has already worked out a deal with the National Principal's Association. The only loose end is a homeschool contingency. He'll meet with them next week. He planned the details of the dinner meeting down to the menu.

"Chanel, stop it. Come here baby girl." Hayman's polished and plump wife Janice, picks up the ball of fluff and walks to her husband. He leans down so she can place a kiss on his check. "I'm so glad you're home honey, even if only for one night. You must be exhausted. How was your special dinner?" She takes his suit jacket.

Hayman walks further into the kitchen and places a hand on both of his sons sitting at the counter doing homework. His oldest son Jamie will graduate from high school at the end of the

87

semester, with the other following a year later. Their youngest daughter is a freshman in high school. She never leaves her bedroom, which is fine with Hayman. The boys turn to see their father. Jamie offers Hayman a plate of cookies.

"No thank you, son. I just came from dinner. It was a very successful evening, and yes, I am depleted. I fly out first thing in the morning. Jackson and I have a conference call with the Canadian Prime Minister in between his dating rounds."

Hayman pulls out a chair beside his youngest son Chad. "I thought you all would be in bed by now. I hope you weren't waiting up for me."

"Jamie has eight hundred fifty points after tonight's game. He's on pace to break one thousand this season. He sealed the deal with an epic three pointer going into halftime." Chad boasts about the brother he worships. Jamie looks expectantly at his father then lowers his head.

Janice puts the boys' glasses in the sink and wipes the counter. "We got home an hour ago, but the boys both have homework to finish. Celebratory snickerdoodles were ready before the game, just in case. Are you sure you don't want one? They are your favorite."

"I can't eat another bite. The cook made apple pie for dessert." Hayman shakes his head in disgust. "I hate apple pie, but I was obligated to eat it so I didn't appear rude."

Hayman stands and walks to the cabinet where he pulls out a heavy crystal glass and a decanter filled with dark amber liquid. He pours himself a drink and leans against the quartz countertop.

"I specifically planned each part of the meal based on the likes and dislikes of my guests. I went over the menu with Chef

Lavalier last week and again on the phone yesterday. He completely disregarded my dessert wishes. I requested tiramisu, but his wait staff walked in with apple pie! People expect more than apple pie when they are invited to a private dinner at the White House." Hayman rubs his temple and continues his rant. "Then he has the audacity to enter the dining room and ask how we enjoyed the meal. When my guests began thanking him for a lovely meal, he soaked in their adoration. That's when I pointed out that I was the one who designed the menu. That stupid cook began speaking in French, and the next secretary of education must also speak the language because the two of them started laughing."

"Oh no," Janice looks at Hayman with rapt attention. "That is so rude. Did anyone translate?"

"That's what makes the story worse. When I asked, Lavalier laughs and says, 'You picking the menu is like the paint salesman taking credit for a painting.' That ungrateful servant!" Hayman snarls while refilling his glass.

"He can't do that Dad." Jamie closes his book. "Jackson needs to fire that guy!"

"Honey, I can't believe someone would do that. It is horribly rude for an employee of his caliber to undermine you like that. You need to tell Jackson. How awful for you."

Chad adds, "You should have thrown his apple pie right at him."

Hayman relishes the support of his family. "I don't want to burden Jackson this week. *Future FLOTUS* is making him increasingly irritable. I will not add a wayward cook to his agenda. I'll address this when we're back in town. I will tell you one thing, Lavalier crossed a line he will regret."

89

~Daughterly Wisdom~

Maryssa helps clean the prep stations. The kitchen staff slowly clears out one at a time. Malik offers to finish the dishes and tells the rest of his staff to leave early. He is banging the pots and pans. Maryssa senses his frustration and comes up behind him to dry.

"Are you okay, Daddy?" She takes the pot from his hands before handing him another one.

"I let Hayman get the best of me tonight." Malik rolls his neck back and forth quickly to release tension. "The lady fingers for the tiramisu were crushed by the delivery man this morning. We had no choice but to change the dessert. I couldn't run it by him because he was traveling and then in back to back meetings. He had mentioned that one of his guests was coming from Martinsburg, West Virginia where apple orchards abound. I thought an apple pie would be perfect and we had some extra jars the distributor sent for testing. I didn't expect a pat on the back from that man, he probably doesn't even do that for his own kids, but his insult went right through me. I insulted him. Which was wrong." More sulking. "He must think I'm a trained seal. He picks the menu and all I to do is execute it. He is a pompous jerk!" Malik rinses off the last pan and dries his hands.

Malik stews as Maryssa watches and patiently waits for him to calm down. They stand in silence other than the sounds from the water.

"Every time Haddie or I were faced with a harsh review, a wise man always shared Proverbs 15:1 with us, 'A gentle answer turns away wrath, but a harsh word stirs up anger'." Maryssa leans her head on her Dad's shoulder. "You are a very kind and discerning man. You always speak in love. Don't beat yourself up for one slip. Pray for gentle words next time you deal with Mr. Barnes. That's the advice you always give us."

90

Malik leans down and kisses his daughter's head. "When did you grow up to be so wise? You are becoming more and more like your mother every day."

"My Dad is pretty great too." Maryssa pulls away and winks at Malik. "Are we all finished here? I could use a ride home. Or I could just ride the Metro. Home. Alone. At night." She flashes her father a hopeful smile.

"So very subtle of you. Of course I'm driving you home." Malik dries his hands then takes the last pot from Maryssa.

She heads for her locker and yells over her shoulder, "Bring that apple pie and we can eat some at my place." She mumbles, "Someone should appreciate it."

~ Reconnaissance~

Jackson stares out the window of his makeshift office at the majestic mountains. He requests that his briefing with Hayman be as early as possible this morning so he has time for one run before his first date of round 3. The first date has Jackson going on a sleigh ride through town with the nurse and the physical therapist followed by a painting class with one of the twins and Susanne. Tomorrow has Jackson ice skating with the model and the other blond twin in the morning followed by a tour of the region in a helicopter with Annie and Haddie.

"Are you even listening to me?" Hayman's gruff voice rings through the speaker on the conference table. "Is he listening to me?"

"Yes, he's listening and writing notes. Apparently he's having trouble writing and talking at the same time. He has that concentration look on his face." Madison covers for Jackson

91

while shooting him daggers. Jackson lifts his shoulders and tilts his head in apology to Madison.

"Hayman, I think I can handle the rest of the meeting. I'm sure you want to take a quick nap before you land. The rest of the agenda is mostly housekeeping items. I can take over and review with Jackson."

Hayman offers a long pause before a reluctant, "Fine, but make sure he's ready for the cabinet meeting tomorrow afternoon." There is a click on the line and silence follows.

"Go, Jackson. We'll cover the rest later. I know you're dying to hit the slopes before the sleigh ride. I haven't seen Haddie walk down the hall yet, so you might catch her if you hurry. Just make sure to tell Hayman we covered everything on this list and don't be late for Sadie!" Madison shakes her head and waves her hand towards the door.

Jackson jumps out of his seat, places a quick kiss on his friend's cheek, and rushes out the door. Shouting, "You're the best Madsi!"

After changing quickly in his suite, he races to the ski rack where he attaches skis and grabs poles. He feels only slightly guilty about using his secret service detail to check on Haddie's whereabouts. He nonchalantly waits at the bottom of the chair lift until she skis over to the base.

Haddie shakes her head when she sees him waiting. Not able to avoid this moment without a blatant blow-off, she makes her way to the lift. "You seriously need to stop stalking me. This is getting ridiculous. Don't think I won't file a restraining order just because you're the president. You still have to follow the law." Haddie bellows as she approaches him.

"Technically, I'm not stalking. I see it as a reconnaissance mission. Word on the mountain is that the ski pro gave you the inside track on all the best trails. I'm just trying to get in a good run before I have to govern the country today. Instead of seeing me as a stalker, you should pat yourself on the back for doing your civic duty for helping the President." Jackson smirks and winks at her.

Haddie takes a deep breath in wary defeat. They both glide over to the chair lift and wait for the next chair to swing around and clip them at the knees, knocking them both into their seats. The lift screeches and squeals as it slowly makes its way up the side of the mountain. The cold air feels so crisp and clean as it hits Jackson's face. He looks at Haddie and stares. Her eyes are closed, her head tilts toward the sun, and she is glowing in the sunrise.

"Wait a minute. Is that? Is that a smile? Yes, yes, it is. You are smiling in my presence. You are not miserable and glowering. I see this as a small victory." Jackson gloats and turns his head forward while peeking at Haddie.

Haddie offers an exaggerated eye roll. "Glowering? Really? I don't glower. Besides, the smile isn't for you, it is for the glorious morning." She pauses, "And also for the silence, which you shattered with your commentary of my facial expressions."

"A smile and a smirk in one conversation. I think I'm growing on you Haddie Robinson."

"Would it be considered an assassination attempt if I helped you out of your chair at this height?" Haddie sweetly smiles at him.

"I believe so. If you wait until we get closer to the top, you could probably get away with a broken bone, but then I'll just guilt you into sitting with me in the emergency room." Jackson retorts.

Haddie attempts and fails to hold in a chuckle. "What makes you think, guilt works on me?"

"Apparently, everyone on this production thinks you are sweet as a peach. I wouldn't know because you seem to hate me for some reason, but I'd be willing to bet that you would feel awful for hurting, even me, and would spend your day nursing me back to health. If not, I could always press charges on you." Jackson stares forward but sees Haddie's shocked expression from his peripheral vision.

Haddie crosses her arms. "First of all, blackmail is a crime, Mr. President. Secondly, I'm positive Priscilla or Rachelle will gladly, and more expertly take care of easing your pain. Maybe a fall would knock some of that smugness out of you."

Jackson sadly looks forward.

Haddie feels convicted by her attitude and turns her head towards Jackson. "I don't hate you. I'm so sorry, I keep giving you that impression. I don't know why I behave like this around you. It's not who I am. I just don't fit into your world. This isn't my thing and I'm definitely not your type but that doesn't give me the right to threaten bodily injury."

"There you go again, assuming you know my type. If you would get to know me, I might surprise you." Jackson scoots to the edge of the chair and holds his hand out in anticipation. "This is our stop. After you."

Haddie and Jackson hop off the chair and slide down the lift slope. Jackson follows Haddie beyond the last row of trees to the west. He stops as he rounds the last evergreen and gasps. The

94

view is spectacular. He notices Haddie again raising her face towards the sun with her eyes closed.

She is remarkable.

A smiling Haddie looks at Jackson before pushing off and shouting over her shoulder, "Last one down, buys dinner for nine people tonight."

Chapter 5

~Closing the Gap~

Haddie and Annie eat ice cream in Priscilla's and Rachelle's room so they can support whichever woman gets vetoed tonight. They split a half gallon of rocky road with whip cream.

"I hate that they paired us against roommates for this round." Priscilla scoops a large spoonful out of her bowl."

"Annie is the only one who doesn't need to worry. Even if she gets the roses tomorrow, Haddie will probably rip them out of her arms and veto herself." Rachelle laughs and the other three women follow suit.

Annie, nudges Haddie in the arm, "On contraire, I think Jackson is quite smitten with our little Haddie. We should have seen it coming. Haddie has been trying to get vetoed, but all she has managed to do is make herself more intriguing. She's the dark horse. I'd hate her, if I didn't like her so much."

Haddie chokes on her bite, then lowers her head in defeat. "I don't know what else I could have done. I have tried everything. The man knows I don't like him. I've been so rude to him. Surely, he must realize we're not compatible. He's wasting his time and energy. I even asked him to veto me and he denied my plea. Maybe I should be sugary sweet and bat my eye lashes next time."

"Either that or tell him you have fifteen cats in your apartment." Rachelle laughs hysterically.

Annie puts down her spoon and looks directly at Haddie. "I don't know Had, the more I get to know him, the more I think you'll like him. You haven't even given him a chance. Don't you

96

at least owe it to yourself, to try? You're already here and you've made it this far, what's it cost to give him a shot?"

"Um, I'm sorry, has she forgotten that she's going head to head with Haddie tomorrow?" Rachelle looks at Priscilla. Priscilla shrugs and eats another spoonful of ice cream. "You're lucky I didn't push you in horse poop today to win." Rachelle laughs as she squirts more whip cream in her bowl.

This launches all four women into a fit of hysterical laughter.

The knock on the door silences the room. Priscilla and Rachelle link arms as they slowly make their way to the door of their room. It opens and the doorman is holding a large bouquet of yellow roses. "Rachelle Guinn, you have been vetoed."

Priscilla places her arm behind Rachelle's back and squeezes. Rachelle takes the bouquet of roses and thanks the messenger. The two women walk back into the room together. Haddie and Annie rush to hug Rachelle. Cameras following them.

Rachelle takes the envelope from the roses and hands the bouquet to Priscilla. Inside is a handwritten, personal note from Jackson.

Rachelle,

It has truly been an honor to date you this week. Your spirit and fire has kept me on my toes. You are so much fun to be around and I've had blast getting to know you. I hope you find a partner who matches your enthusiasm for life. You deserve nothing but the best!

J

"Why does he have to be such a nice guy? The personal note makes me like him even more." Rachelle tries to laugh through her newly forming tears. "Now I really regret not pushing you in horse poop."

Rachelle halfheartedly laughs. She sits on the bed and grabs her pillow. Haddie starts cleaning up the bowls and ice cream as Annie sits beside Rachelle to comfort their friend.

"I never thought winning would feel so bad." Priscilla sits across from Rachelle and Annie.

"I never thought getting flowers from a man would feel so bad. Maybe I'll draw a mustache on your face tonight while you sleep." Rachelle throws her pillow at Priscilla. "I guess now I have more time to eat ice cream and ski with Haddie. One of y'all better win or I'll be really mad."

~Falling Head Over Heels~

Light is creeping in through the bedroom window. Silence fills the hotel room as Haddie stretches and climbs out of bed. She skips skiing this morning. Annie knows that Jackson has been following Haddie on the slopes, but she doesn't want to spend extra time with him on Annie's date day. Annie has left for the salon by the time Haddie wakes. She hits the gym first thing for a treadmill, then jumps in the shower. She pulls on her favorite pair of jeans and a thin, gray wool sweater. She opts for her purple, comfy Converse instead of hiking boots since they will be in a helicopter. Once last look at herself in the mirror. Her mind races as she heads down to Sadie's table.

There is such a heaviness on her heart this morning. She feels terrible for Rachelle. It's also hard knowing that one of her other two friends will feel the same in the next few days. Annie and Haddie stayed with their friends last night until midnight.

Rachelle felt better by the time they left, but it was so hard watching her process the veto.

She thinks about Jackson and wonders if he and Annie are right. Would she like him, or at least give him a chance if he wasn't President Jackson Cashe? Does she really know him or what the media has made of him? As she sits in Sadie's chair, Haddie can't help but feel badly for how she has treated Jackson. He is right, she has been judging him harshly on what she's heard about him. She has no idea who he is as a person. She enjoys the banter between them and his tenacity. This doesn't mean she is attracted to him or that she wants to win the competition, but she vows to be kinder to him. That is how she was taught.

Sadie recognizes that Haddie is quiet this morning. The two women barely speak while Sadie works on Haddie's hair and make-up. Haddie thanks Sadie as always and praises her gift, but her smile is not as bright today.

Sadie stops Haddie before she leaves the room. She pulls a windbreaker from the rack of clothes provided by the show. The wool-lined windbreaker is dark gray with purple and aquamarine stitching intertwined throughout. It is form fitting and well made. "Take this with you. I heard it's chilly in the helicopter. You'll need something over your sweater. Enjoy the view." Sadie smiles.

Haddie takes the jacket and thanks Sadie one last time before heading to the lobby where they are scheduled to meet the car for the hangar.

Annie sits on a leather couch in the lobby with two carry out cups in front of her on the table. She waves Haddie over when she sees her in the doorway.

99

"Here, I got you a vanilla latte while we wait. Sandra just said that Jackson is running a few minutes late. I'm sure it's something involving national security." Annie jokes.

Haddie sits uncomfortably beside Annie, feeling strangely odd around her roommate.

"I love your jacket, the threading is your favorite color mixed with Jackson's favorite, it's adorable." Annie sits back into the couch and reaches out to place her hand over Haddie's. "Is it just me, or is it weird today?"

Haddie sighs in relief. "Annie, I don't know what to do. It's obvious to me that Jackson and I are not compatible. I barely like him. I have asked him to veto me, but somehow, I've made this a game to him. I don't know if I should be mean to him or syrupy sweet and clingy. I'm obviously rooting for you. Every time I try to sabotage myself, I actually make myself more intriguing to him. What do I do?"

Annie turns and smiles sweetly at Haddie. "I don't want to win because you sabotage yourself. I want to win because Jackson can't stop thinking about me. You told me before my first group date that you believe everything works out the way it is supposed to. If you truly believe that, then today will end up the way it's supposed to, for all three of us. Do me a favor though, try to enjoy yourself. You might be surprised." Annie sips her latte and clasps Haddie's hand. "Enough weirdness between us. Break a leg, friend."

Haddie and Annie sit comfortably for a moment longer drinking their coffee when they hear Jackson's voice coming up behind them. "My apologies Ladies, I didn't think my call would last that long. Are we ready to soar above the Rockies?"

Annie jumps to her feet and walks towards Jackson. "I can't wait!"

Sandra ushers the three of them into the back of Jackson's town car where she and Lisa sit opposite of them. The ride to the hangar consists of directions from Sandra and her assistant as to camera angles and headphones. Sandra finishes her lecture as they pull into the small gated airfield.

Annie enters the helicopter first. Sandra instructs Jackson to enter next so the women flank him. Two military pilots secure the three passengers and their guide. Sandra ensures the headphones, mics, and mounted cameras are working before motioning the okay to fire up the chopper blades.

As they rise above the hangar and head higher towards the San Juan Mountains, they all nervously shift and try to take in the view. The sun is shining and the sky is the perfect shade of blue. They fly over gold and silver mine sites, as well as snow covered mountainsides. The most magnificent view is found over the Durango and Silverton gorge. The railroad tresses from the Animas Canyon and Molas Pass are spectacular. They marvel at the beauty below them. The guide shouts into his mic so they can hear him over the intense whirring of the blades. He provides the history of the region and geographic highlights. It is an awe-inspiring trip.

Jackson asks the guide questions. He fills in the backstory for Haddie and Annie based on his passion for American history. Haddie looks at Jackson and it strikes her how excited and childlike he seems. Annie asks follow-up questions to engage Jackson while Haddie watches them both and takes in the exquisiteness beside and beneath her.

As the helicopter approaches the airport, the three passengers are quiet and reflective of their journey. Jackson thanks the pilots and guide for their time and talents. Annie fluffs her hair after removing her headset. The guide gets out to help Haddie down from the helicopter when her foot slips from under her and she hits the ground with a thud and a crack.

~Infirmary~

Dinner that night was small and more intimate with only five of the six remaining contestants. Annie and Suzanne sit to the right and left of Jackson, Priscilla sits to Annie's right with the remaining twin and the model filling the last two spots at the table. Haddie is in the resort infirmary icing and elevating her ankle.

Annie, Suzanne, and Priscilla keep the conversation going. Annie tells of their helicopter ride today and expresses how impressed she is by Jackson's extensive knowledge. Suzanne and Priscilla stay in the conversation by asking questions for Jackson to answer. The model and remaining blond twin glare at each other as they recount their ice skating adventure today, which apparently ended when the two women began pushing each other out of the way. Sandra reluctantly stopped recording only when Rich forced her to. She was excited to possibly catch a cat fight, while Rich was relieved to avoid one on camera. Off camera was a different story. It took Rich and Jackson five minutes to pull those two skinny rails off each other.

As dinner wraps up, the women are directed to their rooms to wait on the daily vetoes. Jackson grabs Annie's hand and asks her to wait a minute. "I know you want to check in on Haddie in the infirmary for a while so don't worry about getting back to your room. I've already talked to Sandra about it. The boss is giving you 30 minutes." Jackson winks at Annie before walking away to speak with Madison.

Annie finds Haddie eating from a chocolate pudding container. Haddie's leg is elevated on pillows and encased in ice packs. There is a tall black walking boot sitting on the floor by the bed. Haddie notices Annie staring at it, and she scowls in disdain at the apparatus.

"I didn't really want you to break a leg, you know. You're a ballerina, you should know that was a term of good luck, not an instruction." Annie reluctantly smiles as Haddie childishly sticks out her tongue.

"While I was plotting ways to sabotage myself, I certainly didn't mean to do bodily harm. This is not the way I want to spend my time at a ski resort." Haddie frowns then throws her head back into her pillow.

"How long are you in this joint?" Annie asks as she takes the seat next to the infirmary bed.

"They're waiting for a doctor to return from his backcountry skiing excursion today. He should be here in an hour or two as long as the snow storm lets up soon."

Haddie and Annie both look at the door to see Jackson standing there with a bouquet of flowers.

Haddie points at Jackson, "Hey! I thought I was supposed to get yellow roses, not a bouquet of daisies. I feel cheated."

Annie shakes her head. "I think those may be for me Haddie. Jackson just told me to come see you. He must have planned to have you soften the blow. Or maybe he's worried I'll throw something at him and he wants to be close to the nurse."

Jackson smiles as he enters the room. "For your information, these are get well flowers not veto roses. You both are stuck with me a little while longer. I insisted that Sandra, well mostly Hayman, allow me to release the ice skating roller derby queens instead and offer both of you a pass. I hope neither of you are disappointed. I just couldn't do another day with that drama."

Relief floods Annie's face and Haddie looks perplexed.

"From the looks of your faces, at least I know one of you is happy." Jackson offers a sad smile and a shrug.

Annie jumps in, "Don't mind Haddie, she's a grump because she has to trade in her Converse for a boot."

Jackson leans on the door jamb of the room and rubs his hand on his chin. "I don't know. I think she's grumpy because she's sidelined from those secret ski trails she found. Or maybe she's hoping she'll miss out on her one-on-one date tomorrow with the President. I hear he's a real jerk." Jackson smiles wryly.

Just then, the nurse walks up behind Jackson and nudges him into the room so she can enter. "I just received a call requesting that I send you back to your room and you to your meeting." The nurse lifts the ice packs from Haddie's ankle and checks the swelling. It looks like you'll need to stay a while longer. I don't like that swelling and doc Mendez isn't back yet. Can I get you anything? Another pudding? Some water?"

"I'll take another chocolate pudding and graham crackers whenever you get chance, Becky. Thank you so much."

Nurse Becky turns to leave. "All right you two, out. I have to be honest, it feels rather powerful to kick out the President. Is that even allowed?" Becky asks Jackson.

Jackson laughs. "In here, you're the boss."

Annie takes Haddie's hand. "Call me when you're released and I'll come down to help. I am dying to see you walk in that thing!"

"Haha. Get out." Haddie smiles sweetly.

~Strategy Session~

Rich assembles Sandra, her assistant, Hayman, Madison, and Jackson in the small conference room next to Chef Maxwell's office. He wants a secure and secluded location. His laptop is open and he is clicking feverishly as everyone finds a seat around the table.

"So, as you all know, we've been showing some of the raw footage to a random test market. We've also been live streaming some random moments throughout the week. The reviews are coming in much higher than we ever could have anticipated. People love my idea!" Rich grins like he just won the World Series.

"Get to the point, hot shot, I'd like to get some sleep tonight." Madison shakes her head.

"The point, is that this is huge for us. Everyone who already isn't a fan, will be by the end of the show." Rich pushes a button on his laptop and the projection screen comes to life with a pie chart. "Jackson has done an excellent job of vetoing the right women."

Jackson drops his head on to the table. "That sounds so awful."

"Keep your morals to yourself. May I continue?" Rich bellows.

105

Jackson lifts his head and nods.

"The women who have polled high are the women Jackson continues to invite back for dates. The only woman vetoed who the viewers like is the news anchor. The test group loves her. Lucky for them they couldn't smell her. We may have to find a way to get that fact into the final cut so that people don't turn on Jackson."

"Absolutely not! We are not going to broadcast on television that a woman uses too much perfume." Madison sits up straight in her chair.

Jackson places his hand on Madison's arm to settle her. "I completely agree with Madison. Every contestant needs to be projected in a positive light. That's a deal breaker."

Sandra pipes in, "Unless they have brought it on themselves." She swivels in her chair to face Jackson. "While I admire your chivalry Sir, some of these women brought the drama on themselves. Their shenanigans is reality television gold and they know it. The party girl from the first night already has offers from MTV and I'm pretty sure the twins have since contacted friends at the mansion. I give you my word that I will protect the virtues of those who have shown virtue, but the others deserve to be shown on their own merits. Trust me, I know what I'm doing. This is exactly why you chose me."

All eyes are on Jackson. He nods in acceptance and looks at Rich.

"Sandra and I will work together on figuring out the news anchor issue. The only other issue is Suzanne. The testers like her, but there is something about her that bothers them. Hopefully, we'll catch something on film that can help us figure out her flaw. We can't get data on it, but it's hanging out there in all the feedback. As for the remaining four women, you can see here that Annie rates the highest. The cat fight on ice today was a double gift for us. The ratings will be great for this episode and we didn't have to choose between the top two women."

"*We?* Rich, you mean *I. I* didn't have to choose. You are not the ones who have to let these women down, it falls solely on me. Let's try to remember that key fact." Jackson pushes back from the table and begins pacing.

Hayman sits up in his chair as he rubs his hand through his hair. "Thank you Rich. This information is very helpful. You and I will sit down after this meeting and work with Sandra on some of the details. Everyone, be ready to fly out tomorrow night. We will leave after Jackson's last individual date so it will be a late night. There, we will have a full briefing on Air Force One. The following morning starts bright and early for us with a breakfast meeting on the education bill. Jackson, I managed to negotiate a truce with most of the major players. We can review the meeting agenda tomorrow. The crew and final three contestants will follow us in two days on a charter flight after finalizing interviews and getting last minute shots. Let's finish for tonight. We'll meet back up in the morning before the individual dates. I think Jackson needs a break. Maybe a snack."

Jackson doesn't look back as he leaves the room. He is tired of this and ready for it to be finished. He walks down the narrow, hotel hallway, towards Chef Maxwell's office. He sees the plump man holding a plate of cookies while trying to turn out the lights and close the door. "Chef, may I help you?"

Startled, Chef Maxwell turns. "Oh, President Cashe, I didn't see you. Yes, please." Chef Maxwell hands Jackson a plate of peanut butter cookies. "My very wise wife calls me a fool when I attempt to multitask." He chuckles at himself. "I just finished for the evening when I heard about Miss Haddie. I am on my

107

way to see her in the infirmary. Peanut butter cookies seem to be her favorite so I grabbed a few for her. I thought she could use a special treat." Chef Maxwell decides to keep secret his calls from Malik this week checking on his niece. If Haddie and Malik are keeping it quiet, they must have a reason.

"That is very thoughtful of you, Chef. Maybe I'll walk with you and she'll share a cookie with me. These are my favorite as well." Jackson winks.

Chef Maxwell pauses to study Jackson's face before making a decision. "I'll tell you what, if you promise to give Miss Haddie my best regards, I shall let you deliver the cookies for me. That way I can get home to my wife."

Jackson smiles conspiratorially at the man and says, "You have my word, Chef. Thank you."

Chef Maxwell pats Jackson on the shoulders as he turns to walk away, leaving a robust laugh in his wake.

Hayman watches Jackson turn the corner and closes the door to the tiny conference room. He pointedly looks between Rich and Madison. "We need to keep the specifics of the show from Jackson. Our jobs are to take care of these details so he doesn't need to process such information. So far, his decisions have mirrored our projections, the one exception being the odorous anchor. We only need interference if we notice he's making the wrong decision. Sandra, do you feel confident that you have enough footage of the women to craft a story for each of them? The stories will represent Jackson in the best light and the women reflective of his decisions?"

"Yes. I just need a few leading interviews with some to finalize pieces. Like I explained earlier, most of the women panned out exactly how we thought they would and we have the material to show them in their full glory. The drunk church girl from day one was unexpected, but her hypocrisy should rate well. I just need to get her to talk about her religious background more. I know you want an unreasonable turnaround time so I have a team working non-stop on editing. The final cuts for the first few rounds should be ready by Sunday evening. We will start the next phase of dates on Monday."

"Sandra, I want Rich working with you on final edits. Obviously, I have final say. I'd like to get this on air within the next two weeks so Jackson's new girl gets a full news cycle after the show finishes. We need to ride this wave as far as it will take us."

"My job is done for tonight." Rich closes his laptop and stretches in his chair. "I'm headed for the bar, anyone interested?" Rich looks directly at Sandra's twenty-something assistant, who blushes.

Madison hits him on the back of his head. "Let's not have a repeat of Boston. One drink, then to your room....alone!"

"Yes, mom."

~Poker~

Haddie groggily rubs her eyes as she tries to remember why she is in this strange room. She looks over and sees Jackson Cashe flipping through a magazine. He looks up at her with a broad smile when he sees her stirring.

"Hi there, sunshine."

"I must have fallen asleep. What time is it?"

"Per Nurse Becky's report, you've only been asleep for about an hour." Jackson says while looking at his watch. "I think I heard that the doctor has finally returned and will be in shortly to see you."

Haddie tries to sit up in her bed and winces in pain. Jackson picks up the ice pack that falls on the floor and helps Haddie by wedging her pillow behind her. Once she is settled, he sits on the edge of her bed. Haddie spies the cookies on the table beside her bed and looks at Jackson quizzically.

"Chef Maxwell made you peanut butter cookies. I am merely his delivery service. No tip necessary, it was my pleasure." Jackson flashes his smile as Haddie rolls her eyes.

"Do your cheesy lines really work for you? Or do women put up with them because you're so powerful?" Haddie feels badly as soon as the words come out of her mouth.

"Ouch." Jackson stays seated and contemplatively looks at her for a minute. "Honestly, it's you. I'm really not a cheesy line kind of guy, but you seem to bring them out in me. You knock me off my game."

"Well, I'm reassured you actually have some game." She smirks.

Jackson studies her for a minute.

"What? Do I have chocolate pudding on my nose or something?"

He hands her a cookie. "Do you play poker?"

Baffled, Haddie quietly responds, "No." She takes a bite of her cookie.

"Rich and I play poker once a month with a group of guys we've known forever. We've played so long together that we know each other's tells. Rich has a terrible poker face. He never wins. Our buddy Michael folds too early so we always know when he has a good hand. Spencer always bets too high and crinkles his eyebrows when he has a good hand. You, you I can't figure out your tells. I can't seem to get you out of my mind. I think about you all the time. You intrigue me. You are witty and smart and thoughtful towards others. Everyone around here sings your praises. Yet you treat me like a piranha. Those aren't cheesy lines, by the way, it's honesty. I say cheesy things because I'm nervous around you. So, I'm upping the ante the next round. Double or nothing. No cheesiness. No pretenses. I'm laying all my cards on the table and I'm calling your bluff. I think you don't want to like me, but it's getting harder. I'm starting to grow on you. I just called, now it's your play."

Haddie looks like a deer caught in headlights. She holds her cookie in midair, swallows, and gapes at him. Jackson gets up from the bed, grabs a cookie and takes a bite as he heads for the door.

"Goodnight Haddie, sweet dreams."

~And Then There Were Three~

Annie opens the door for Priscilla and Rachelle who carry ice cream, bowls, and spoons. Haddie sits up in her bed with her ankle elevated and iced. Her boot is sitting on the floor beside her. She just returned from her individual date with Jackson and the women all gather to compare stories.

Rachelle starts scooping ice cream. "All right ladies, make me jealous about your fabulous dates today."

Priscilla laughs as she sits on the edge of Haddie's bed. "Well, you've already heard about mine. There really isn't much to tell. We went snowmobiling. While the scenery was spectacular, the snowmobiles were so loud we couldn't talk. Afterwards we drank hot chocolate by a remote fire pit on the side of the lodge. It was an incredibly romantic setting, and I totally torpedoed myself talking about work." She drops her head into her hands and offers a low, painful groan.

Haddie spits out while laughing, "I'm sure it wasn't that bad. Besides your job is fascinating!"

Priscilla looks at Haddie with embarrassment in her eyes. "Yeah, to a med student, not as stimulating date conversation. I was so nervous that I rambled on and on about things I've seen at work when I cover ER shifts. I couldn't stop talking. I felt like I was watching someone else take over my body and I couldn't make them shut up. At first, Jackson seemed interested. He was asking questions and listening intently. By the end, I noticed he looked a little green. I realized I had crossed the line and started telling some pretty gnarly stuff involving bloodily fluids. I apologized but it was too late. It was awful. Truly awful. I wanted to veto myself." Priscilla hangs her head low and falls back onto the bed beside Haddie.

"Oh no P. I'm so sorry. I'm sure it wasn't that bad. You've had great dates with him all week. He'll take those dates into consideration." Haddie, still laughing with the others a little, reaches out and rubs Priscilla's arm.

"How was your date McFracture?" Rachelle squirts whipped cream in Haddie's bowl.

"I don't even know how to explain it. It was like speed dating on steroids, but completely one sided." Haddie takes a bite of her ice cream and tries to remember everything. "We went to a

112

pottery painting shop since I obviously can't walk well. We both picked out platters and began painting. He told me that he didn't know anything about me since I've been mean and closed off all week so I owed him personal scoop." Haddie rolls her eyes while the others pointedly look at each other.

"That kicked off a deluge of questions. It was ridiculous. He started with my first memory, then asked me about every teacher I had in elementary school. My voice was hoarse by the end of the date. He had to be bored. He was probably hoping for more excitement." She rests the bowl beside her on the nightstand and readjusts the ice and pillow, obviously uncomfortable with the attention. The hotel room remains quiet as they wait for more.

"It actually took a sad turn when I told him about my knee and then my sister." Haddie pauses for a moment reflecting. "Once we reached the part of my life story where my ballet career ended and my sister was diagnosed, well, it was strange. I don't usually like to discuss that time period, but I couldn't seem to stop. He watched me and didn't say a word, so I just kept talking. I explained how those life changing events inspired me to learn more about medicine. When I finally finished, he told me about his mother. I had no idea his mother died of thyroid cancer." Haddie looks up and realizes her friends have stopped eating and are watching her intently. She shakes the emotion off and attempts to move the attention off of herself. "So, see P? My date consisted of sad family memories. He probably longed for more hospital gore. At least I gained a pretty platter out of the deal." Haddie picks up the bowl and eats more ice cream.

The women sit in silence for a moment. Everyone thinking what Haddie cannot see. Annie senses Haddie's desire for change.

"Well, my date seems like a combination of both of yours." Annie props herself up more in her bed and pulls the blanket

113

tighter. "We went for a gondola ride to the top of a mountain and had breakfast. The view was spectacular. We were so high and could see for miles."

"Thank goodness I didn't have that date, I would have hyper ventilated and passed out from my fear of heights!" Rachelle laughs.

Annie chortles and continues her story. "He asked me questions the entire time too, but we mostly talked about my work. I couldn't stop talking either. I talked about data and research the entire breakfast. He seemed interested and kept asking me question after question so I rambled on about everything and anything. I was exhausted from talking so much but he kept the conversation going by giving me ideas and angles to study. It wasn't very romantic, but it was definitely exhilarating." Annie gazes into thin air as she recounts her date.

Priscilla covers her face with her arm. "At least you didn't talk about gaping wounds and triage methods....and I don't even work in the ER, I just help out occasionally." She woefully groans. "Maybe you'll be one of those power political couples that are attracted to each other's minds. You could rule the world together. I will be stuck sewing up your adversaries." Priscilla speaks into the crook of her arm.

Annie contemplates Priscilla's insight for a second. "I wonder how Suzanne's date went today, has anyone heard? I don't think I know what they were doing."

"I heard they went horseback riding and had lunch. There is something weird about that chick. She doesn't talk to anyone all day, but acts like a social butterfly around Jackson. I don't think I've spoken a word to her this entire time. Maybe she's one of those cookaloo crazies who has been sabotaging us all week. She could have been squirting perfume on the anchor every day in the

114

hallways." Rachelle snorts and stands up. "Who wants more ice cream?"

There is a knock at the door and their eyes shoot all around to each other quickly. Annie rises to answer the door while Priscilla sits up and follows her slowly. Lisa, Sandra's assistant is standing there holding a tablet and her phone. Annie releases the breath she is holding.

"Sandra needs everyone in the big lobby by the main fireplace. You'll be filmed so freshen up if you need to. You have thirty minutes. Sadie is waiting." Lisa walks off to knock on Suzanne's door.

Annie rushes to the closet and pulls out different outfits. Priscilla rushes to the door and heads for her room. Rachelle cleans up the ice cream mess while Haddie slowly reaches down for her boot.

After a quick stop at Sadie's table, Haddie stands in front of the fireplace watching the crew race around performing their jobs. There are four bouquets of roses sitting on a table, three pink, one yellow. Annie and Priscilla arrive and begin fidgeting with their clothes and hair. Suzanne stands off by herself until Sandra orders her over with the other three to test the lighting.

Annie attempts to engage Suzanne in conversation to which she is greeted with a glare instead.

Suzanne leans close to the three women and speaks in a quiet, menacing tone. "Ladies, I'm not here to make friends. I'm here to win. I spend every day competing with smarter people than you and I never lose." She straightens up and flips her long, strawberry blond hair.

115

Haddie, Annie, and Priscilla look at each in shock. One, by one, they begin laughing uncontrollably. Just then Sadie comes over to give the women one last look. Suzanne brushes off Sadie's attempts while Annie and Priscilla chat about Rachelle being so funny. Haddie's eyes water as Sadie hands her a cane that has been simply, but elegantly decorated in purple and aquamarine fabric.

"Sadie, you are so very thoughtful."

Sadie makes a "shushing" motion then walks back to her station.

Jackson walks into the room and stands by the table. He smiles at all four women as Suzanne jumps into Annie's and Priscilla's conversation like they are old friends. Sandra calls everyone to attention and gives brief directions. The cameras begin to roll.

~Sunday~

The sun rises over DC as Air Force One descends. The team is exhausted from the Colorado trip and only manages a couple hours' sleep on the flight. In an effort to remind anyone watching that Jackson is still working at full capacity while dating fifteen women, Hayman schedules a few meetings on Sunday. Rich and Madison head to their apartments to change before spending the day with Sandra's team. Jackson heads to the residence for a shower and Hayman makes a quick stop to his house.

Hayman arrives back at the White House early and heads directly to Malik's office to review details. The kitchen is busy with activity preparing for their breakfast meeting. Hayman turns the corner and sees Malik's door closed and locked. There is no light from under the door. Frustrated, Hayman turns to look for Malik.

After an unsuccessful search, he spots Oscar, Malik's right hand man in the pantry. "Where is Malik this morning? Certainly, he's not late on our first day back to DC."

Oscar looks quizzically at Hayman. "Mr. Barnes, today is Sunday. Chef Lavalier doesn't work on Sundays. I think he's at church right now. He stayed late last night to prepare everything for this morning and left me detailed instructions. We've been working all morning. Is something wrong? May I assist you in any way?"

Hayman storms out of the room and reaches for his phone. He dials Malik's number as he heads to his office.

Malik answers on the second ring. "Mr. Barnes, is everything all right?"

"No Malik, it is not. When I tell the head chef about an important breakfast meeting scheduled for Sunday morning, I expect the head chef to be here, doing his job. Can you explain to me why Oscar is preparing my breakfast instead of you?"

There is a pause on the other end of the line. "Mr. Barnes, it is in my contract that I have off on Sundays for church and family time. I prepared everything in advance and have full confidence in my team. If there is something amiss, I can address it with them tomorrow morning but until then, Oscar is fully capable of meeting your needs."

"No, he's not!" Hayman is shouting now. "This meeting is very important to me. I expect you to be here within the hour."

"With all due respect, Mr. Barnes, no, I will not be in today."

"What did you say to me?"

"Today is Sunday, a day of rest according the Bible. I am on my way to church with my daughter. I have the contractual right and religious freedom to worship today. If you have anything further to discuss, I will be in tomorrow morning. Have a nice day, Mr. Barnes."

The line goes dead. Hayman reaches his office and slams open the door. He throws his phone into the cushions of his silk stiped, champagne colored couch. He slams the door behind him and paces.

Madison cautiously knocks and opens the door. "Hayman? Is everything okay? Do you need me to do anything?"

Hayman continues pacing and glares at Madison. "Malik Lavalier is unbelievable! I command the head chef to prepare a breakfast and he defies me so that he may to go to church? He is choosing fantasy over the business of the President of the United States! In ancient Rome, I could have him beheaded and impaled!"

Madison attempts to calm Hayman. She speaks soft and slow, trying to placate him without riling up his irrationalness. "Okay, Hayman. Is there a problem in the kitchen or with the breakfast that only Chef Lavalier can fix? May I help in any way?"

Hayman shoots daggers at Madison, "Tread lightly, young lady."

There he goes with the young lady crap again. One of these days I'm going to tackle him. I have more political experience than he does. Argh!

Madison calms herself and steadfastly continues. "I was on my way to see you so you could review the meeting agenda. I made the changes you requested and Jackson also has a few

118

suggestions for the brief speech afterwards. The guests will be here within the hour. Jackson will meet you after the breakfast portion. We need to decide where the photo ops will take place and go over Rich's talking points for the press. Do you have time for that now, or shall I come back later?"

Hayman gruffly sits at his desk and holds out his hand for Madison's paper. "Call Rich and close the door."

~Spotlight~

The dark SUV with blacked out windows, turns down a quiet side street in Washington, DC. News vans and a satellite trucks line both sides of the narrow road. Haddie, Annie, and Suzanne arrive at the Washington & Lee Bed and Breakfast. Greeting them is a swarm of paparazzi and reporters. Sandra has security guards outlining a pathway up the stairs of the colonial style home to the front porch. She turns to face the women in the back seat.

"Ladies, welcome to reality television notoriety. It's only going to intensify this week. We've been hyping this show while filming in Colorado and the live streams have been insanely popular. The whole world knows the names of all fifteen women, but your names specifically, were leaked by someone from the resort. There will be no hiding for you all. Just because your names are public, you still are bound by the confidentiality terms of your contracts and the no outside communication restrictions. You may smile as we're walking in, but do not stop for questions. Keep it low key. Once we make it inside, I'll give you all an hour to get settled before we meet in the parlor for a production meeting."

Sandra studies the women in the backseat. "Do you have any questions?" She waits as all three women nod. "Get ready ladies, it's show time."

The shouting begins as soon as the doors to the black SUV open. Journalists and photographers are edging each other out, pushing and shoving into security. Annie and Haddie follow quickly behind Sandra. Annie supports Haddie as they walk up the stairs. Both women smile politely, but remain focused. Annie turns to see Suzanne posing like she's walking a red carpet.

"So much for keeping it low key." Annie sighs as she walks in the door.

Sandra whispers so only they can hear, "She needs all the help she can get." Haddie and Annie look at her in surprise. Sandra shrugs. "She's not popular with viewers. Apparently everyone but the president sees through her charade." Haddie and Annie follow Sandra into the bed and breakfast while thinking about what she just revealed to them.

The women settle into their rooms. Haddie's window overlooks the flower garden behind the house. It is filled with rose bushes and various plants and shrubs. The evergreens are covered in twinkle lights. There is a walking path that leads to a large wooden swing tied to the branches of a broad oak tree. The garden is barren under the cold winter sun, but Haddie imagines how beautiful it will look in a few months. It must be stunning at night when the lights are lit and sparkling in the snow. She stares for a few more minutes as she hears Lisa talking in the hallway.

Haddie grabs her favorite pashmina wrap and walks to the door. She entwines herself in the soft lavender fabric and feels the warm embrace of familiarity. Annie's door opens just as Haddie lifts her hand to knock. Both women glance at each other and begin giggling.

"Great minds." Annie smiles warmly

As they walk down the wooden staircase and across the foyer, Haddie admires the original woodwork and craftmanship of the carpenter. Her boot making a thud with every other step. They pass a gorgeous study lined with built-in bookcases surrounding a large mahogany desk. The room is a flurry of activity with Sandra's crew staging lights and speakers for the individual interviews this week. They enter the parlor in time to see Suzanne giving Lisa and Sandra detailed instructions on how she expects to be filmed so as to highlight her best angles. She glowers at the women as they sit on an antique rose colored settee. Suzanne sits opposite Haddie and Annie with a huff.

Sandra points at Lisa's tablet as they talk quietly. Lisa heads across the hall to the study while Sandra finds her way to the wing backed chair next to Suzanne.

"Ladies, we have a lot of ground to cover this week so we can make our production deadline in 6 days. Tomorrow will consist of three individual dates. Suzanne, you and Jackson will have breakfast, followed by Annie's lunch, then Haddie for dinner."

"Absolutely not!" Suzanne angrily interrupts. "I want dinner, not breakfast."

Sandra authoritatively extends her hand, effectively cutting off Suzanne and continues. "There will be a veto bouquet sent tomorrow night. The final round will consist of individual dates; one in the morning and one in the evening. The dates will entail the finalists and Jackson touring a multitude of DC attractions. The footage will also be used for a tourism video so dress accordingly. You will each finish the day with private Jackson time as he either gives you pink or red roses. Any questions relating to the details of the dates?" Sandra dares Suzanne to argue with a piercing gaze.

The women all nod in understanding. Haddie is still processing how she ended up in the final three.

"You all will remain at the Washington and Lee until Friday for final interviews and extra footage. You will be sent home with strict instructions for privacy until all episodes have aired. We will spend Sunday with President Cashe's team reviewing the final cut. The First episode will air on Monday followed by a new episode every night during primetime with the finale on Sunday. Immediately after the finale, we will broadcast a reunion special with the fourteen vetoes. Rich Miller will work directly with the winner on how to handle the relationship PR. You are no longer my problem after the reunion special. I know this is a lot to squeeze into two weeks. Do you have questions at this point?"

Sandra pauses and waits for questions. Suzanne pulls out a paper with a list of questions. "Lisa!" Sandra yells facing the study. She rises and walks towards the door. "Lisa will handle the rest of your questions."

Haddie spends the afternoon reading in the sunroom. She loves the collection of books amassed in the study. She looks at her watch. Annie should be returning soon. Haddie heads to her room and jumps in the shower so they have time to talk before Haddie's date.

Haddie stares at her clothes, trying to decide what to wear. She chooses a dark grey sweater dress. She listens to Green Day on her phone as she dresses. She slips on one of her favorite tall black boots and puts in her pearl studs. One last fluff of her hair and then a quick check of the contents in her black clutch. After waiting for as long as she can for Annie, Haddie realizes they may miss each other. She heads downstairs to find Sadie.

She grabs two sugar cookies from the hall table and hands one to Sadie as she sits in the chair. "I'm ready to be your canvas, have your way with me."

Sadie shakes her head and smiles as she graciously takes the offered goody. "These cookies are dangerous. I can't resist them. I'm going to gain ten pounds before we leave on Friday."

"You and me both! The cranberry breakfast scones don't help either."

Haddie and Sadie talk about the history of the Inn and how they love the accurate period furnishings. It turns out that Sadie is quite the history buff. The women talk and laugh comfortably like old friends.

As Sadie applies her finishing touches, she stands in front of Haddie and quietly speaks. "Haddie, I'm probably overstepping my bounds and for sure could get reamed out by Sandra, but I have to share something with you and I hope you're okay with my two cents."

Haddie nods for Sadie to continue, curiosity growing.

"I have spent quite a bit of time with President Cashe over the past two weeks. I also hope I'm assuming correctly that you and I have become friends?"

Haddie smiles and nods in agreement.

"President Cashe seems to be a good man at heart. He has been kind to me and the others and not just when the cameras are rolling. He listens and asks very thoughtful questions. He never speaks poorly of the other contestants, and let me tell you, he has had plenty of material." Sadie thoughtfully pauses. "I know from the beginning you didn't want this and you're still wary about it

123

now, but I hope you rethink your position on it. I have heard the way he talks about you. I have seen the way he looks at you. I have seen a side of him that has never been portrayed in the press. I don't think he's the same person his advisors want portrayed in the media. I guess what I'm saying is that you two are more alike than you think. For the first time in a long time, I have faith in a politician. I think the two of you together can do great things. It's weird and comforting. I feel like I'm watching a movie that has been perfectly planned from the beginning by like a master author or something. Anyway, I just wanted to share that with you."

Haddie takes a deep breath and considers Sadie's words. "Thank you for your honesty and your friendship, Sadie. I promise I will go into this date with an open mind. I'm still not sure if he is attracted to me because he thinks I'm playing hard to get or if he is genuinely interested. I do know that he has been very persistent and seems authentic. I at least owe him a chance."

Haddie takes Sadie's hands in hers. "Thank you, Sadie."

Lisa breaks the silence. "Haddie are you ready? Your car will be here in fifteen minutes and we want to film your pre-date thoughts."

"I'm as ready as I'll ever be, let's do this."

Chapter 6

~Surprises~

The sun is setting over Washington, DC. Reds, oranges, blues, and purples merge together with wispy clouds. Jackson stares out of the window as he waits to begin a quick meeting in between dates. Hayman has some important topic he needs to address so he can negotiate some issues with the education reform bill. He turns as he hears Madison enter the room. She joins him at the window. She studies her friend.

"Are you nervous?" Madison looks disbelievingly at Jackson.

"Maybe." Jackson fidgets with his shirt sleeve.

"That's so cute. I don't think I have ever seen you this way. Definitely not towards Vanessa. I'm not complaining, I really like Haddie. She is refreshing in our world of politics and celebrity. There is just something about her."

"Should I be worried? Do you want to date her?" He turns to look at his friend with a smile.

"Stop it. You know what I mean. You obviously see it too. I'm just trying to say that I like seeing you this way. It's nice. I hope your date goes well tonight."

"Thanks, Madsi. Me too. I'm taking her to the ballet tonight. I asked Sandra to arrange a private performance by her old ballet company. I thought maybe seeing her old friends would put her at ease and she will finally open up to me, but now I'm nervous. Is it too much?"

Madison plasters a huge grin on her face. "There is no such thing as a gesture that is too grand in this situation. I think it's absolutely perfect. I'm very impressed. She'll love it."

"Who will love what?" Rich strolls into the residence behind Jackson and Madison.

"Your mom will love the condolence flowers Jackson sent her. He wanted her to know how sorry he feels that she has you for a son." Madison saves Jackson from Rich's ribbing. He squeezes her arm in thanks as they walk towards the couches.

"Will you three knock it off! Sometimes I feel like a chaperone in high school. We have work to do before Jackson's next play date." Hayman says gruffly as he follows in behind Rich. He drops some folders on the coffee table and directs everyone to sit.

"Hey! These 'play dates' as you call them, were your idea. I didn't ask for any of this." Jackson retorts.

Per usual, Madison wrangles everyone back to task. "We only have about fifteen minutes, so let's get started gentleman." She walks over to sit in front of the historic window in the West Sitting Hall.

The other three follow her lead and find spots on the couches surrounding a round coffee table. Hayman passes out the folders for the three to review. "You are right, Jackson, about whose idea it was, and it was a good one. The hype for this drama is helping your approval rating to sky rocket. The tourism numbers and economy stats are steadily increasing, and the show hasn't even aired yet. Mark this under the 'Hayman is always right' column and let's get to work."

Madison takes her folder and leans back into the formal floral couch rolling her eyes behind Hayman's head. Jackson winks at her.

"What is so pressing, Hayman?" Jackson flips through the folder.

"While you were in Colorado, I met with the power players who can impact the education reform bill. Union reps, higher education leaders, private and charter school advocates, and the largest homeschool association in the country. We hammered out some of the deal breaker aspects but we still have a few items to tackle. To date, everyone is on board with the bill and, with a few tweaks, will openly endorse us and it. The homeschool crowd has been the most difficult, but I'm working some alternative angles. They are the only group not concerned with money allocated to them, but they also don't want any restrictions. Hopefully, I'll have worked out the kinks with them before the next meeting. In preparation, I'd like to review this plan as a final draft. If the homeschool advocates are not willing to work with us, we need to focus coverage on the negative aspects of it. In addition, this folder also has detailed examples of homeschooling gone bad. There are truancy statistics, reports of abuse and neglect, as well as studies showing the negative social impact on homeschooled children."

"We've seen these before, the good statistics far outweigh the negatives and the homeschool advocates also have studies that support their agenda. The more we shout *bad*, their side will outcry the *good*. How does this help us?" Madison questions.

"The other side doesn't have Rich Miller. We will ensure that all media outlets see this as a public outcry for help; 'These poor neglected children are being denied basic education.' The only national player who will cover their plight is Fox News. We'll make them look like pariahs by the time we're finished with

127

them. If they can't play ball and negotiate, they will be removed from the game." Hayman sits back in his seat and closes the folder.

"So basically, we're attacking the homeschoolers because they don't agree with us?" Madison asks Hayman.

Hayman glares at Madison.

Jackson breaks in, "What is their major concern with the bill specifically?"

"Religious freedom and propaganda for their belief system. It's mostly the closeminded evangelicals who home school. They want less oversight, more freedom to cover religious teachings, and the elimination of some core science topics. Basically, they don't want any evolution or big bang theories covered on standardized testing and want to be able to cover their own version. I think it's called creationism or some such nonsense. Allowing this alternative and false teaching, hurts our standings in the scientific world. We need more scientists, not priests."

Jackson writes notes on his folder to study later. "What do they want in exchange for their support? Is there anything else holding up an agreement?"

"They are asking for an allocation of money dispersed to states to cover their individual costs for educating their children. The argument is that they spend more on individual education for their children that the state offers. This is similar to the demands for school choice, but the private and charter school assemblies are being cooperative and negotiating with us for other subsidies and benefits we can offer. There simply isn't enough money to do what we need to do, while offering school choice options to appease their advocates. The goal is for public education to keep the lion's share of the money. They also want a national Tebow Bill without restrictions."

"So, we're playing chicken with the entire education reform bill because you don't want to give homeschool parents the ability to teach what they want and allow their children to participate in extracurricular activities?" Madison startles herself with her brash response.

"The states will turn on us if we take money from them and allocate it to private citizens. They will also be furious if we affect their graduation rates and testing scores because homeschool students can't pass the science benchmarks. Also, we can't allow star athletes to pick and choose which schools they want to play for, that's encouraging an unfair playing advantage. We can't cater to religious freaks at the expense of education." Hayman turns towards Madison, "You are being very argumentative this week, Miss Lyn. Do we have a problem?" Hayman scowls at her.

Jackson jumps in quickly to avoid a war between his advisors. "Hayman, this is a lot of information to process tonight. It's been a long two weeks. My mind is not clear right now. I'd like more time to review the folder. Let's take the night to think about this and try to be creative with a solution. Remember, my grandmother spent her life teaching in public schools. I have the utmost respect for public education. Hayman, I would like to be involved in future meetings regarding the education reform bill."

"Yes, Sir." Hayman nods, watching Madison and Jackson acutely. "Miss Lyn will ensure the next meeting is added to your schedule."

Jackson closes the folder then stands. "Now, if you'll excuse me, I have a 'play date' and I don't want to be late." He raises his right hand to usher out his guests before he takes one more look in the mirror.

~Beauty of the Dance~

It is a chilly February night in Washington. The almost full moon brightens the sky. Outside of the American Theatre, Jackson opens the car door for Haddie as they climb in after watching the ballet. They sit quietly in the backseat of the town car as Travis tells the driver to go. Haddie looks at Jackson with glistening eyes, damp with emotion. She studies him for a moment before softly speaking.

"I can't believe you did that for me. It was so sweet and thoughtful. I loved seeing so many old friends. They were magnificent. I loved it. I've been so busy with school and the show, I haven't seen them this season or last. It was a wonderful surprise, thank you Jackson." Haddie says shyly.

Jackson beams brightly at Haddie. "I'm so happy you enjoyed yourself. I know you think I'm over confident about everything, but I was very nervous about this idea." Jackson reaches over and holds Haddie's hand tentatively. "Sandra told me I wasn't allowed to ask for the entire show in addition to dinner or 'Suzanne would flip out on her for unfair advantage'." He chuckles. "You look breath taking, by the way. I can't remember if I told you that or not before the show."

Haddie smiles back at Jackson. They drive in silence, hands softly touching in a perfect fit.

The convoy stops on the main street of a small neighborhood in front of a café type restaurant. A deep red canopy hangs over the door. The scroll letters eloquently naming the establishment, *Ristorante Italiana.*

130

Jackson timidly explains to Haddie that this restaurant is the closest thing to Little Italy he had found in Washington, DC as they climb out and walk to the door.

"My mom used to take me into Boston for special occasions and we would eat at this amazing restaurant called Philips. It would be a date for just the two of us. The ambiance of this place reminds me of the restaurant, and her. Those are some of my favorite memories of my mother. She could never resist authentic, homemade pasta. I hope you like it."

As they enter, the smell of roasted garlic and tomatoes fill their senses. They both smile at each other as they catch the other one breathing the aromas in deeply. The hostess fawns over Jackson and leads them to their table in a back corner. The restaurant is empty with the sounds of Italian music quietly piping through the sound system. Haddie recognizes the sounds and smells of home. Secret service agents are in plain sight surrounding them but remain at a distance from the table. The waitress brings over two plates of appetizers. There is fried zucchini straws and bruschetta.

"Not to sound like a chauvinist jerk, but I had to choose the menu ahead of time so the food could be checked. I hope you like it. I chose baked ziti and chicken parmesan for dinner. Tiramisu for dessert." Jackson looks tentatively at her, waiting for her approval.

She smiles. "I couldn't have chosen better myself."

A different server comes over with a bottle of wine. The surfer looking waiter opens it at the table and Jackson expertly admires, smells, tastes, and approves the selection. Both glasses are filled with a sweet red wine. Jackson holds up his glass and offers a toast. "Here's to two people getting to know each other and enjoying the company. Cheers."

"Salut!" Haddie clinks glasses with Jackson and takes a sip.

"Ah, it seems you know a little bit about Italian cuisine too; Or at least Italian toasts." Jackson chuckles. "Although I'm not Italian, I've always been fascinated by the immigrant growth in the eighteen and nineteen hundredths. Irish, Polish, German, it's all fascinating to me. Usually the men came first and would send for the rest of their families once they found work. Entire communities and neighborhoods formed around the influx of immigrants. They found work in factories and coal mines and they supported each other. The historic immigrant culture really exemplified the 'it takes a village' sentiment." Jackson stops as he notices Haddie giggling. "What? Are you bored? Sometimes I get on tangents about historical topics. Madison warned me not to bore you with my trivia facts. I'm sorry."

"No, that's not why I'm laughing at all." Haddie smiles broadly. "My grandmother would be very impressed. You've just described her childhood. My great-grandfather came from San Giovanni, Italy. He followed his brothers over here to work in the coal mines. My great-grandmother sailed over six months later and had intense sea sicknesses. She was turned away at Ellis Island because of an eye infection. She had to make the journey back and tried again a year later. She was reunited with her husband a year and half later after three rounds of sea sickness and one eye infection. My grandmother says I have her mother's tenacity. My Mama calls it stubbornness."

"Now that, I have seen firsthand. You definitely are stub.., I mean tenacious." Jackson chortles.

"Trying to impress my mother and grandmother by agreeing with them, you are a very smart man."

"Tell me more. I'm completely enraptured by your story and now I really want to meet your grandmother."

132

"You might regret that, she is one tough lady. She has endured so much in her lifetime and she doesn't take any sass. I should know, I learned not to curse with a bar of soap in my mouth and don't get me started on her wooden spoon." Haddie stares off remembering her grandmother. "The town where my family is from, are all related. I think the entire village came over and settled in the area. When someone new came into town they lived with families from the village until they could find their own place. When there wasn't work, they moved to other areas in groups as well. I have an entire faction of my family in Detroit. Two aunts moved with their husbands and cousins followed to find work. That's how I ended up in South Carolina. My mother followed my aunt. I guess that's what I did too, I followed my cousin to DC and here I am." Haddie quickly changes track, she isn't ready for Jackson to know her connection with Malik. She is surprised he doesn't already know, but for some reason, she wants to keep that to herself for now. "You know Senator Marchio?" She waits for Jackson's nod. "His grandfather lived with my great-grandparents until his wife came over from Italy. My grandmother used to babysit him."

"This is amazing! Tell me more." Jackson leans in and places his chin on his fist.

Haddie and Jackson fill every second with talking, only stopping long enough to take bites of food. Jackson tells Haddie about his childhood and his mother. He talks about his grandparents who taught him the value of hard, physical labor. He had to chop wood every winter before he could go skiing. Haddie now understands why everyone keeps telling her that she has more in common with Jackson than she realizes. They both had very strong mothers who taught them independence and humility. Their grandparents were examples of the American Dream and the drive it takes to get it. Jackson shares more about his mother's sickness and Haddie tells him about Chloe and Beau. She shares more about her dreams after medical school.

133

They talk for hours like they were the oldest and dearest of friends.

As they leave the restaurant, Jackson takes Haddie's hand and links it into the crook of his arm. She leans into him as they walk. They continue talking as he opens the door. Flashes of light blind them and startle Haddie into a frozen form. Jackson instinctively responds quickly and protectively. He wraps one arm around her shoulders while keeping the cameras at a distance by waving with the other. Travis helps guide her into the waiting car as Jackson tries to block her from the cameras by giving a last minute turn and wave.

Travis sits in the front as he turns to face them, "I'm sorry Sir. Someone from the restaurant must have called and alerted the media."

"It's fine Travis, I'm not surprised." Jackson turns to Haddie, "Are you all right?"

"Yes." Haddie seems frozen and somewhat startled. "I guess I should have been prepared after yesterday, but I wasn't expecting that. I think I forgot for a minute who I was with and what I was doing." She is flustered momentarily.

"It must be my sterling conversational skills. You forgot time and place." Trying to break the tension with a corny joke, Jackson squeezes her hand. They ride in silence.

Arriving at the Inn, Jackson turns to her. "I know I'm supposed to escort you through the press mess to the front door, but maybe we can walk through the gardens in the back for a few minutes?" He is nervous and anxiously awaiting her response.

She frowns, "I don't know, it's really late. I should probably get some sleep."

"Just five minutes. I don't want to end our date with photographers and paparazzi." Jackson looks at her longingly, hoping she'll say yes.

She nods in agreement. "There is a swing in the back, we can sit there for a few minutes."

Jackson looks to Travis who nods his approval. Travis begins speaking quietly into his wrist. Jackson waits for an agent to open his door. He climbs out to more flashes of light and reaches out his hand for Haddie. She climbs out while keeping her head down to watch where she is going, the lights are so bright and scary.

Jackson walks Haddie to the shadows of the front door of the Washington and Lee. He opens the door and steps inside briefly knowing he will see her again soon. Jackson leans in and places a lingering kiss on her right cheek. He thanks her for a lovely evening then turns and walks down the stairs towards Sandra and Lisa who are waiting outside the production van. He hands them a card for the veto roses and offers one last nod to the media. He gets into his car which discreetly pulls away from the motor cade and drives to the back alley of the bed and breakfast.

Haddie stealthily walks through the old home and sneaks out the back door into the garden. The night air is chilly, but not cold. The moon is big and shining brightly above her. It reminds her of the movie her aunt used to watch non-stop. "Bella Luna" she says to herself, "beautiful moon!" She walks to a wooden swing covered by a canopy of vines and lights hidden in the back corner of the garden. She sees Travis enter first followed closely by Jackson.

Jackson watches her, trying to gauge her mood. They sit quietly on the swing as they rock back and forth. He thanks her for sharing the stories of childhood, attempting to rekindle their great conversations from earlier. "I really would love to meet your grandmother. Stories like hers inspire my work today. I think that's why I'm so passionate about immigration now. Our country was founded on immigration. None of us would be here without it."

Haddie frowns. "Jackson."

Oh no, that doesn't sound like a good 'Jackson.' Damn photographers!

She turns toward him in the swing. "This is our problem and one of the reasons why I've kept my distance. I shouldn't admit this to you, but you're starting to grow on me so I feel the need to confess." Perplexed, she continues. "I feel drawn to Jackson, the person. Since your ultimatum in the infirmary, I've kept an open mind about you and, well, you're not so bad." She smirks at him. "The problem is that I'm not a big fan of President Cashe and definitely not his political party. Don't forget, I'm a South Carolina girl. After the last two elections, I learned a lot about people and politicians. No offense, but the Separation wasn't caused by the division of the people, it was caused by decades of politicians and journalists telling us how divided we are and that the other side is the ultimate evil. People like you did this to our country. We forgot that we were founded on freedom. In an effort to fight for values, people forgot to respect the values of others. Somewhere along the way, we lost the art of communication and compromise. Instead, we turned into what both sides hate, intolerant dictatorships. The middle ground lost its voice to extremism." She sighs, "Now it's my turn to apologize for the tangent." Haddie pauses and then looks directly at this man holding her hand. "Its time I'm honest with you, Jackson." She waits, trying to find the courage. "I didn't vote for you."

136

Jackson looks shocked and appalled. "What? I can't believe it. I thought you were so normal. I didn't realize you were one of those crazy conservatives!"

Affronted, Haddie pulls back her hand and begins to stand.

"Haddie, relax, sit down. I am joking." Jackson gently pulls her back down to the swing. "I'm sorry. I hear what you are saying, I promise. I make jokes when I'm nervous. I wasn't trying to make light of this."

Haddie sits while crossing her arms and pulling her sweater tighter around her shoulders. Jackson takes off his gray blazer and drapes it over her shoulders. Her eyes glisten with moisture. "Jackson, I…"

"Listen, Haddie. There must be a way to work this out between us. I'm completely smitten with you. I've never believed in feelings so strong that it can make opposites attract, but my parents are the perfect example. My mother pulled out every good and generous quality my father has, he was drawn to her. I feel that way about you. I can't explain it. You have such a strong pull on me. You make me want to be a better man, a better leader. Your words help me to see another side of me that I didn't know I had. The past two weeks, I've seen things through new eyes. It's like you've softened my heart. Help me to see the other side. Help me to understand. I can't stop thinking about you. You're my straight flush. All my chips are on the table. It's your call now."

Jackson reaches out and wipes a tear that escapes from Haddie's eye. Then he takes her hand in his and raises it to his lips for a sweet kiss.

"I'm going to leave you now. It's late and we have a long day of being tourists tomorrow." He smiles warily at her. "Think

137

about what I've said and we can talk more about this tomorrow evening. I have another special surprise for you."

Haddie nods. Jackson stands and offers his hand to help Haddie off the swing. He keeps hold of her hand as they walk to the back door. Jackson leans in and offers a chaste kiss on Haddie's cheek. He turns and walks through the garden out the back gate. As he climbs into his waiting car he nods at Travis, who again speaks softly into his wrist. An agent stationed inside the with Sandra nods. Sandra waves to a man behind her who walks upstairs to the guest rooms, with a bouquet of yellow roses and a card.

~If You Can't Take the Heat~

The White House kitchen is a hub of activity today. Things have picked up since the President and his staff returned. The sous chefs are busy organizing inventory that has just arrived. Martin is helping in the pantry while Oscar is in cold storage. The soundtrack from Moonstruck softly drifts from Malik's speakers. He chops fresh tomatoes, peppers, and herbs while his kidney beans soak in water. Madison met with Malik about the menu for tonight. Jackson wants a dinner featuring Haddie's favorite foods and a dessert which celebrates South Carolina. Malik knew just what to make. After sneakily obtaining his brother-in-law's famous chili recipe, he worked with Martin on the perfect dessert. Malik hopes he gets a peek at Haddie tonight. He hasn't seen her in over two weeks. He's been keeping tabs on her, but the production crew keeps the women on complete lockdown.

Malik turns as he hears loud voices behind the kitchen wall, coming from the pantry. He walks back there to find Oscar refereeing an argument between Martin and the delivery man. Oscar tries to calm Martin while directing the tall and lanky delivery guy.

"Hey Mike." Malik waves a greeting to the man. "What seems to be the problem here guys?" Malik tries to break the tension while assessing the situation.

"Malik, this guy went onto my truck to get that box while I was in here unloading the produce. You know that could get me into trouble. I have a system and I have to follow it so I don't lose track of my cargo." Mike turns to Martin, very frustrated. "Man, you can't do that. I've been doing this a long time. I know where to put everything. Don't go onto my truck. I have to scan that box in order or it messes up my print outs at the end of the day!"

The men start arguing again. Mike tries to take the box, marked Green Tree Acres, from Martin. Martin turns to pull the box farther from Mike's grasp. Oscar steps in between both men trying to mediate. The tensions is escalating.

Of all days. All I wanted was some calm and quiet while my chili cooks. Malik rubs the back of his neck. He knows this will end in one of two ways, and fighting in the White House kitchen is frowned upon so he steps into the fray.

Malik puts his cutting shears on the stack of boxes Mike has already unloaded. He raises his voice slightly and leans in towards the three men. "Martin! Let's give Mike the space he needs to unload the boxes. Once he's finished, you can get whatever you need." Malik looks at the box label and starts to understand. "Sorry Mike. Martin is still new and this box is from his special distributer." He then turns back to Martin and tries to give the man the benefit of the doubt. "Martin, we take procedures very serious here and Mike has a routine that must be followed. Here, I can take the box and help Mike straighten out the rest of the shipment." Malik holds out his hands for the box Martin is holding.

All eyes are on Martin as he stares back, contemplating what to do next. He reluctantly hands the box to Malik and walks back to his station. Oscar quietly apologizes to Malik and Mike as he turns and walks towards the cold storage room to arrange the boxes Mike has already unloaded.

Malik shrugs at Mike dumbfoundedly and tries to change the tone of the kitchen. "How is that new baby, Mike? Are you and Anna getting any sleep? You better have pictures to show!" Malik places a hand on Mike's shoulder as they walk out towards the delivery truck and Mike pulls out his phone and starts bragging. All is right in the kitchen.

~Honesty is the Best Policy~

It is a beautiful, sunny day in the capital city. The sun is bright and the skies are clear blue. The temperature could cooperate more, but the portable heaters are helping to warm the filming area. Considering it is still February, it could be much worse. Sandra is grateful it's not snowing while Annie just wants to avoid wearing a heavy coat over her patriotic outfit. Lisa talks into her headset then pulls Annie away from the heaters to an open space where the cameras are all pointing.

Annie is standing at the base of the Washington Memorial surrounded by two camera crews and a photographer. The *Future FLOTUS?* crew is there along with a crew filming for the tourism ads. Annie fidgets with the tie belt on her navy, wide leg trousers. Her red crop blazer pops over her white top with navy stripes. She combs her fingers through her hair. She nervously waits for Jackson to finish at Sadie's make-shift station in a trailer by the road. She smiles at he approaches.

Jackson has an awkward, but sweet smile across his face. He takes both of Annie's hands in his and kisses her cheek. "You look absolutely beautiful today, Miss Annabelle."

140

Annie blushes and shyly smiles. "Thank you, Jackson."

"Do you mind if we sit for a minute before we start our day?" Jackson looks to the side, away from all the prying eyes.

Annie nods in agreement and Jackson walks them over to one of the long concrete benches outside of the memorial. The benches are usually packed with tourists waiting for their time slot to visit. Today, they are empty and silent.

"Annie, I know we're supposed to wait and do this tonight at the final veto session, but I would feel dishonest if I didn't talk to you now." Jackson looks downs at her cold hands resting in his.

"Jackson, it's okay. I know. I have seen you with Haddie. I've also seen Haddie change over the past three weeks. I might be more upset if I didn't love Haddie. She's an easy person to fall for so I can't blame you." Annie wipes a solitary tear from her cheek and looks back at Jackson with a sad smile. "I won't say I'm not disappointed, but I appreciate your honesty. Something tells me, this is new for you too. Something also seems to have changed in you over the past three weeks. Whatever it is, it's endearing"

Jackson absorbs Annie's words and squeezes her hands. "It has truly been mine honor to get to know you, Annie. So much in fact, that I have a proposition for you. I've thoroughly enjoyed our time together. You're a fascinating and intelligent woman. Although we're not a romantic match, I am attracted to your mind. I'd really like to offer you a job in my administration as a strategist. I'm intrigued by the work you do with your partner and I need your skill set as I navigate this new reality. Please say yes?" Jackson waits patiently for Annie's reply.

Annie sits up straighter and offers a smile. "Well, I definitely did not see that coming. Obviously, I'm honored, but I'd like

141

some time to process the offer, Mr. President." Annie sweetly releases Jackson's hands and looks at him for another moment. Steeling herself, she stands up and straightens her jacket. "Now, let's go see this monument! I've heard sunrise is unbeatable at the top." Annie stands and puts her hands in the pockets of her full pants.

Jackson places his hand on her back and leads her towards the security doors as he launches into a history lesson about the Washington Memorial.

Sandra looks at Hayman and Madison with shock all over her face. She quietly growls into her mouthpiece, "Lisa! Get me the execs on the phone asap! This changes everything! This has been a nightmare! First, last night's shenanigans. Now, this. I'll gladly go back to those pampered, psycho housewives after this! Did we at least have them mic'd up for that conversation?"

Hayman turns towards Madison with a scowl on his face. "What was that? Did you know he was doing this?"

Madison shakes her head "no" while trying to conceal a grin.

"I don't know what has gotten into him this week. This girl would have locked down support in California. I know the dancer is hot, but she's from South Carolina. I just included her in the line-up to show open mindedness. I didn't think he would pick her." Hayman shakes his head in disgust. "You're dealing with Sandra. She's going to have a lot to say about this. I'm going back to do some actual work. Keep a close eye on him today. No more surprises!"

Madison smiles broadly towards Sadie as she watches Hayman pout off down the long walkway to his waiting car. Sadie beams back and gives an excited wave in response.

The bed and breakfast is relatively quiet this morning. Haddie spends the morning reading and walking in the hibernating garden. She thinks about her time here last night with Jackson. She heads to her room to get ready. Her mind flooded with all that has transpired. Slowly, members of the production crew return in shifts to regroup before the next location shoot. The noise of the others helps her refocus.

Haddie leaves the Washington and Lee before getting a chance to see Annie. She didn't see her last night either. When Haddie returned to her room, Suzanne was throwing a fit in the hallway hitting her yellow rose bouquet on the walls and furniture. Rose petals and leaves were flying everywhere and Suzanne was cursing everyone in sight. Security swept Haddie into her room and kept watch by Annie's and Haddie's doors all night. Suzanne finally stopped around one in the morning.

Sadie tells Haddie that Suzanne had been moved off site and will be monitored until the reunion show. Haddie thinks that Sadie is acting weird but keeps her thoughts to herself. Sadie rambles on about tourism in Washington, DC and how she used to come here with her grandparents as a child. Haddie listens to Sadie's stories, but her mind wanders to Annie and Jackson. She wants so badly to be sitting around the kitchen table with Uncle Malik and Maryssa sorting out her feelings. This is such an overwhelming time. A whirlwind of activity and emotions. Sadie finishes Haddie's look and adds a spritz of vanilla. Haddie admires Sadie's artistry and stands to hug her new friend.

"You've come a long way Haddie Robinson. I'm glad I was able to come along for the ride."

"Sadie, you are a true gem. My life is better for knowing you." Haddie smiles warmly.

The door opens, Lisa calls from the trailer door for Haddie to get her mic and be put into position. Haddie follows Lisa to the front doors of the National Air and Space Museum. She watches as Jackson goes into the trailer to see Sadie as a mic is clipped to the back of her lavender and gray wool sweater. The waist band of her black, stretch, twill ankle pants securely holds the receiver. Haddie's heart beats a little faster and her hands shake.

What is wrong with me? This is ridiculous. I've spent three weeks with this man. Why would I be nervous now?

Haddie can see that Lisa is speaking to her, but her mind is still on the trailer.

"Haddie. Haddie." Lisa waves her hand in front of Haddie's face.

"I'm so sorry Lisa. I don't know what's come over me today. I feel so out of sorts." Haddie smiles and tries to redirect. "I heard you, I think. We are hitting some of the Smithsonians first, then dinner at the White House. Of course, we'll probably only get through the Air and Space because of my walking boot. Did I get it right?"

Lisa grins at Haddie and nods. She straightens Haddie's sweater and fluffs her hair. "All right, so you were listening. Do you have any questions?"

Haddie directs all her attention towards Lisa and smiles. "Yes, how is your mom feeling since her fall? Did she end up with a cast or a lovely walking boot like me?" Haddie holds out her foot while twisting the large black boot back and forth.

Chuckling, Lisa responds, "She opted for a hot pink cast, making her the talk of her quilting club. She even had my little sister bejewel it. I'll show you pictures later. We're a very entertaining family."

"Now that's a great idea! Maybe your sister can bejewel this hunk of metal too."

The two women laugh as Jackson approaches. He is beaming as all his attention focuses on Haddie. Jackson stares at her and takes in her beauty. "Haddie, you look absolutely stunning. As always."

Haddie smiles back and blushes. Jackson reaches out and takes Haddie's hand in his and tucks it into the crook of his elbow. "I can take it from here Lisa."

They hear Sandra yelling from inside the building. "For the love of all that is holy, please start recording before he talks this time!" Jackson chuckles to himself while Haddie looks questioningly at him.

"So, I've been thinking about what you said last night."

"Shouldn't I be saying that to you?" Haddie questions.

"As I was saying, you made an interesting point last night which sparked a thought."

"First, I thought I everything I said was interesting. Secondly, you *thinking* makes me nervous." She smirks at him.

"You are a difficult date sometimes, you know that?" He squeezes her hand. "What I have been trying to say, is that I understand what you mean about dating Jackson verses dating President Cashe. Here's the thing, I won't always be President Cashe, and I'd like to find out if Haddie and Jackson work. So, when we enter this door and the cameras start rolling, let's be

145

Haddie and Jackson, tourists on a date, not President and dating show contestant. If you like Jackson enough to date him, we can sit down and negotiate the rest. I would guess that you are a formidable negotiator. Deal?" He looks at her like a child asking for a puppy.

She considers his proposal and takes a deep breath, "Deal, but I probably still won't vote for you next election."

With hearty laugh he responds, "I would expect nothing less, Miss Robinson."

Madison turns to Lisa, "Hayman is not going to like that conversation being on film." She rubs her temples as Lisa pats her shoulder.

"Probably not, but Sandra loves it." Lisa nods her head towards her boss who is beaming with satisfaction.

The doors open to the National Air and Space Museum. Sandra waves her arm and the cameras continue to roll. Jackson leads Haddie into the large room and heads towards the US Mail exhibit. "Let me woo you with my extensive knowledge on all things air and space. I wanted to be an astronaut, did I tell you that?" Jackson launches into the history of the postal services and cargo planes.

~Nerves~

Maryssa paces impatiently in her father's small office. Malik opens the door and hugs his favorite daughter. Maryssa's dark brown, tight curls are pulled back into a pony tail. She is still wearing her jacket from the cold of the night.

"Baby girl, I told you that you could not be a server tonight. President Cashe doesn't even know we're related to Haddie. It

146

would be dishonest for you to pretend you don't know her and even more disruptive if you hug her like you haven't seen your best friend in three weeks." Malik leads Maryssa to a chair. "This is her night. Whatever is meant to be, will happen. You can not interfere. Let her enjoy this night. You'll have her back in a couple of days."

Maryssa walks to her father's desk and plops down into his chair. "I know. I know. I just can't believe this is happening. I never thought they would mesh. Miss young republican, Sunday school helper dating the poster child for everything democrat she voted against." Maryssa wrings her hands together and continues pacing. "Honestly Dad, I've been praying they wouldn't kill each other this entire time. I just wanted her to have a break to ski and rest. I'm dying to talk to her to hear this story. I'm going out of my mind. I know I can't serve tonight, but oddly, being in the same building makes me feel closer to her. Like I'm supporting her off stage like we used to when we danced."

Malik crosses the room to Maryssa and envelopes her into a long hug. "I love how close you two are and I have no doubt that she feels your presence. Remember what we always say about how life works?" Malik holds Maryssa at arm's length.

She takes a reassuring breath and smiles. "We know there is a bigger plan, we must always trust the plan in front of us even the road is crooked. Focus on the fruit, not the pruning. Surely goodness and love will follow us all the days of our lives." Maryssa stands to hug her father tightly then pulls away to sit at the table. "Go. I'm fine. I have homework. Keep me posted?"

"Of course. If you get bored, you can help Martin." He winks at his daughter as she rolls her eyes. "Boy, you really don't care for him do you?"

"You should be happy that I find him creepy." She laughs and throws a crumpled paper at her father.

~The One~

Madison meets Jackson and Haddie at the entrance to the residence. Cameras following them and standing behind Madison. They are laughing and holding on to one another. Both of them glowing and beaming with red cheeks from the cold air.

"Well, it looks like the Smithsonians were a huge success." Madison quizzes them.

"Smithsonian. Singular. Everyone was worried about me walking slow, but the real concern was Mr. history professor giving lectures at every exhibit. The flight simulator was hilarious. Don't ever get into a plane with him! We're all lucky, he's not an astronaut or a pilot." Haddie laughs while giving Madison a hug.

Jackson watches the women embrace like old friends.

She is amazing. How does she make everyone feel so special after such a short time?

"Oh, I would believe it. I've heard fourteen years of his lectures. You're lucky you didn't tour the capital building or the Supreme Court, you would still be in the lobby. He gave our Con Law professor fits in class with his questions and trivia knowledge."

"Excuse me, dear friend, I'm trying to impress my date. You are supposed to help me look good." Jackson softly pinches Madison's arm.

148

"There is only so much I can do with the material I have to work with, Jackson." Madison snorts in his direction.

"She's snorting now, this can only go downhill for me." Jackson directs Haddie towards the couches. "Is everything ready?" He looks at Madison.

She nods and winks. "The table is set. I'm assuming you can serve your guest the main course?"

Jackson places a chaste kiss on Madison's cheek. "Thanks, Madsi."

Madison walks away and stands behind the scenes with Lisa. Jackson takes Haddie's coat. "Miss Robinson, I have a special treat for you. I must confess, I involved a few people in my conspiracy to woo you. I needed to find out some intimate details about your food tastes without tipping you off to my plans. I had your favorite meal prepared for tonight's dinner. We are having chili and honey cornbread. I believe, the Cheerwine is a cherry soda type of drink, so I've been told."

Haddie looks at him unbelievingly. "Yet again, you never fail to amaze me. I am moved by your thoughtfulness. That explains why Madison was asking so many questions about family meals at my house. However, I should warn you that I'm a bit of a chili snob. My father has a secret recipe that he'll take to his grave. No one has topped it yet so don't be offended if it's not my favorite."

Jackson leads her to his private dining room and pulls out her chair. The baroque table and chairs have a regal feel. The mahogany table has extravagantly curved legs and intricate carvings that were obviously crafted by hand. The golden fabric on the chairs is hand stitched and boasts of gorgeous scroll work. The table is set for royalty with sparkling crystal goblets and gold filigreed china. Tapered candles in golden candelabras shine a soft light. A large bouquet of purple roses, Asiatic lilies, and purple daisies fills the middle of the antique table. Haddie takes in the sight and releases a deep sigh. "This is stunning, Jackson. I have to admit I'm overwhelmed and humbled by the enormity of this room."

Jackson takes his seat. "I feel the same way. I hope I never forget the honor of this privilege." Jackson ponders the view. "Let's hope the chili also impresses you."

Jackson lifts the lid off the white china serving bowl and scoops out chili. The sweet, savory, and spicy aroma fills the air. He passes her a bowl of grated cheese and a plate of crackers. "I have no doubt you will tell me if this passes your test." Jackson grins at her.

Haddie lifts the spoon to her mouth, takes one bite, closes her eyes, and smiles deeply.

Uncle Malik finally got my Dad to spill his secrets. He is always one step ahead of me.

"That smile looks like a good sign. Does it pass your test?"

"You get an A plus for planning, implementation, and thoughtfulness." Haddie takes another bite while Jackson passes her a basket of warm cornbread. They spend the entire dinner talking about family recipes and traditions. Jackson's mother used to make homemade chicken and dumplings with real bone broth. He hasn't found anyone who makes it like she did. Haddie shares stories of working in the kitchen with her grandmother and learning recipes from the old country.

Sandra leans towards Madison and Lisa while whispering, "Is it just me, or does it feel as if they've forgotten they're in a room full of people and cameras?"

Madison's smile grows even bigger.

"This is television gold." Sandra beams with excitement.

Lisa and Madison steal a glance at each other and both sigh as Sandra ruins their moment.

~Syrupy Sweet~

Maryssa watches her father walk pass the open door again and again then in and out of his office twice. "Are you pacing now? I thought we weren't supposed to worry." Maryssa flashes her father an ironic smile.

"You are not as funny as you think you are, dear one." Malik offers a halfhearted laugh. "I am cleaning my station while Martin finishes the peach cobbler and I seem to be missing my favorite cutting shears. I feel as if I'm going crazy."

"Too late for that, Dad." Maryssa chuckles at her own joke. "All right, let's find your shears. When did you last use them? You made chili, right? I'm guessing you used them to chop herbs into the pot? Did you do anything after that?"

Malik pauses to think then kisses his daughter's forehead. "Thank you, my very smart child. What would I do without you?" Malik walks out of his office and towards the cold storage room with Maryssa in tow behind him.

They pass Martin finishing the cobbler at his station. Maryssa notices a bowl of freshly whipped cream sitting next to him.

Whipped cream on peach cobbler? Interesting choice. I would have gone with hand churned vanilla ice cream. I must remember to ask him why he chose that.

151

The busyness of the kitchen is starting to slow. Most of the staff left after the table was set and the food placed. Oscar manages the remaining staff while they clean and prep for tomorrow. Malik loves the ebbs and flows of a kitchen. A busy kitchen reminds him of watching his girls dance. The staff moves in and out together like a ballet ensemble. Each with a specific job while bringing the bigger picture to life.

Malik reaches the door of the storage room and looks around the boxes. The large, shiny blades catch his eye on the floor by a stack of boxes. "Ah, there they are!" He turns and explains to Maryssa, "I must have brought them with me when I dealt with an argument between Mike and Martin today."

"What? Who would have an issue with Mike? He's such a great guy." She leans in towards her father and whispers. "See, creepy."

Malik catches an unpleasant scent as he bends to retrieve his favorite shears. He searches his surroundings looking for the offending source. He passes the threshold of the cold room and peaks on the other side of the wall. Everything on the metal pantry rack looks normal. He glances quickly at the items on each shelf and notices a box flap peeking out from underneath the bottom shelf.

"Who did this? This is a health violation waiting to happen. Everyone knows not to put anything directly on the floor. It must have been shoved during the scuffle today."

Malik leans down and pulls the box out from under the shelving unit. He pulls hard as it is jammed towards the back. He opens the box to find three jars of canned peaches, but something seems off to him. He inspects the jars closely and realizes the metal lid is puckered up instead of down which means the seal is broken. He unscrews the metal screw band and the lid pops off like a soda lid that's been shaken. Bubbles cover the peaches. Strangely, the smell of rotten fruit isn't as strong as he anticipates. It is masked by a sweet, syrupy smell coming from the jar. He quickly closes the lid and brings the box out of the room with him and heads directly to Martin's station. Martin is gone.

"Dad, what's wrong? You have your thinking face and it's making me worried."

Malik inspects Martin's station. He sees a clean canning jar sitting by the sink. *That's odd. Why would he stop to clean the jar while he is still working?* Everything else looks normal. Sugar, flour, salt, milk. He picks up a mixing bowl and smells the contents.

"I saw the bowl of whipped cream. I was going to ask him tomorrow why he used that instead of ice cream. Do you know why he chose whipped cream?" Maryssa inquires of her father.

"This isn't whipped cream. It's a marshmallow type of meringue." Malik sees the empty box for a culinary torch near the jar. "He must have used a burnt marshmallow topping. I'm not sure why he did that. The smell of the roasted marshmallow would drown out the sweet smell of the fresh..."

Hundreds of conversations and visions flash into Malik's head at once. His face goes pale white as the bowl crashes to the ground.

"OSCAR! Where is Martin?" The kitchen comes to a screeching halt as everyone has all eyes on their always calm Chef.

"I think he went up to help serve the cobbler. He said something about an added touch. Why? Is something wrong? Did he not let you taste it first?"

Malik runs from the kitchen at full speed while yelling loudly over his shoulder. "Call Travis and make sure they don't eat that cobbler. And do not let Martin leave this building!"

Malik bolts up two flights of stairs and bursts through the door of the dining room. Shocked, Haddie stares at her uncle. Her spoon sitting in a partially-eaten bowl of cobbler. She is alone.

"Where is the President?" He shouts.

Confused, Haddie explains that Jackson just excused himself to go to the bathroom suddenly.

Travis busts into the room and looks between Haddie and Malik. Everything happens in an instant. Malik tells Haddie to check on Jackson and for both of them to try to vomit up what they just ate. He then directs his attention to Travis. "We need to get a doctor here immediately and we need to find Martin Smith. I think he just tried to kill the president."

Chapter 7

~Admission~

The camera crew has cleared out completely. Madison is speaking softly on the phone in the corner. Secret service agents are scurrying in every direction. Jackson and Haddie are sitting beside each other on a floral couch in front of the famous half-moon window in the West Sitting Hall. Nurses have finished taking blood samples and the doctor concludes his exams. Another nurse enters with two syringes resting on a silver tray.

The gray-haired gentleman removes his glasses and places them inside his left suit jacket pocket. He reminds Haddie of her favorite professor at the conservatory. Dr. Miller has a wealth of knowledge in his eyes. He seems kind and nurturing, but focused and dictatorial. "Well, you two are very lucky. Based on the evidence from the food and an initial examination, it's very likely that you both were exposed to foodborne Clostridium botulinum from the peaches. While not romantic or pleasant on a date, vomiting up the cobbler was the best thing you could have done in this case. I'll want to evaluate you closely for the next 24 hours, but it seems that the poison was evacuated before any nerve damage was caused. I understand why you don't want to be transported to a hospital, and I will agree, if you allow the nurses to monitor your vitals and range of motion every hour. I will also give you an antitoxin injection which should attach itself to any remaining toxin in your bloodstream and prevent it from attacking your nerves. In addition, I would feel better keeping you hydrated and nourished via an IV bag."

Jackson and Haddie, both still in shock, nod in agreement. Jackson rolls up his navy-blue gingham shirt sleeve. The nurse directs him to make a fist as she ties a rubber tourniquet around his arm. Haddie pulls up her sweater sleeve and waits for her turn. She rolls her shoulders to relieve some of the tension, but it doesn't work. Her mind races with the events over the past hour. She wishes Uncle Malik would have stayed with her, but she knew he had to help Travis.

Madison walks up behind Dr. Miller with a concerned look on her face. "Haddie, are you okay staying here tonight? We didn't make up a bedroom because neither of you can sleep for the next 12 hours, but I have arranged for the theatre room to be ready for you two to binge watch movies or TV shows. Is there anything else I can do?"

Haddie can't think straight. She only shakes her head from side to side slowly.

Jackson takes his unoccupied hand and rubs Haddie's back. She looks at him with sadness and confusion on her face. Jackson worries this will push Haddie farther away from him. There is no way to separate Jackson, the man, from the presidency after an assassination attempt. "I can get you some sweats to wear if you want to be more comfortable or Madison can send someone to get clothes from the hotel or your apartment."

Haddie barely speaks over a whisper, "Sweats will be fine." She holds her arm out for the nurse and watches as Jackson walks into a bedroom and closes the door.

"There, all finished with your injection. We'll hook up the IV bags once you both have changed and are comfortable. The poles are easily portable, but the tubing can be a nuisance." The nurse's black hair pulled low into a tight ponytail. Her scrubs sport a pattern of stars and moons. She tightly covers the cotton ball with a plain band-aid to prevent the puncture spot from bleeding. She squeezes Haddie's arm and smiles warmly.

Jackson opens the door and emerges wearing navy blue sweat pants and a fitted matching hoodie. Haddie hadn't noticed how

156

fit he is before now. He looks like a guy she would hang out with at a gym or from class. Nothing pretentious, just a normal guy.

"Haddie, I left some clothes on my bed for you to try. If they don't fit, I can grab something else. I'm sure you'll swim in them, but they should work." Jackson hesitantly shrugs.

Haddie rises without a word and walks across the room. She closes the door behind her. His room is exactly how she would have imagined. It's a strong room with dark wood and decorated in blues and grays. The furniture is more modern than the rest of the residence. Bold, straight lines with little to no detailed woodwork. She pulls off her sweater, careful not to knock off the band-aid. The charcoal gray sweatshirt is so soft and smells of Jackson. It surprises Haddie how comforting the smell is to her. She rolls up the cuffs on the sleeves so they don't swallow her. The sweatpants have a long elastic band at the bottom so they don't drag, but they are way too big and remind her of parachute pants. They are obviously not your run of the mill sweats. The soft cashmere reminds her that she is the guest of Jackson Cashe, III, of the New England Cashes.

When she finally opens the door to the sitting room, everyone has cleared out and Jackson stands alone in the center of the room staring. He looks nervously at her and holds out both hands in surrender. "I asked for everyone to give us a minute. The nurses are setting up in the theatre room so we won't have to carry the IV poles." He pauses for a minute. "So much for me being a good date." He jokes, worry fills his face.

She's going to bolt. She looks like she can't find an exit quick enough.

Haddie rushes across the room and throws her arms around Jackson. She holds him tightly and breathes in his scent. Jackson feels her tremble as she starts to cry.

157

"Hey. Hey. It's okay. We're okay." He pulls her away slightly so he can see her face. He wipes away a few tears and holds her by the shoulders. "How are you feeling?"

She wipes more tears with her hands and stares into his eyes. Suddenly she breaks the contact from his right hand to her shoulder. She swings her fist around and gently punches his shoulder. "Don't ever scare me like that again! I'm still mad at you for making me like you, now I have to worry about people killing you! This is the worst date ever."

Jackson beams, "You just admitted that you like me. It must have been the chili."

They both laugh as he pulls her back to his chest.

~Treason~

Hayman slams down the phone in his home office. He stomps into his kitchen and starts banging around cabinet doors looking for a glass. Janice walks in holding Chanel and the boys turn their heads from the television on the other side of the open concept room.

"Hayman, dear, are you all right?" Janice asks puzzled. "Do you need something?"

Hayman finds what he is looking for and heads to the liquor cabinet at the edge of the kitchen. He pours himself a drink and takes a long swallow. "Everything is going to hell in a hand basket." Hayman barks. He takes another drink. "There was an assassination attempt on Jackson's life tonight while the television crew was filming. This is the last thing I need!"

Hayman fills his glass again as Jamie and Chad walk into the kitchen to listen to their father.

"Oh my, poor Jackson. What happened? Is he all right?" Janice caresses the dog in worry.

"He is fine from what I know. Dr. Miller is monitoring him throughout the night. My problem is keeping this from the media. Thankfully, I had the entire production crew sign confidentiality agreements, and there was a limited amount of people in the residence when it happened. I have to get that woman to edit this portion of the film out and destroy the evidence before this gets out to the public. An assassination attempt at this juncture will kill our agenda and momentum."

"Who did it and what did they do, Dad?" Chad takes a seat at the counter.

"The kitchen staff!" Hayman nearly shouts his indignation. "Some crazy man who was hired as a cook belongs to a militia from Georgia. The group is denouncing his actions and trying to disassociate but their fanatical evangelical doctrine was found all over his apartment. He was caught along with an accomplice working at a fruit canning company in Georgia. Both men are being questioned now. Something about rotten peaches containing a deadly bacteria were found in the food. They caught it quickly enough to stop the bacteria from spreading." Hayman takes another long drink. "I blame this on Malik Lavalier. He failed his post. Such smugness from such a small man. He must have a part in all of this. That man needs to learn his place."

"You need to fire him, Dad!" Chad shouts. "He is a treasonous insubordinate. You need to make an example of him."

"Chad is right, Dad. You can even spin this in your favor. If that producer woman has Mr. Lavalier on tape at all, she can show the food and him. You can crucify him in the court of public opinion. He would become persona non-grata. You know the story is going to leak somehow on social media about the attempt.

159

Use it to your advantage. Watch all the footage and craft your own version of what happened. The man will never work again and will hopefully be arrested. You could destroy his life. That would serve him right."

Janice takes the empty glass from her husband and walks to the sink. "The boys make sense Darling. How can a successful chef not know that rotten peaches are being served? Let me do some research and work my connections. We can start poisoning the water about him now. By the time the story breaks, no one will be surprised."

Hayman's scowl turns into a sly sneer. "I'm going to call Sandra."

~White House Secrets~

After watching *Singing in the Rain* and two vital checks later, Haddie's rear end is getting tired of sitting. She stretches and looks around at the theatre chairs. The two nurses are sleeping in their recliners and Jackson twists in his seat to stretch his back. Travis is sitting by the door, he refuses to leave Jackson's side until morning.

"I don't think I can sit much longer, do you think we can walk around a little before our next checkpoint?" Haddie stands and reaches her arms as high as she can without pulling on the needle in her arm. The IV bags were disconnected an hour ago, but the catheters will remain until Dr. Miller's final check.

Jackson looks at his watch and gives Haddie an ornery look. "I have an idea. You can't tell anyone what we're going to do, but it's so much fun. I have never shared this with anyone. Can I trust you?" Haddie shyly smiles and nods. Jackson grabs her hand and they head out of the room.

He winks at Travis who follows them down the hallway, up a flight of stairs, and down another hallway. Jackson opens the doors to a large, empty ballroom. He holds out his hand inviting Haddie into the room. Moonlight streams into the windows almost completely lighting the vast expanse. "The Roosevelt children used to roller skate in this room. So did Amy Carter, and she actually left a mark in the wood floor that was only recently repaired." She smiles at his cuteness.

Jackson kicks off his slippers, releases Haddie's hand, and starts running full speed into the moonlit room. The running stops and he glides on his socks twice as far as he ran. His contagious belly laugh fills the room as he does the same thing towards the western side of the room. He grabs a serving cart in the corner, one with wheels on the bottom and pushes it over to Haddie. "Your turn."

She sheepishly looks around and contemplates what he is asking her to do. Haddie takes a deep breath and nods. Jackson lifts her up under her arms and places her on top of the cart. He takes off at a sprint as they slide together the entire length of the room. They both laugh like children.

A few more passes later, they clear out of the room and slowly walk the halls of the White House. Jackson gives her a history lesson at every turn and she listens intently asking questions along the way. Only breaking to make a pit stop for the nurses and to rest Haddie's ankle.

Jackson opens the foot rest of Haddie's recliner and props her ankle with a pillow. He helps her take off the large, black boot. A nurse hands him an ice pack before she goes back to her seat in the far corner of the theatre. Once Haddie is comfortable, he settles back in his chair and watches her.

"Penny for your thoughts." He nudges her arm.

She smiles in return. "My Nunnie Mary says that all the time."

"It must be a grandmother thing. That is how mine started conversations." He reaches out to hold her hand. Their fingers entwine into a perfect fit.

"Although I'm having a wonderful time, I have this horrible feeling about Annie. She's probably so worried, not to mention this is very unfair that I get extra time with you. I think it's only fair that you spend private time with her too. She's really wonderful." Haddie frowns and focuses on her ankle.

Jackson pushes a strand of hair behind her ear so he can see her face. "There you go again assuming I'm some kind of player. Haddie, I choose you. It's only been you the entire time. I've been enchanted by you since you blew me off in the cooking class." Jackson laughs softly. "Annie knows it too. In fact, we talked about it yesterday. I haven't kept her around because I am attracted to her. I have been getting to know her for other reasons." He pauses. "I'm hoping she's the newest member of Rich's team. You can ask her if you don't believe me. I agree with you that she is wonderful, but I'm only drawn to her professionally. Annie is happy for us, though I'm sure you'll feel better after speaking with her yourself."

He places a finger under her chin and turns her face to his. "Haddie, I've already told you that you're the one. Neither one of us wanted to do this ridiculous contest, yet here we are. It's like the plan was to get us together the entire time. The choice has never been mine, it's always been yours. What do you say? Are you willing to take a chance on me?"

Uncle Malik's words of wisdom float through her head. *We know there is a bigger plan, we must always trust the plan in front of us no matter how twisty the road.*

162

Haddie looks deeply into his eyes, tears filling hers. She leans in and places her forehead against his. "Yes."

~Morning~

Dr. Miller clears his throat as he enters the theatre room effectively waking up Jackson, Haddie, and the nurses. "Well, it seems my wife isn't the only person who ignores my requests. So much for staying awake all night." The nurses jump to their feet and scurry to take vitals. "At least your security detail assures me that regular check-ins occurred all night and that sleep only just arrived within the hour."

Haddie and Jackson sit up in their chairs and try to shake the sleepiness from their eyes. One of the nurses picks up Haddie's ice packs and helps her with the walking boot. Jackson rubs her back. "Dr. Miller." He nods at the gentleman.

Dr. Miller pulls a chair in front of them while pulling out a small flashlight from his pocket. He flashes the light into their eyes as he begins speaking. "We'll perform another round of bloodwork to be tested, but the rushed results from last night showed a miniscule amount of the toxin. I believe we successfully beat it to its intended target of your nervous system. The nurses shall continue monitoring you during the day. I strongly urge you to directly report to me any symptom we discussed last night." The stodgy physician turns to the new nurses who have arrived to relieve the night shift. "Let's take more samples then remove the IV ports. We need to get them on their way this morning before Hayman Barnes has a heart attack. Miss Robinson, I have been told that you are to return to the Washington and Lee with a nurse attendant. I will write a conclusive report and send it to you swiftly Jackson. Until then, any questions for me?"

163

"No, thank you for everything, Dr. Miller. I am very interested in your official findings." Jackson shakes Dr. Miller's hand. Dr. Miller offers a slight head bow to Haddie as he turns to leave. The nurses begin their quick work as Jackson and Haddie sit in silence, each reviewing the events of the night in their thoughts.

As the nurses finish and leave Jackson and Haddie alone in the theatre room, he turns and places his hand on her cheek. "Well, I wish our date could have been more romantic, but I won't lie and say that I didn't enjoy our extra time together which included your subsequent confession of love."

Haddie rolls her eyes.

"I'm going to talk to Sandra and Hayman today. I don't want to be away from you for an entire week waiting for this show to be broadcast. I am leaving tomorrow for a ten day summit in Canada. Come with me. I was supposed to wait until tomorrow due to filming, but that's not an issue now. We can fly up tonight and have a romantic dinner. We can spend the entire week together."

"I do have a life you know." Haddie smirks as Jackson frowns.

"Please."

"Jackson, really, I can't. I have been out of pocket for three weeks with the show. My classes have already started and I need to catch up with my assignments. Plus, I'm scheduled to work at the library this week. Not to mention that I need time to think about everything that has happened. You've kind of turned my life upside down. Lastly, I'd rather stay out of the limelight for a while, at least until I'm out of this contraption." She giggles and knocks on her walking boot.

"I hate to break it to you, but your days out of the limelight are long past. You've seen the craziness since we've arrived back in DC. Once you're revealed as my girlfriend, you will be paparazzi gold. I've asked Madison to work on a security plan for you with a private agency. I'll pay for it, of course."

"See, this is exactly what I mean. I need some space to process all this. It's been a lot to absorb."

"That's what worries me. I've finally worn you down, I don't want you to go home and make up reasons why you think we're incompatible. You'll watch President Cashe in the media and start hating me again, I can't risk that." He looks nervously at her.

She giggles at him. "This isn't the 1700s. We can text and call each other every day. I promise I won't watch the news if it makes you feel better." She lightly plays with his fingers which are now entwined in hers. "I've already given you my word. I just need some rest and to catch up on classes. We can see each other as soon as you get back into town from presidenting."

"Presidenting? That's a new one. All right, I understand. Just remember, I have the resources of the entire government. If you try to run, I will find you." He caresses her cheek with his fingers.

Marcus knocks on the doorframe and clears his throat. "I'm very sorry to disturb you Sir, but Mr. Barnes is insisting on seeing you. I've held him off for as long as I can. He needs to walk through your itinerary and you have a meeting with the education reform committee."

Jackson continues looking into Haddie's eyes. "Thank you, Marcus. Can you arrange for Miss Robinson to get back to the

Washington and Lee discreetly? Do we have tracking devices we can attach to her phone?"

"Sir, I'm sure that's the worst dating idea you've had, and you've had some doozies. Respectfully, Sir."

"Marcus, I think you have the toughest job in this whole building." Haddie smiles broadly.

"Thank you, Ma'am. You have no idea the difficulty."

The white production van comes to a stop in the alley behind the Washington and Lee. Sandra climbs out of the back first to look for reporters or paparazzi. She motions to the van and Haddie slinks out next wearing Jackson's oversized sweats. The two women briskly walk through the garden to the back door. Waiting in the back sunroom is Annie.

Annie walks right up to Haddie and envelopes her in a big hug. The hug speaks volumes of unspoken words. Only these two women understand the overwhelming experiences that have transpired over the past three weeks. They have been on a roller coaster of emotions from beginning to end, together. They have formed a bond that no other can appreciate.

"Ladies, I hate to break up your reunion or congratulations or condolences or whatever exactly this is, but I need you in the parlor for a production meeting. Now." Sandra frustrated, strides out of the room.

Annie gives Haddie one last squeeze then links her arm in Haddie's. "It seems we have a lot to talk about."

They walk silently to the parlor, waiting to share their secrets in the privacy of their rooms. As soon as they turn the corner to enter the parlor, Haddie feels Suzanne's icy cold stare shooting daggers in their direction.

"Well, well, look at what the cat dragged in this morning. So much for miss prim and proper Haddie Robinson, angel of the President's eye. You could have at least had the decency to change before your walk of shame. I knew your little 'play hard to get' performance was just at act. Aren't you the most scheming of us all?"

Haddie's face drains white as she stands shocked and dumbfounded by Suzanne's attack. "I, um, no, I."

"Enough Suzanne! We've all heard plenty of your venom the past two days. You lost. Get over it." Sandra snarls. "Haddie. Annie. Sit. Look people, this has been one disaster after another since day one. I've had to deal with a bachelor who didn't want to be matched, a resort with less than discreet employees, fist fights, drunken falls, a sore loser, and a national security crisis. My agent warned me this would be too boring and guarded. This has been more adventurous than the all my seasons in reality TV combined. Now, everyone, listen up and focus so we can wrap this up today and start editing. Lisa!"

Lisa hands Sandra a cup of water and two pills. Sandra rubs her temples and begins the schedule for the day. "Immediately following this, I want individual interviews with the three women, starting with Suzanne. I swear Suzanne, if you don't take it down a notch about unfair play, I'm going to show your most unflattering moments on every teaser this week. I'll make you look like a fool. Annie, you'll go next with Haddie last. Obviously, we won't have a final veto tonight since Jackson took it upon himself to mess with all reality TV rules and conventionality. He broke the cardinal rule which is don't mess with the producer. I will have to edit the entire project differently so I can spin this." Sandra talking more to herself than the cast and crew.

"Lisa, we'll need to map out some additional scenes we'll need to stage. Maybe a recreated veto for Annie or Annie narrating the scene outside the monument. I'm not sure yet. Just remember, you are mine today. I will cram in as much as I can to get this wrapped tonight. Lisa will be working with you all on your final departure schedules tomorrow morning, but you'll want to start packing tonight. We'll want to get you home before the wolves attack your apartments, if they haven't already."

Sandra gets up and walks out of the room. "Move it, people! We only have one day!"

Suzanne glares at Haddie and Annie then storms out of the room. Annie grabs Haddie's hand and drags her up the stairs. She pulls them into her room and closes the door. "All right, spill everything."

Haddie flops back onto Annie's bed and sighs. "I don't even know where to begin Annie. This has been the most surreal experience of my life, and that says a lot. I don't even know what happened. Two months ago I was studying for finals. I didn't even know the president had a party let alone the drama that enfolded with his fiancé. I was plopped into this dating competition completely under duress. I spent the entire two weeks talking about the awesomeness of you, Priscilla, and Rachelle. Now look at me. I'm spending the night in the White House, stopping assassination attempts, and completely in over my head with this man!" Exasperated, Haddie drapes her arm over her face and tries to focus. She sits up quickly. "Annie, I'm so sorry about all of this. I know how much you wanted it. I feel like such a fraud, but I never intended this to happen. You believe me, right? You know I'm not what Suzanne said, right?"

168

"Seriously Haddie? I've watched the whole thing transpire. I think I've known for sure since the helicopter ride. After I left the infirmary I realized that every conversation I ever had with Jackson was intellectual and academic. He never looked at me the way he looks at you."

Annie sits beside Haddie and holds her hand. "What are you going to do? Do you love him? Wait, I already know the answer to that. The better question is, have you realized you're in love with him?"

Haddie hesitantly nods, reality hitting her in the head, and flops back down on the bed. She covers her face with both hands. "Annie, everything has happened so fast. I need to process everything. I need to breathe. My life is completely going to turn upside down just when I need it to be structured and focused. I have classes and work. I start med school in a few months. I don't have time for a relationship, and I certainly don't have time for 'this' relationship."

"Calm down, friend. Since I have met you, you have preached to me that everything is part of a master plan. You can't doubt that now, can you? If so, you're not the woman I thought you were all this time. You need to take some deep breaths and look at this from an outside perspective. You're taking all online classes, right?" Annie doesn't wait for a response. "Most online classes I've taken are self-paced. From what we've experienced this week, I'm assuming the media attention will only increase so I'm guessing you'll be barricaded in your apartment for the next week. You could potentially knock out most of your assignments in one week. Instead of binge watching a new show, you can binge on school work. I'm sure it's just as fun." Annie chuckles at herself.

Haddie lays on the bed processing everything her friend just said.

"Come on, Haddie. You're the most positive person I have ever met. Pull yourself together and rethink this. I mean, really. I'm the one who got dumped and then got a job offer instead of the guy. Besides, you even have me believing in this master plan thing, don't bail on me now."

Haddie sits up and looks at Annie. "Oh my gosh, I'm such a horrible friend. I haven't even asked you about you yet. Are you going to take the job? What is the job? Are you really okay with Jackson and me?"

"I'm still considering the job offer. I need to sit down and talk things through with my business partner. We've worked so hard to build our company. I'm thinking maybe I could work more as a consultant. I could work part time in DC and part time in Santa Clara. Just like you, I'm processing everything. It definitely has been a whirlwind adventure for sure. All right, enough about us, let's talk about Suzanne. Wow, is she a lunatic! She has been screaming and throwing things since her veto. She really lost it when she heard about you having to stay the night with Jackson. She threatened to call the media and cry about unfair advantage and breach of contract issues. Poor Sandra had to bring in the network lawyers to talk to her. I'm surprised Sandra hasn't stroked out yet. It's been awful. I've stayed in my room this whole time to avoid her. She is scary."

"I know! I can't believe she attacked me like that. It's not like I wanted to be poisoned. Good grief! I can't wait to ask Jackson what he saw in her. I don't see how he picked her over Priscilla or Rachelle."

Haddie and Annie laugh. They both talk about their dates with Jackson and how crazy this entire experience has been. Lisa knocks on the door and calls Annie down for her interview as Haddie heads to her room to take a shower. The beginning of a plan forms in her mind.

170

Madison and Rich knock on the door to the Oval office. They enter the room to the sound of whistling. Madison smiles.

"Uh oh. Please tell me I'm not hearing the sounds of love. I might vomit." Rich looks disgustedly at Jackson.

"Hey! I would like to remind you that this was all your idea. No one is more surprised than I am, Rich. Haddie Robinson is amazing and yes, I'm in love. Madison, did you arrange the flowers? I worked all morning on the card." Jackson grins like a Cheshire cat.

"Yes, sir. They went out about an hour ago. I spoke with Sandra this morning and the women will all be departing the Washington and Lee shortly. The women who remained in Colorado, were sent home early since the finalists were leaked. She's ensured that the women all have adequate protection, especially Haddie and Annie. Rich and I will be spending the rest of the day with Sandra and her team editing and getting ready for the first episode to air. Hayman will fly out with you today. We've prepared an extensive briefing packet to get you up to speed on everything that was placed on the back burner the past two weeks. Rich and I will take the red eye and be with you first thing in the morning. Do you have any questions for us before you leave?"

"Make sure that Haddie is the star of the show." Jackson stresses the point.

"Kill me now. It's worse than I thought. You're a goner." Rich slaps Jackson on the back. "I guess we're going to need to fill your spot at the poker table."

"Again, your fault." Jackson replies as he shoves Rich's arm and laughs. "You two get going, now. I need to read this packet and get ready for Hayman. I'll see you tomorrow. Thanks Madison for helping with the flowers."

"You are very welcome and I'll make sure Haddie's shown in the best light."

Jackson pulls out his cell phone and texts Haddie.

```
Safe travels home today and good luck with
classes tomorrow. I miss you already.
```

He smiles like a kid on Christmas morning. He sits on the golden couch and spreads the contents of the briefing packet out on the coffee table in front of him. His phone vibrates.

```
Shouldn't you be busy presidenting?
```

He laughs out loud at her response and quickly pecks out his own.

```
I am never too busy for you. Do you miss
me?
```

He holds the phone in his hands, waiting nervously for her reply

```
A little 😊
```

Jackson laughs, puts down his phone, and starts reading.

Chapter 8

~Reality After Reality TV~

Lisa and Haddie stand in the sunroom of the Washington and Lee. Haddie's bags are packed and ready for her ride. Lisa gives Haddie the official departure directions. "You are free to resume your normal activities, but please be discreet over the next week. I'm supposed to also remind you that contractually, you cannot speak to anyone about the show until the final episode airs. Remember, the show airs tonight and consecutively for the next ten days. After the finale, you're on your own. I'm assuming President Cashe's team has a plan in place for PR and marketing your relationship. You two can talk and text this week, but again, under the utmost secrecy and discretion. Do you have any questions for me?"

"No, Sandra gave us all a stern talking to last night. She let us go to bed after an hour while she stayed and went over the fine print with Suzanne." Haddie chortles.

"It was easier to get Annie and Suzanne out of here because they went straight to the airport. We arranged for you to be smuggled out of here in a catering van, but I'm sure reporters are already camped outside of your apartment building. You may consider staying somewhere else or making sure you can sneak in a back door." I have really enjoyed getting to know you, Haddie. You are a special person." Lisa hugs her.

"Thank you so much for everything Lisa. You were the backbone to this whole operation. I appreciate all of your help and patience with me. The pleasure is all mine."

Sadie walks into the kitchen. "Hey! You can't leave without a hug from me too!" Sadie embraces Haddie. "Now that you are tabloid fodder, make sure you never leave your house without make-up and your hair fixed. If you need a full time make-up artist as FLOTUS, you better call me."

"Who else would I even consider? You're a magician!" Haddie wipes the dewiness from her eyes and stares at her two new friends. "Thank you both so much! I'm honored that you both consider me a friend. Now I need to get out of here before I start blubbering like a fool."

A knock at the back door breaks up the farewell moment. A security guard opens the door and tells Haddie it's time to leave. She follows him out of the door and into the waiting catering truck. She calls Maryssa as soon as the doors close her in the back of the van.

"Aaaahhhh!!!!! I've been waiting for your call. It's been killing me not talking to you. I can't believe you were a finalist. I saw you all over the news with those other two girls. Where are you now? Do I need to come pick you up? Our building is under siege. There are reporters up and down the block. Not to mention a florist from the White House came earlier and delivered fourteen bouquets of roses. He brought them in boxes and set them up here so the reporters didn't see. I'm guessing that means that you're the one, but I can't believe it. Are you the one?"

Haddie smiles so big her cheeks almost burst. "I have missed you too Maryssa. How much caffeine have you had today?"

"It's all nerves. I've been on pins and needles waiting to hear from you today. Are you coming home now?"

"I was planning on it, but now I'm nervous. I can't deal with all the press and I definitely don't want to be held prisoner all week. Maybe we should stay with Uncle Malik."

"Dad suggested the same thing. I actually packed some of your things just in case. I have your laptop too. Text me things you can't live without and I'll meet you at the house."

"Thanks. I'm so overwhelmed right now. Leave the flowers but take pictures for me. I'll see you soon. Love you."

"Love you."

Haddie hits end then sends a text.

```
I hear you set up a flower shop in my
apartment. Have you ever heard of overkill?
You are lucky Sandra didn't find out.

I'm the leader of the free world, she
doesn't scare me…..well, maybe a little.
Have you seen them? I can assure you they're
not nearly as breathtaking as you.

Flatterer

Honest

Sweet

I miss you

Me too

I'm in a meeting. I'll call you later. XO
```

Haddie smiles broadly as she places her phone on her lap. She knocks on the window of the van and provides new directions to the driver. She relaxes as they drive through the city.

The savory aroma of garlic and tomatoes fills the air. The water for the pasta is boiling and the garlic bread is dressed and ready to go under the broiler. A pitcher of sweet tea sits on the counter with three glasses next to it. The table is set and Malik works busily in his kitchen.

He hears the front door open and walks out of the kitchen to see which of his girls came home first.

Haddie sees her Uncle Malik, drops her purse at the door and runs into his arms. She begins to cry. Malik holds her tight as he watches a man in a dark suit carry her bags into the doorway, waves, and turns to leave, closing the door behind him. Malik rubs Haddie's back as she cries.

She finally pulls away and looks at him. He wipes the tears from her eyes and waits for her to speak.

"I'm so sorry. I think I'm just exhausted. I don't know up from down and everything in my life has changed. I feel like a hot mess."

Malik pulls Haddie to his side and walks her into the kitchen. "I can only imagine, sweet girl. As Nunnie Mary says, nothing is so broken that some food can't fix it. Come, help me make the salad while I finish the baked ziti. We can talk about anything you want."

Haddie breathes deeply and then exhales relaxing her shoulder muscles. She leans into Uncle Malik and squeezes his side. "I've missed you so much. It smells amazing."

The two work at chopping vegetables together in the kitchen. Malik asks how she is feeling since the poisoning. He gives her the details about the arrest and his side of the night. Malik, sensing that Haddie isn't ready to talk, fills the conversation with updates from his and Maryssa's weeks without Haddie.

Once the ziti is in the oven and the salad is ready, Malik pours Haddie a glass of sweet tea and pulls out a chair for her at the table. He sits beside her at the large round table. "All right, Haddie, it's your turn. Are you ready to talk?" She nods. "I kept tabs on you the entire time. From what I heard, you tried as hard as possible to keep Jackson at bay and uninterested in you." Haddie nods again at her uncle. "I also heard that you were yourself with everyone else causing them to fall in love in with you."

Haddie starts to protest the compliment, but Uncle Malik holds up his hand. "I already know the answer to that one." He smiles. "You broke your ankle falling out of the helicopter and Jackson spent the evening with you in the infirmary?" She nods again, in amazement that he knows so much. "Although I try not to assume anything, based on the amount of flowers at your apartment and the fact that Jackson had me make your favorite dinner, he fell in love with you too." Haddie slowly nods as her eyes fill with tears again. "So, I guess the question is, how do you feel?"

"I don't know. I mean, I do know, but I can't process everything. It's all so overwhelming and scary. I didn't want to love him. We're so different. We couldn't be more different. It will never last. I didn't even vote for him. If it weren't for you, Maryssa, and med school, I wouldn't even live in this country." Haddie drops her head into her eyes and sighs.

"Haddie Robinson, I can't believe what I'm hearing from you. You, of all people." Malik gently scolds her.

Haddie looks up at her favorite uncle, worry and confusion on her face.

177

"We don't believe in coincidence or chance. We believe in Romans 8:28 and Jeremiah 29:11. Everything that happens to us is part of a bigger plan and purpose. You would never have put your name in for that show, but you were meant to be there for whatever reason. You tried your hardest to get kicked off the show, but didn't. Now here you sit, questioning how you got here and why. We may never know the why, but let's focus on the basics of the situation. You met a guy that you really care for and he cares for you. He is a nice guy. He is successful. He has a florist at his house." Malik winks at her. "Haddie, look at everything our family has gone through over the years. The good, the bad. We have always had faith in His plan, why on earth would you doubt that now? Instead of worrying and stressing, focus on the beauty of life in front of you. Love is a wonderful, life changing event, enjoy the ride." Malik squeezes Haddie's hand. He gets up to put the bread in the oven, allowing his niece to take it all in and think.

After a minute, Haddie wipes her eyes and takes a sip of her tea. "I still can't believe Daddy gave you his chili recipe. I about fell out of my chair when a took my first bite."

Malik returns to the table and looks at her strangely. "Didn't Jackson tell you?" He continues as he sees her confused expression. "He called your dad for the recipe, not me. Madison told him how special the recipe is so he had her track down their number and asked them to keep the secret. I think Esther cross examined him on the call too. Can you imagine poor Jackson on that call? I doubt he got a word in at all." Malik laughs hysterically.

"I can't believe he called them. I can't believe Dad gave him the recipe." Haddie laughs and tears up again, in wonder. "I called them on the way over, but they were so concerned about my ankle and the poisoning, they didn't talk about anything else. I'll have to call back later and get the scoop."

178

The front door swings open, and Maryssa bursts into the room. "Haaaaddddiiieeee!"

~The New Normal~

The end credits flash on the television screen as Haddie's phone begins to ring. She takes a deep breath of relief now that the first show is finished. The show was tastefully edited and it was nice to see the faces of her friends and Jackson. Haddie was on pins and needles the past two hours. She looks at the number on her phone, California.

"Hello Annie." Haddie smiles. Maryssa and Uncle Malik head into the kitchen to bring their dessert plates to the sink.

"Haddie! It's all of us, we're on conference. Priscilla and Rachelle are on too."

Rachelle starts talking before Annie even finishes. "All right, you have to tell us the Suzanne story. Annie texted today that good ole Suzi is a loony toon. I want details."

The four women discuss the show. Sandra did a fantastic job of accentuating the character flaws of the blondie twins and the cheerleader. The drunk girl angle from day one was the main focus of the third half hour. Haddie feels badly for Sophia, especially since they all know the real reason was high altitude and nerves, not drunkenness.

"I spoke with Sophia yesterday. She seems to be in good spirits. She was nervous about how they would portray her, but she has a good support system. I'm going to text her later." Annie shares with the group.

179

The first hour of the show introduced the world to the fifteen contestants. Haddie, Annie, Suzanne, and Priscilla had the most air time.

"I can't wait for the episode to show Haddie busting it while climbing out of the helicopter. Now, that will be fun to watch." Rachelle laughs uncontrollably.

"Hey!" Haddie laughs in response.

Priscilla groans, "I just hope they edit out my graphic medical stories. I will never live that down at work."

"On the bright side, my business is blowing up with requests since my name was leaked." Annie brags, "I may have been dumped by a guy, but my career is sky rocketing."

"Lucky you. I actually had an elderly client come in with her grandson today. She found out I was single from the show and wants me to consider dating him." Rachelle laughs.

Priscilla asks if he is cute.

"Oh, he's hot....and he starts college this fall."

"Cougar!" Priscilla shouts. They all burst into roaring laughter once again.

Haddie's phone beeps and 'restricted' comes across the screen. "I hate to break up this reunion, but I really need to take this call. I miss you all so much. Keep talking, don't let me stop you."

After the goodbyes, Haddie switches calls and smiles down to her toes before the first words are spoken.

~Politics As Usual~

After four days in Canada, Hayman flies back to Washington to continue work on the education reform proposal. He leaves Madison and Rich this morning with detailed instructions for handling Jackson. Surely, they can survive without him for twenty-four hours. This will be a short and jam packed trip. The car picks up Hayman at the airport and drives directly to the White House.

His secretary meets him at the door and hands him a stack of folders. They set off in a direct path to his office. He drills her on the details for today's meeting as they walk. She assures him that no stone has been left unturned and that the meeting will go off without a hitch today. The wait staff is setting up the conference room with breakfast foods and juices as they speak. He asks about the egg and spinach soufflés and she explains that the menu has changed to mini quiches. Hayman stops in his tracks and snarls at her.

"Sir, I've been assured the change is to your benefit. The mini quiche will allow guests to work and eat, whereas the soufflé would entail larger plates and a formal table setting." The young woman cautiously reports. "I personally spoke with the head chef when I heard of the change, sir."

Hayman growls. "It's too late now to change, but in the future, no changes shall be made without my approval first. I would have thought that was the law around here anyway. Apparently, the cook thinks he is more intelligent that I am. I will address this with him when the Canada trip is finished. As for you, do not allow this happen to again, or you will be on the streets looking for work. What I say, is the final say. Do you understand?"

"Yes, sir. I'm very sorry." She bows her head in defeat.

He assesses her demeanor. "Very well, let's move past this and get to work today. Have any of our guests arrived?"

"We're waiting for the last two now. The nominee for Secretary of Education is waiting in your office now. I can let you both know when everyone has arrived."

"Make sure they start eating before we enter the room. I want them at a disadvantage and feeling relaxed before we begin this morning. I have much ground to cover and I don't need any dissidents in that room. Bring plates for us in my office so we can eat beforehand." Hayman huffs as he opens the door to his office.

"Yes, sir. I'll check on them now."

"Ronald, great to see you." Hayman walks directly to his friend with an extended hand. His secretary closes the door and goes to fetch their breakfast.

Forty-five minutes later, and both filled from their private breakfast, they walk to the Roosevelt room. Hayman and Ronald enter to guests filling their plates or already at their seats just beginning to eat. The guests stop what they are doing to stand and greet the two men. Hayman smiles at his plan.

"Good morning! I see you all are enjoying this hearty breakfast. I'm sure it tastes as wonderful as it looks. Please, sit and continue. We can eat and work. Let's get right to business, shall we?" The attendees scurry to arrange their plates, folders, and agenda.

"Last time we were together, we were able to hammer out some of the bigger sticking points. I hope you all have had time to speak with your organizations about the details. Barring any unforeseen events, Ronald will be confirmed this week as

Secretary of Education and we can present a unified bill as early as Monday. I would like to start with continuing education requirements for teachers. Susan, I trust our negotiation attempts were successful and appealing to the teacher unions?"

Susan, a smart woman in her early fifties, has a mouth full of food. Quickly chewing, she wipes her mouth and looks at her notebook beside her plate. "Yes, we are amenable to that as long as you agree to the extended time requirement of three years for completion."

"Wonderful, Susan. You are a remarkable leader for educators! Moving on to school choice initiatives. The Private School Collaboration has agreed to tax breaks for families instead of a national voucher system. In exchange, private schools will have less restrictions on academic and athletic scholarships. Is this agreeable with everyone at the table."

Susan, who has now pushed her food to the side, clarifies. "The teacher unions are only agreeable if a scholarship cap is implemented and enforced. This is a deal breaker for us." She sits up straighter in her chair.

Hayman condescendingly laughs. "Of course, Susan. We obviously want to keep a fair playing field for athletics. No one wants to see unequal parings. My son plays lacrosse at Westondale Prep, it gets boring when the public school teams can't make it a game of it." He laughs at himself as Susan discreetly rolls her eyes.

"I understand your position, but I would like a cap in place before we leave today, none the less." Susan retorts.

"Susan, you drive a hard bargain but we already have some figures calculated. Carol submitted some suggestions on behalf of the Private School Coalition. My team added some comments

183

and recalculations. The information should be in your packets. Look at the figures and let me know by tomorrow morning if there are concerns. Carol, thank you for your work on behalf of private school institutions."

"We are happy to be a part of the conversation, Mr. Barnes. We are pleased that school choice initiatives are still part of the conversation in the new United States." Carole, a tall woman with red hair, replies.

"Let's not get political now, Carol. We've worked well together so far. Let's keep the streak going forward." Hayman gently scolds the thirty-five year old, well dressed woman.

"This is fantastic! We are moving right along this morning. The last issue we need to agree upon is the national testing standards. To recap, the President would like an independent testing company to create a national standard for all students. Susan, let me save your energy while you enjoy this lovely breakfast. We have all agreed that teachers and schools will not be penalized for low scores until a standard has been set. We will revisit that point in five years. Is that still affable with the unions?"

"I would like it in writing that we reserve our right to review the testing process in two years." Susan spits out before Hayman begins talking."

"Yes, yes. That stipulation is noted, as discussed. I think that is all we need to finalize for today. My secretary will send copies of the final bill to your offices today. I expect formal statements of support from each of your groups this week. Once the confirmation is official, we will introduce the joint bill to congress. Thank you all for…"

Hayman is interrupted after speaking over a man at the other end of the long table. "Mr. Barnes, please allow me a moment to speak." Paul Shelton, a tall man in khaki slacks and a buttoned-down plaid blue shirt, practically shouts over Hayman.

Hayman leans back in his chair and folds his arms over his chest. "Mr. Shelton, by all means, please share your thoughts." Hayman is annoyed.

"The Coalition of Homeschools is not ready to submit our approval or support for this bill. I have tried to contact your office all week, but have not been able to share my concerns. After speaking with everyone this morning, it seems that maybe you were too busy negotiating with the other groups. I'm hoping that you just hadn't gotten to me yet." Paul stands his ground in the room full of politicians and lobbyists.

"Frankly, Mr. Shelton, I'm surprised that anyone from your group has cause for concern. You are receiving more benefits from this bill than you have at any time in history. You have a seat at the table. Your Tim Tebow initiative will be made a national mandate so any homeschooled child may enjoy the benefits of the public school athletic system. You are getting regulated testing so that local school boards can't insist on additional testing. You are starting to sound ungrateful. I'm intrigued to hear your concerns." Hayman smugly sits in anticipation.

Paul sits forward on the edge of his chair. His placement towards the end of the long table is a message to him that he received loud and clear. He leans in so that he can see the other leaders at the table. "Please don't mistake my concerns for ungratefulness, sir. With all due respect, offering a few crumbs under the table, doesn't equal a seat at the table. It has been a humbling honor to serve on this committee and I am grateful that homeschool families were offered the opportunity to participate.

185

With that said, there are two major stipulation that we're insisting on if you want our support and not our disapproval." Paul continues before Hayman has the chance to interrupt. "You see, the initiatives we're receiving are long overdue, but the added restrictions are still unacceptable and shines a negative light on homeschooling. We have a tough time understanding why a "C" average is acceptable for participation in school activities and above failing allows students to advance to the next grade in public, private, military, and parochial schools, but it's eighty percent in both for homeschoolers."

Paul continues as Hayman stares in disbelief at the show of assertion. "I am the pastor of a church which hosts the largest homeschool co-op in the country. The lowest individual score in our co-op is higher than the average score of the two public schools in our county, but one third of our students wouldn't be able to participate in sports and extra-curricular activities because the guideline is higher for them. If you want our support, we need the requirement lowered to sixty-five percent, which is still remarkably higher than the standards for traditional schools. We also insist that the science portion of the national testing instrument not violate the religious beliefs of some homeschoolers. Specifically, big bang theory and evolution subjects being tested. At the very least, we request these items not be included in the test or an equal number of questions be included about creationism. These are deal breakers for us, sir."

Silence takes over the room. Susan writes down her concerns on her notepad, but she is afraid to speak. Everyone waits for Hayman to blow. Eyes dart back and forth between both men.

Hayman stands and places both hands on the table. "Mr. Shelton, your support is not needed. The mission of the United States of America is to ensure that every child receives a quality education regardless of race, sex, geographic or financial status.

186

By choosing to isolate your children, you are already taking away money from the public school system."

"Isolate? Really, Mr Barnes? The public school system model does not fit the needs of every child. If you would have returned my calls, I could have shared with you statistics and examples to support this fact. What about children on the autism spectrum who are denied services because their grades and test scores are so high? The public school system is happy to use their scores, but won't provide the basic therapies they need to help them cope in the community. Or the dyslexic child who isn't tested because it's too expensive for the school and they don't have the personnel to teach them strategies? Don't get me started on the children who are homeschooled to protect them from bullying and aggression, by other students and teachers. You call it isolation, I call it protection and intervention." Paul takes a deep breath as Susan swiftly sits up in her chair, ready for a fight. "I apologize for my frustration. My intention is not to denounce the public school system. In contrary, I am advocating that all children do not learn the same way and to urge this administration to equally support all avenues of learning, not only the government run, bureaucratic based system. If your goal is truly to meet the needs of every student, then we need to start thinking outside the box and looking at how people learn, not how we can force square pegs into round holes."

Hayman holds up his hand to silence Susan before the entire reform bill implodes. "That was a very theatric speech, Mr. Shelton. I'm sure the other members of this committee would love to debate your claims. However, it boils down to this, if you do not support this bill, we will need to rethink the other initiatives being offered to your group. Now, unless there are any other reasonable requests to discuss, we will adjourn. Thank you all for your time."

"I'm sorry to hear that, Mr. Barnes. We will be making a statement this week, but it will not be in favor."

"Your funeral." Hayman briskly walks out of the room and down the hall. He walks passed his secretary's desk, she follows with her notepad. "I want to know every statistic we have on homeschools. Especially the number associated with churches." Hayman spits out the order and slams his door in her face.

~Nightmares~

The bedroom in the suite is dark, moonlight steams in through a crack in the curtains. Jackson wakes with a start. His heart is pounding and he is damp from sweat. He looks around the room trying to gather his bearings. He is still in Canada. The clock on the nightstand says four in the morning. He tries to calm his nerves.

The nightmares began the day after the assassination attempt. He wakes at the same part in the dream every time, Haddie laying in a hospital bed. Jackson shakes his head and goes to the bathroom. He splashes water on his face and takes a long swig from a water bottle on the counter. He stretches his sore muscles. He is tense during the dreams. They seem so real. Jackson walks around the suite trying to clear his head. He walks to the desk and flips through the briefing folders left by Hayman. One folder falls to the ground. Jackson picks it up and realizes that it is the security report from the poisoning. He grabs a hand full of pretzels from a bowl on the coffee table and sits to read the report.

The details from that night, presented by secret service in the report, are staggering. The would-be assassins had planned the attack for months. They created a super botulin toxin that should have been completely untraceable until it was too late. The grower infused the toxin into a jar of peaches.

188

Once they put the pieces together, the agents reopened the car accident of the previous pastry chef. They discovered a hole in the break line. Martin killed the pastry chef and begged his cousin to get him an interview with Malik. Oscar was found innocent, but according to the report, he was interrogated for over twelve hours. Their intricate plan was essentially fool proof. If Malik hadn't been so perceptive, Jackson and Haddie would have been paralyzed in forty-eight hours and dead in seventy-two. Jackson drops the report on the couch beside him and rubs his hand across his chin. Thinking of a world without Haddie sends shivers down his spine.

He checks the clock. It's five in the morning. He picks up his phone to text Haddie. She should be getting up soon to do yoga before working on her classes. His desire to make sure she is okay outweighing his guilt for waking up his love.

Good morning, sunshine. I wanted to be the first person to greet you this morning.

His phone quickly vibrates as a smile bubbles from deep within him.

My cousin's snoring woke me a little while ago. You are a much cuter wake-up call.

I couldn't sleep and I missed you.

You just caught me. I was trying to talk myself into getting out of bed for yoga. Now that my foot is back to normal I need to start exercising again. You are the perfect distraction.

I'm glad you're not sick of me yet. We talked until midnight then I start texting at five. I promise I'm not a stalker.

I was getting worried.

Nope, not a stalker, but a little crazy in love.

You're so cheesy.

I've been called a lot of things by republicans, but never cheesy.

I seriously just LOL'd.

Am I too cheesy or just the right amount?

I'll get back to you on that.

I'll be home in five days. Will you meet me at my house? I need to see you.

You mean the People's House?

Yes, that one.

I'll be counting the days.

I'm going to think of you doing yoga all day now.

Stalker

Love you more

Jackson places his phone on the side table. His mother would love Haddie. He falls asleep on the couch thinking of the two of them baking in the kitchen together.

Knocking on the door startles him awake, but he's smiling this time. Hayman enters the suite and looks at Jackson questioningly. "I look better than you and I was on a plane at five this morning. Late night?"

"Something like that." Jackson rubs his eyes. "I need to jump in the shower before the rest of the gang shows up for meetings." He sees the security folder on the table and begins to think. "Hayman? What should I do if I want to honor someone for extraordinary patriotism in their job?"

Hayman smiles, "Anyone I know?"

Jackson responds absentmindedly, "I'm not sure yet, I'm just thinking at this point."

"Well, I would begin by a special presentation of the Presidential Medal of Freedom for the person and honor them with a day of national celebration. I mean, off the top of my head. I'm sure I can come up with other ideas."

"Hmm, yes, have Madison check on details for me. We can talk about it when we get back to DC."

"I will present a plan for you by tomorrow. On another note, we have something serious we need to discuss. There is a small fraction of the population that is causing more division in the country. With the fragile rebuilding state that we are in, we must take every threat as an attack on the country. This group has been opposing every initiative we have put forward. They are a hate group who encourages discrimination. According to information I received yesterday, they are trying to kill the education reform bill based on religious freedom, which is Ludacris. Most importantly, they are behind your assassination attempt last week."

"I thought the assassination was linked to a small militia group in Georgia. Who are these people? Have they been on our radar before now? I'm confused."

"That's why you have me, Jackson. This group needs to be stopped. The majority of them disaffiliated with the Allied States, but there are some who live in the states that remained with us. Georgia is one of their main states, along with the other southern states. One of the assassins lived in New York before the Separation. He relocated here to launch the plan, but he is from the south. Based on my calculations, about one eighth of the population remains loyal to this extremist group. We must monitor them and shut them down before they cause more damage. I have some preliminary plans and numbers here for you to consider. I would like for you to sign an executive order today alerting the nation to the threat."

"Who are they? Let me see your report." Jackson reaches out for the folders and flips through the contents. "Wait, Hayman, this is madness. Surely, you're not suggesting we target the entire Christian faith."

"Absolutely not, Jackson. Half the population relates to that religion, or at least call themselves Christians. No, I'm suggesting that we put an end to the extremist faction that follows an Evangelical philosophy in which they spew their doctrine to others. They are the extremists of the extremists. They have nothing in common with our purpose as a nation. They are the reason behind the Separation. They should have left with their people. Their agenda boasts intolerance, separation, and exclusivity. They tell others that they own the afterlife and their god is the only real god. I'm worried for your safety and those around you if we don't stop them now."

Jackson's fears about Haddie rush to the forefront of his mind. "What exactly are you proposing? We must be careful not to alienate any more citizens. The goal is to win back states not lose them. How do we monitor without decreasing our population?"

"It's all outlined right there in the executive order. Evangelical churches and their leaders must submit detailed descriptions of their programs and sermons monthly to a newly formed government agency that will enforce laws and prevent discriminatory rhetoric and separation propaganda. Likewise, any Evangelical school or homeschool must do the same. We must ensure that children in our care are receiving a quality education, not made up jargon. Think of it as a public safety directive. This is merely a monitoring program to prevent assassination attacks and safeguard the safety of The People."

Jackson stares out the window and contemplates Hayman's plan. Visions from his nightmares flash through his mind. He thinks about Haddie being poisoned. "It's just a monitoring program? What about the first amendment?"

"This is about protection of others, not freedom of speech. We cannot allow them to spread their propaganda and hatred. This order establishes a monitoring system for this one group."

"This is the group who attempted to poison Haddie and me?"

Hayman nods.

"All right. I'll sign it."

"Jackson, you're doing the right thing. Here is the order. Sign it now, so it goes into immediate effect. I'll work out the details. We can make an official statement when we return next week. I already have a few names of who should lead the monitoring agency. I'll brief Madison and Rich while you're in the shower."

"Thanks." Jackson heads for his room and closes the door.

Jackson's phone lights up and vibrates on the table. Hayman briefly looks at the screen and sees Haddie's face pop up with a text

Hayman rolls his eyes. *This one won't last long. They never do.*

~Purpose~

The laptop screen blurs. The words all smoosh together. Haddie rubs her eyes and closes the lid. She stands at her desk and stretches on her tiptoes, reaching high towards the ceiling. She arches to the left, right, then backwards. She rolls her shoulders, her neck follows. She rolls her ankle which is stiff but feeling much better. She looks at her desk and room from high school. Nothing has changed at all. Maryssa is still sleeping in her twin bed on the other side of the room.

Uncle Malik painted the room a pale shade of gray. Haddie's side was accented in purple while Maryssa's had lavender and shades of pink. Haddie grins as she remembers the intense negotiations over decorating their room. Maryssa and Haddie went from having their own rooms in their own houses in South Carolina to sharing one bedroom in Uncle Malik and Aunt Ruth's brownstone. While the two were best friends, their decorating styles were completely different. Maryssa's snoring fills Haddie with gratitude over their apartment, which Haddie misses desperately. Hopefully she'll be able to go home once the hype of the show dissipates.

Haddie walks downstairs to the spacious kitchen. What the brownstone lacks in bedrooms, it makes up for in abundant open space. The coffee calls her name as she takes cream out of the fridge. She pops a mini muffin in her mouth as she stirs her coffee. She leans on the counter and enjoys the aroma coming from her oversized mug.

She picks up her phone and sees Jackson's face smiling at her. His navy blue sweatshirt bringing out the blue flecks in his hazel eyes. She will see him in person in three short days. The time passes quickly. He has been busy in meetings and her with classes. They manage to talk and text throughout the day. She can't resist texting him after seeing his picture.

I know you're really busy, but I'm taking a study break and I just wanted to say hi. So, hi.

Her phone immediately bings.

Hi. I'm pretending to be checking my schedule on my phone right now. I'm smiling inside but I probably look like I'm scowling at the prime minister.

Don't ruin relations with Canada on my account. You can text me back later.

No, I'm so happy you texted! I picture you sitting at a computer wearing sweats, hair in a bun, and very very lonely for me.

Haha! You have the sweats and bun part right. I'm actually enjoying my piping hot cup of coffee. My laptop was making my head spin. I'm thinking about taking a walk.

Please be careful, if you do. I worry so much about you.

I'm a big girl, and no one knows where I'm staying. Not even you 😊.

Which still doesn't make sense to me. I'm dying to know your secret whereabouts. You know I can get the FBI to find you, right?

I told you, I need to tell you in person. It's not bad, but you'll be surprised.

Are you married?????

Yes, and I have twenty kids. Is that a problem?

Only the part where I have to share you. Uh oh, I have to go, Hayman has steam coming from his ears. Tell your kids I said hi. Ps-I miss you!

Me too

Haddie puts down her phone and sits at the kitchen table staring out the patio door leading into the small, enclosed sunroom. Aunt Ruth used to sit out there every day when she did her Bible study. She said the bright yellow color and the sunlight streaming in, helped her to focus on the bigger picture. Haddie misses Aunt Ruth and Lizzie so much. She wonders what they

196

both would think about Jackson and all this drama surrounding her. Lizzie was all about attention so she would have loved being the American Pippa Middleton. Haddie giggles at the thought.

The front door opens and closes loudly, startling Haddie. Uncle Malik storms into the kitchen and throws his keys onto the counter. He is mumbling loudly to himself and very agitated.

"Uncle Malik? Are you okay?"

"No, I'm not, and neither are you!"

Haddie is worried and runs to the window looking for reporters. "You're scaring me, what's happening?"

"Where is Maryssa? It's nearly ten, is she still sleeping?"

Haddie nods.

"This is no time to sleep, this is a time for action!" Malik continues mumbling to himself and pacing around the kitchen.

"Uncle Malik, please, tell me."

"This has to be all Hayman's idea. Jackson would never do this." Hayman talks louder but still to himself. He sees the worry on Haddie's face and he sits at the table. He takes a breath then places his hands on hers as she sits across from him.

"An executive order was signed two days ago by President Cashe. The order targets Christians."

Haddie shakes her head back and forth. "No, he wouldn't do that. You must have misunderstood."

197

"No, sweetheart I didn't. I heard it directly from his personal secretary who goes to my church. Hayman had it ferried over from Canada yesterday. It won't be announced until next week, but it is legitimate. The order calls for all Christian churches and schools to submit sermons, programming, and educational tools monthly to a government monitoring organization as well as Christian authors and song writers. Anything which spreads the Gospel in any form. Monitors will determine whether information presented by Christian groups is appropriate and positive for everyone. Those deemed 'extreme,' the order labels them as 'extreme Evangelicals,' need surveillance and possibly detained or encouraged to move to the Allied States."

"That's crazy, are you sure? Jackson would never do anything like this." Haddie is in denial. Panic starting to settle over her.

"I wish I was wrong, but I verified it with sources in Canada. Hayman had a private meeting with the President and came out with the signed document. "This has Hayman's fingerprints all over it. He is an outspoken atheist and has written me up for not working on Sundays. I also heard that he is battling right now with a pastor over the education reform he's been trying to push forward. This is exactly something he would do. I'm wondering if Jackson has any idea what the order entails. You need to talk to him, Haddie. You need to convince him that Christians deserve the same religious freedoms as every other religion in this country."

Haddie stands and starts pacing now. It's her turn to talk loudly to herself. "I can't. How can I do that? We just starting dating. We made a truce to not talk about politics. Hayman is his most trusted advisor. I think Jackson is actually a little scared of him, if I'm honest. I can't go against Hayman Barnes, he would eat me for lunch. We barely have time to text, let alone have a serious conversation about an executive order he signed. I can't even go to his house without his invitation. How would I even bring it up, when?" Haddie paces and considers the ramifications.

Malik walks to Haddie and takes her hands in his. "Haddie, maybe this is the reason everything has happened the way it has with you two. Maybe the plan is for you to be the voice in Jackson's ear for such a time as this. Think about it. Hayman keeps Jackson secluded from outside influences. He is even shields Jackson from the media. Jackson only knows what Rich and Madison tell him and that is all filtered through Hayman first. Haddie, you are the spokesperson for our people. You must fight for our right to worship and pray as we are called to do."

Haddie walks away from Malik and sits back down at the table. She tries to calm her breaths and heartrate.

How can this be happening? I need to talk to Jackson. No, I need to figure this out before I talk to Jackson.

A million thoughts rush through Haddie's overwhelmed head and heart. Malik sits beside Haddie and waits for her to process and respond. He has watched her grow through many trials during her lifetime. So many emotions. He knows how strong she is and knows that she will do the right thing. He waits.

Haddie looks up resolutely. "We need to pray about this. Pray for the timing and the words. If this is part of His plan, it will unfold the way it should." She pauses, "Call Nunnie Mary and tell her to give up her chocolate for the next few days. She loves to fast. We have some praying to do."

Maryssa saunters into the room, still in her pajamas. "What are you two talking about so loudly. You could wake the dead." She rubs her eyes.

"I think we just did." Malik laughs at his daughter who is yawning.

Chapter 9

~Threads in a Tapestry~

Maryssa helps Haddie sneak into their apartment early one morning by causing a distraction arguing with the garbage man. Stan, the garbage man, is the brother of the building super Dan. Both Stan and Dan were happy to help for free pizza and wings. The reporters were so busy laughing at Maryssa in curlers trying to add a bag while they were emptying the bin. Haddie slips right into the back fire entrance being held open for her by Dan. She is able to spend the next two nights in her own bed.

The next three days fly by with both Jackson and Haddie texting when they can. Jackson has had back to back meetings. Haddie crams three exams into one week so she can finish early. She had to cancel her shifts at the library because reporters found out about her job and began harassing students for their credentials. This saddens Haddie. It's a reminder of the life she is giving up and the spotlight now shining right at her. She tries to focus on classes and avoids looking out the windows. The only time she watches television is to watch *Future FLOTUS?*.

Jackson returns tonight. Haddie is resolute in her plan. Her emotions feel like a kaleidoscope all blurring together. Anticipation, worry, frustration, but longing for Jackson shines the brightest. Their texts haven't been enough and calls have been impossible. Uncle Malik reminds Haddie that he and Aunt Ruth fell in love by writing letters to one another. Haddie didn't realize so much information could be shared via text messages. Jackson seems so open with her and he brings out the same out in her.

She loves that he asks about her classes and dreams. He wants to know everything about her and she enjoys learning who Jackson is, breaking the Presidential illusion she held for the past year. His emotional depth and quest for learning inspires her. She wishes more people knew his heart instead of his politics. More things would be accomplished if all politicians voted their conscience and common sense instead of along rigid party lines.

Haddie spends the morning studying then hatches the first phase of her plan. She opens her laptop and dials Jackson's number into Google Hangouts, and waits. She knows he is on Air Force One with Hayman and that a video chat right now is very risky, especially for a new relationship. She nervously waits as the chimes ring.

Jackson's face pops onto the screen.

He's not smiling.

"Hey! I thought I'd take a chance and video chat. Is this a good time?"

"Wait, just a minute." He stares in another direction. She waits with bubbles rumbling in her stomach.

He smiles. "Hey there, yourself! This is quite a surprise!"

"A good surprise or a bad one?"

"Your face is like a mirage in the dessert. Hayman isn't so happy with you right now, but you're not dating him so it doesn't matter. You're a sight for sore eyes, so yes, a good surprise."

"There is the flatterer I know." Haddie giggles.

"You took a risk by calling. I could have been hosting a dignitary or cabinet member. You could have interrupted a national security briefing. I could have you arrested."

"I know a good lawyer."

"Who?"

"Umm, you. Unless you won't represent me."

"I think we can negotiate a fee. I could use a good shoulder massage after ten days of tenuous Presidenting." Jackson smirks at Haddie.

"How about a nice tiramisu? I needed a study break today so I made my grandmother's special recipe straight from San Giavonni, Italy."

"If I didn't know it before, I definitely know it now. You are the perfect woman."

Haddie laughs so hard she snorts. "Hardly, I'm just waiting to show you all my flaws."

"I don't believe you. You don't have any flaws. Now about this tiramisu?"

"My grandmother always says that the way to a man's heart is through is stomach, she must be right."

"She seems very wise, I can't wait to meet her."

"Oh, she's very interested in meeting you too. My mother gave her glowing reviews about you. Apparently, you charmed my parents during your brief conversation with them. I'm still in shock that my dad gave you his secret recipe."

Jackson offers a deep laugh. "It wasn't easy. He told me that if I hurt you, he would take back the recipe right after he hunted me down and shot me. He effectually scared the daylights out of me and I have the secret service on my side."

Jackson loves watching Haddie heartily laugh. Her eyes scrunch up and her entire face lights. He watches her intently, his own smile taking over his face.

"We take our family recipes very seriously." Haddie continues laughing. "This tiramisu recipe is a tightly guarded secret too, I hope you like it. You should invite Hayman since I interrupted his meeting. Do you still want me there as soon as you get back?"

"I wanted you here with me now." His look intensifies. "I don't think I can travel without you anymore. Your presence brings me comfort."

Jackson can see Haddie's cheeks blushing through his phone screen. "Sweet talker." Haddie moves on before she loses her nerve. "I'll be waiting in the residence with tiramisu and three plates. I hate to break it to you, but I won't be able to stay long. I have two finals early tomorrow morning. The good news is that I'll have plenty of time after that."

"I'm holding you to that promise. I'm disappointed that I can't see you long tonight, but I'll take what I can get."

A knock at the door breaks Jackson's gaze from the phone. Hayman walks in and explains that they need to get back to work. "I hate to end this, but I'm being summoned. That presidenting thing and all." He winks at her.

"I understand. Besides, I need to go study. I'll see you in a few hours." She shouts loud enough for Hayman to hear. "Hayman, I'm so sorry for interrupting. I've made a peace offering. Please join Jackson and me for homemade tiramisu when you all land. It's a special family recipe."

"Tiramisu is my favorite dessert. Thank you very much Miss Robinson. Now, if you'll excuse us."

204

Jackson winks at Haddie and blows her a kiss before the screen goes black.

~Tiramisu~

The phone rings as soon as the final episode of *Future FLOTUS?* finishes. Haddie hears Annie, Priscilla, and Rachelle talking even before she says hello. She smiles. The four of them weren't able to talk together after the last two shows. Rachelle and Priscilla had television interviews following the episodes of their vetoes. Annie opted out of interviews tonight since she was offered a job by the president and hadn't finalized the details. The women have three nights of episodes to critique.

"Boy, you weren't kidding about your date Priscilla. All you talked about were gruesome medical procedures." Haddie teases without skipping a beat. All four women break out into a roar.

"I told you! It was awful. I was cringing the entire episode. I'm never going to live this down at work tomorrow. I got four texts during the show already. I guarantee gory soundbites will be floating all over the hospital before my morning shift." Priscilla half-heartedly laughs.

"How about the cat fight!" Annie cracks up as she starts talking. "We heard it was bad, but they really went after each other. The only time I've ever seen that much blond hair swinging in the air is when my mom watches classic rock videos on VH1."

Priscilla jumps into the conversation. "My favorite part was Jackson's face. He looked like a deer caught in headlights. He was probably afraid he would be next! It was obvious by that point, who the front runner was for him."

Haddie blushes. "Stop, that's not true. You all had great dates with him. I was still rooting for one of you to win."

"All right, not to sound mushy, but the ballet, really? Haddie, if that didn't seal the deal I don't know what did. That was the sweetest gesture I've ever seen outside of a romcom. Who knew President Jackson Cashe had such a romantic side. If you don't end up with him, people will think you're heartless. That made me want to vomit more than scenes from Priscilla's date." Rachelle warns lightly.

Annie adds on to Rachelle's observation. "Seriously Haddie, that was so adorable. Then the romantic Italian dinner. You had this thing in the bag from your first group date. It's no wonder why Suzanne stares daggers at you. If I didn't like you so much, I'd be really ticked!"

Rachelle jumps into the conversation. "Have you been trolling the Internet? There is so much speculations about what happened once the cameras left after the assassination attempt. Sandra did a great job of telling the story without many details, all while flourishing the dramatic angles. Everyone assumes you went to the hospital but no one can confirm your whereabouts that night. Plus, Suzanne dropped a little nugget of unfair sleepovers in her exit interview. Unless something else breaks in the news, you'll be tabloid gossip for a while. I hope Jackson's PR team is on the case."

Haddie feels defensive. "We were trailed by two nurses all night. I'll be glad if I never see Suzanne again in my life. Ugh. You know I'm just as shocked about this as you all. I tried so hard for him to not like me. I even asked to quit in the infirmary, but that's when he egged me on to give him a chance."

"I knew I shouldn't have left you alone that night!" You can hear the sarcasm in Annie's voice. "Haddie, it's obvious that you two were meant to be together. We all felt it there and according to social media and the press, the world sees it too. Don't feel bad or guilty. Enjoy it."

"When are you coming back to DC? I need more Annie wisdom in my life." Haddie chuckles.

"I'm always a phone call away, dear friend. As for the job, I'm still deciding what to do. I've worked so hard to build my business. I think I have a plan, I just need to discuss it with Rich. Hopefully, I'll be there soon." Annie's smile shows through her words.

"Well ladies, I hate to cut this short, but I have a date with the President." Haddie confesses.

Grunts and groans follow her announcement.

Rachelle talks over the others to tease her friend. "Thanks for rubbing it in, Haddie!"

"Trust me, it won't be all sunshine and roses. Hayman is joining us."

The laughter is so loud, Haddie holds the phone away from her ear.

Marcus meets Haddie at the receiving door. Security scans her and her tiramisu. She has flashbacks of her last night together with Jackson as she walks the halls. The smile grows from her heart to her face. The White House is starting to quiet down, but there is still much activity. She can feel the reverence in the building. People smile knowingly at her as she passes them in the hallways. Haddie feels awkward knowing that these people have seen such intimate sides of her that she typically keeps private. She politely nods and smiles back as she follows Marcus up to the residence.

They walk down the center hall of the residence and into the private living room. The greyish beige of the walls gives the room a warm feeling. The dark cherry furniture is masculine and sturdy. The couches and chairs are black leather. Haddie takes in the room. It looks like a man cave that was decorated by a professional designer. It's obvious Jackson spends a great deal of time in this room. It has his personal books laying on the table and a dart board on the wall. It warms Haddie's heart to see this side of him.

"Miss Robinson, please make yourself at home. The President wants you to know that he will be up in a few minutes." Marcus waves Haddie further into the room.

"Marcus, please call me Haddie and thank you." Haddie smiles softly.

Marcus returns her smile and nods, "Miss Haddie."

Haddie looks around the room trying to determine what to do now. She walks over to the large round table behind the seating area.

This would be the perfect table to do a puzzle.

Haddie remembers the countless hours she would put together puzzles with her sister and mother when they were little. The table is big and sturdy but small enough for four chairs to intimately share an activity. She rubs the table and admires the beauty of the wood. Marcus walks back into the room with a tray that he places on a matching side table. The tray holds crystal glasses, a pitcher of water, plates, cloth napkins, and silverware.

"Miss Haddie, I thought you might need these. Is there anything else I can get for you?"

"No, Marcus, this is wonderful. Thank you so much. Would you like to join us? I can't promise it's the best, but I'm a decent baker."

"Thank you, Ma'am, but I couldn't." Marcus pats his stomach. "My nephew is getting married this summer on Fire Island, I need to shed a few pounds before hitting the beach with family."

Haddie chuckles, "I totally understand."

"His secretary just called up to say he is on his way." Marcus nods and leaves the room.

Haddie starts cutting slices of tiramisu and placing them on the china. She hears Jackson and Hayman talking as they enter the room as she serves the last piece. She turns in time to see Jackson fly across the room to pick her up and swing her around once. Haddie squeals then laughs. He puts her on the ground and places a longing kiss on her lips. He holds her tight for a moment before Hayman clears his throat.

"Sorry Hayman, I just can't help myself. She has enraptured me."

Haddie pulls away and holds out her hand. "Hello, Mr. Barnes."

Hayman nods in greeting, "Miss Robinson, it is wonderful to see you. Thank you for the invitation."

Haddie motions for the men to take a seat around the table. "I hope it tastes as good as my grandmother's. You all can be honest. I can't learn to make it better, if I don't know what it has

209

too much of or what it's missing." She is bashful. "Travis seemed to like the piece he tested."

"I'm sure it's perfect, just like you." The three of them sit down around the table. Haddie passes the plates and silverware. Jackson takes a bite and closes his eyes in awe. The decadence melting in his mouth. "Haddie, you are an angel. I'm sure of it." Jackson takes another bite.

"I must say, Miss Robinson, this is quite a treat. I do love tiramisu. I find it difficult to discover an authentic piece. You've done a marvelous job. My wife will be jealous she didn't get to enjoy a piece."

"Oh, you must take her home a piece. Surely we can find a plastic container in this building. I definitely don't want to take it home. I've been snacking and studying all day. I don't need the temptation."

"Yes, Jackson said something about you taking online classes. I know from my eldest son the importance of self-motivation while fulfilling online responsibilities. I hope filming didn't interfere too much in your education."

"Not at all, thank you for asking. In fact, this week of solitude allowed me to push through most of my course load. At this rate, I should finish a month earlier than the semester ends. That will allow me extra time for work study hours."

"That is very impressive." Hayman studies the woman.

Jackson shares stories from their week in Canada at the summit. Madison closed the Prime Minister's wife's hand in a door. Jackson has tears rolling down his cheeks as he tells the story. Hayman rolls his eyes indignantly.

Hayman finishes the last bite of his dessert and wipes his mouth on the cloth napkin. "Thank you again for this wonderful treat. I really should be getting home now." He rises and pushes back from the table. "Jackson will fill you in on our plans to debut your relationship to the world. Rich has some ideas about an exclusive interview during primetime. We should schedule time to sit down tomorrow with the team and Sandra. The ratings were the highest in network history, so it seemed to work out on all fronts." Hayman leers at Jackson and Haddie.

Hayman makes Haddie sick to her stomach, but she keeps a smile plastered on her face. She stands, places the lid back onto the container for the tiramisu, and stacks the dishes and silverware. "Mr. Barnes, please take this home to your family."

"Hey!" Jackson protests.

Haddie looks at Jackson and snickers. "You are so cute. I'll make you another one. In fact, tomorrow I'm making butterscotch, chocolate chip brownies. Mr. Barnes, please join us again tomorrow night and we can talk then about your plan over brownies and milk."

"Homemade desserts two nights in a row? Why do I feel like I'm being buttered up for something?" Jackson stands and pulls Haddie to his side. "Just ask, I'll give you anything you want!" Jackson places a kiss on Haddie's head.

"Maybe I'll tell you tomorrow." Haddie offers a quiet laugh then leans her head into Jackson. She can smell his body wash and breathes deeply. "I actually need to leave now too."

Jackson's face falls and he pleads with Haddie to stay. "You can't leave. You just got here and we haven't seen each other for days. Please, stay longer." He stares into her eyes begging her to stay. She etches every inch of his face to memory. Tomorrow

211

may be their last time together. Her feelings are undeniable now. She needs to leave before she starts crying and blows the entire plan.

Haddie squeezes Jackson's hand. "I really can't. I have an online study group in an hour and I still need to email my portion of the outline. I'll text you when I'm finished. Maybe we can video chat if you're not too busy presidenting."

Jackson laughs as he pulls Haddie tightly into his chest. "Yes, I have an exciting night reading through a stack of briefs that Hayman has prepared for me." He breathes in her amazing scent. The lavender and mint always make him feel calm when she is near. Hayman rolls his eyes in the background and heads for the door.

He places a soft kiss on her lips then stares into her eyes. "Until tomorrow. I'll walk you to the door."

~VIP Invitation~

Hayman's wife and two sons are sitting in the family room. Janice reads a magazine while petting her pampered dog. James and Chad watch a basketball game on television. No one notices Hayman walk in the house. He places the container on the kitchen counter. Chanel picks up her head and barks softly, too lazy to offer more. Janice turns and sees Hayman.

"Hello, darling. I didn't hear you come in. How was your day?"

James and Chad both shout a greeting to their father over the TV.

Hayman walks into the traditionally decorated living room. He sits in the only non-floral chair in the room. He insisted on

212

having one leather recliner in this room. Janice picked it out, but respected his one request. Hayman is smiling broadly.

"I was invited to Jackson's quarters tonight by the winner of the FLOTUS show, Haddie. She personally invited me for a piece of homemade tiramisu. It is a family recipe of hers. She offered me the rest to bring home for you all. It is in the kitchen."

"Oh, how sweet of her. I was hoping he would choose Suzanne all week, but I do like Haddie. She seems very nice."

"She's super hot!" Chad barks.

"And flexible!" They showed shots of her practicing yoga one morning during the finale. "I'm not surprised at all that Jackson chose her." James derides.

"Boys, please." Janice scolds. "We want Jackson so find a nice girl. Do you like her dear?"

"I do, so far. Jackson has been less focused the past three weeks, but my hope is that it is just the unusual circumstances. Tomorrow is a normal day at the White House. I should be able to get him to refocus. We have a demanding schedule. Haddie invited me tomorrow evening as well for another dessert and to discuss how to introduce the new couple to the media. I am pleased that she wants to hear my opinion on the matter. That does bode well for her."

"And she's hot." Chad interjects once more for effect. All three men haughtily laugh.

"What time will you need to leave in the morning? Will you have time for cook to make you eggs? I can text her to be here early in the morning, if so." Janice inquires.

213

"No. I'll grab something on the way tomorrow. I need to arrive early. I have meetings to finalize the education bill and then an appointment with the chief usher to discuss the firing of Malik Lavalier. I will not abide by his lack of reverence towards me." Hayman spits out the last words in disgust.

"Firing is too good for that man, Dad. He should be arrested for his role in the assassination attempt. The country needs to know that he is public enemy number one. You should smear his name all over the media."

"I'm with Chad. He is a disgrace and a traitor to the new government. You need to hang him in effigy so that he'll be lucky to get a job flipping burgers. You can't let him get away with his outward defiance, Dad. Show him whose boss!"

"Dear, the boys have a point. He has been very defiant as of late. Jackson doesn't need that kind of insubordination at a time like this. You always take care of Jackson, and this is no different. That man needs to be taught a lesson." Chanel barks in agreement.

Hayman rubs his chin in thought. "You all have a point. I'll have Rich make some calls to reporters tomorrow night to leak the story in a few days after the official assassination report is released. The media won't even bother to read the entire report. They'll just go with what we feed them. By the time this is finished, Chef Lavalier will be crucified on every cannel. People will always wonder if he played a role in the assassination attempt."

Hayman broadly smiles at his plan. "Now, who wants some future FLOTUS tiramisu?"

The boys jump out of their seats.

~Preparation~

The sun rises over the Potomac. The water is calm, the streets are just beginning to wake. Clouds swirl quickly overhead. Reds, pinks, oranges, and purples entwine together fading in and out of each other like they have been painted on a canvas. The vibrant colors reflect off the dark glass water. The air is crisp and cold.

Haddie sees her breath as she runs for the first time in weeks. Maryssa keeps step beside her. Both moving in silence. Maryssa understands the heaviness of the task ahead weighing on her cousin. Haddie's chest rises and falls as her feet pound against the sidewalk. Her heartbeat fast, but steady. The sun rises higher revealing a bright blue behind the darkness of night. The clouds look like wisps of cotton candy stretching across the horizon.

Morning is Haddie's favorite time to run. DC rises early. It reminds her of the orchestra pit before a performance. Musicians tuning their instruments. The cacophony of individuals working alongside one another. Each one preparing to do their part for the greater good, desiring to play in unison for others to hear and feel. Sadly, the notes haven't sounded in tune for years. It's as if each musical group is playing their own melody instead of listening to the other instruments.

Haddie slows as they get closer to their apartment building. The private security guards Jackson hired run ahead and behind them. The media attention doubled after the final episode aired revealing Haddie as the President's girlfriend. Haddie's entire street is consumed with news trucks and reporters. Security holds them at bay while Haddie and Maryssa skirt into the side of the building.

The day blurs around Haddie. She goes through the motions of her daily routine, but her mind races. She talks to her parents on the phone. They encourage her and remind her that she is an overcomer. Her Nunnie Mary calls to pray with her and reminds her to text as soon as it's all over so she can eat chocolate again which makes Haddie laugh. She tries to study but can't focus. She does some stretches with Maryssa. Afterwards she tries to read her favorite Francine Rivers book, but her thoughts always turn to Jackson. They text throughout the day. He misses her and can't wait to see her.

Her favorite part of the day is a video chat with Chloe. The four year old bounces up and down the entire time. She turns the tablet sideways and upside down while talking. Haddie laughs and makes faces at her. Chloe gets off when her dad calls her in for lunch. Her brother in law blows her a kiss and says he's praying for her.

After lunch, Haddie pulls out all the ingredients for her favorite brownies. She turns on some music and starts measuring. Baking always makes Haddie feel grounded. The precise measurements, the steady mixing of textures, the smell of butter and sugar melting together. Baking brings back sweet memories of Aunt Ruth and Lizzie. What she wouldn't give to talk to them today.

So much has changed in five short weeks. She is the girlfriend of the world's most eligible bachelor. She is the most sought after celebrity for reporters and paparazzi alike. As if all that isn't enough, she is caught up in a political war between her boyfriend's respected advisor and her faith. It's still unfathomable to her how she ended up in this position.

For I know the plans I have for you. Plans to prosper you and not harm you. Plans to give you hope and a future.

The oven buzzes and the savory smell of chocolate wafts through the air. Haddie pulls out the pan and checks the brownies.

Perfect.

~Unraveling~

It seems the Oval Office has an open door today. As soon as one meeting ends, another begins. Rich and Madison come and go all day leaving agendas and paperwork in their wake. Jackson takes calls, personal meetings, and strategy sessions with his team. After a particularly long and taxing phone call with the Speaker of the House, Jackson welcomes a few minutes alone with his senior staff to have lunch.

Jackson smells the aroma of tomatoes, basil, and melted mozzarella as he opens the door of the Oval Office, Hayman behind him. He hears Madison and Rich talking as he walks through the small corridor to the President's Dining Room. The rich cream wall color warms the room as sunlight peaks through the tall, south facing windows. The long oval table is set for four.

Madison takes a sip of her iced tea as Rich stirs creamer in his coffee. They both look at Jackson as he walks into the room and sits across from the white mantled fireplace. Hayman is talking on his phone to one of his sons, Jackson can't remember which one called this time. Madison hands Jackson a folder and tells him to read it before their morning meeting with the housing and infrastructure team. All Jackson can think about is Chef Lavalier's lasagna. The smell is making his mouth water in anticipation.

Food is being served as Rich begins talking. "It is imperative you and Haddie discuss your PR plan tonight. We are behind the eight ball with this one. We should have nailed down a plan before we left for Canada. I know you want to protect her privacy, but that ship sailed the second she agreed to be on the show, brother. I can try my best to curtail the paparazzi, but you two need to give me something to work with first. Hiding her away is only making it worse."

Hayman cuts off Rich. "We will be meeting with Miss Robinson this evening after our dinner with the Secretary of Education. I will meet with you both afterwards to discuss the details. Rich, you can make some preliminary calls to determine which media outlets will be most favorable and appropriate with the story. Madison, will work with Sandra to acquire footage from the show to use as highlights. We definitely want the coverage of Jackson carrying Haddie to the infirmary after her fall from the helicopter to be the primary clip. It perpetuates Jackson's gentlemanly persona."

Jackson listens as Hayman and Rich hash out details and brainstorm ideas as he takes his first bite. The collective masterpiece of spices, noodles, sauce, and cheeses explodes in Jackson's mouth. He closes his eyes in appreciation.

Mmm, that man is an artist. How does he do this?

Jackson remembers the last time he saw Chef Lavalier and the wheels in his head start turning over the events that night. He waits for a break in the conversation to launch his own agenda.

"Hayman, do you remember when I asked you about honoring someone?"

Hayman broadly smiles and nods. "Yes, I have people on the award as we speak."

"I'd like to attend the next press briefing today to announce my gratitude and plans to honor the men."

"The men? I'm confused Jackson. I thought you told me you wanted to honor one man in particular." Hayman looks wary.

218

"I do, but I also want to honor the two FBI agents who made the arrest."

Rich jumps in, "What are we talking about?"

Jackson puts his fork down on his plate and takes a drink of his iced water. "I want to present medals to the two FBI agents who cracked the assassination plot. I also want to award the highest honor for civilians to Chef Lavalier for saving my life."

Madison chokes on her tea as she looks at Hayman. The older man opposite Jackson has gone pale as a ghost and is crestfallen.

"I would like for the agents and Malik to attend the briefing with me so I can thank them in person. I would also like to arrange press interviews with the men to make the rounds and receive the accolades they deserve." Jackson rubs his chin. "Hayman, this is very important to me. Will you personally work out the details? Call the bureau and have the agents come here as soon as possible. Malik is obviously here since we're eating his magnificent lasagna. We can go to the briefing room as soon as everyone is assembled. It is perfect timing with the report being finalized and released this week. These men need to be honored for their service to their country."

Hayman pushes away from the table and stands to leave. He is perplexed and unusually contrite. "I shall get started now so that we have ample time before the next news cycle. Madison, after lunch you notify Chef Lavalier. I would assume he will want to change from his whites. Excuse me." Hayman leaves his cloth napkin on his chair and leaves the room.

Madison and Rich stare at one another. Both knowing the disdain Hayman has towards Chef Lavalier, but neither knowing how to handle the situation. Jackson is lost in his own thoughts as he continues eating his favorite food and talking about the next agenda item.

Chanel barks wildly as Hayman enters the front door. James, Chad, and Janice rush to the front hallway to meet him. They have been glued to the television all afternoon watching the press briefing and subsequent media reports honoring Malik Lavalier and the two special agents.

"Dad, what happened? How did that mad man get away with this? Is he bribing Jackson?" Chad infers.

"Oh, honey. I'm so sorry. What an awful day you must have had." Janice takes his briefcase from him as she keeps Chanel at bay.

Hayman walks down the hallway and across the living room to the bar. He quickly fills a glass with his favorite amber liquid and shoots it down his throat. He fills the glass again and sits, loosening his tie. Shaking his head back and forth trying to process the day.

"Darling, you're worrying me. Please say something." Janice pleads with her husband of twenty-nine years.

"I don't have time to rehash this right now." Hayman is brisk with his response. "I need to get back to the west wing. I ran home for a new tie. Ironically, I spilled marinara sauce on mine and then coffee on my back-up tie while supervising Lavalier's press junket this afternoon." Hayman is in a state of shock. "I must get back in time for a dinner meeting then dessert with Jackson and Haddie."

Hayman stands and walks dejectedly to the stairs, his family watching him in silence. The driver knocks on the front door to let him know it's time to leave. Hayman sighs as he continues his mission to retrieve a tie.

Once back in the west wing. Hayman walks directly to Madison's office. He interrupts her working dinner with Rich and some junior staffers. She places her carton of take-out fried rice on the coffee table they are sitting around as she stands.

"Hayman, do you need me?" She is reluctant and unsure of his mood.

"Is everything ready for our dinner with Ronald? I need this education reform bill on its way by tomorrow morning. We do not need any more surprises."

Madison nods. "I personally checked the President's Dining Room and placed updated folders at each of your seats. Would you like me at the meeting? I can wrap up here if you need me."

Hayman snidely rolls his eyes at his deputy chief of staff. "Thank you, Miss Lyn, but I'm quite capable of running a business meeting myself. I've been doing so since before you were in diapers." Hayman brashly turns and heads to his dinner. The room is deathly quiet as Madison and Rich stare at one another, for the umpteenth time today.

Ronald is already waiting in the President's Dining Room. He stands as Hayman enters, the two men shake hands. Ronald looks at him and look wearily.

"Have you heard from the homeschoolers yet? Are they planning on following through with their threats to boycott this bill?" Ronald asks nervously.

Hayman responds by shaking his head. "I'm not worried. We have everyone else on board. Jackson only needs to hear the

221

highlights from the negotiations with the other groups. Don't linger on that topic, we'll focus on all the agreeable parties."

Ronald adds, "My assistant has attempted to reach Shelton for two days. He is either playing a game or completely oblivious on the art of negotiation."

Both men turn as they hear President Cashe walk down the corridor from the Oval Office.

"Secretary Shaeffer, that has a nice ring to it, doesn't it? It's so nice to see you. Thank you for joining us." Jackson pats Ronald on the back as they shake hands.

"Mr. President, thank you for the invitation. I look forward to our discussions this evening. I have a good feeling our preparations leading up to this meeting will please you."

The three men pull out their chairs to sit around the table. Food is served as Hayman begins explaining the details of the folder to Jackson. Ronald and Hayman take turns filling Jackson in on their negotiations and private conversations with the major players in education. Jackson reads the packet, listens to the men, and asks questions. His mind creates a blueprint of the education landscape as the two men speak. He adds suggestions as Hayman makes notes. Ronald jots down action points for his assistant to accomplish in the morning. The three men walk through the entire plan over steak salad with blue cheese crumbles. By the time the last crouton is eaten, things are almost finalized.

Jackson flips through the folder one last time. "I'm pleased that you worked closely with all parties involved to make a well balanced reform. However, I noticed neither of you mentioned Mr. Shelton from the NHA. Were you able to work with him on this bill? I remember there being some sticking points."

Ronald looks to Hayman to field this question. The air being sucked out by the elephant who just enters the room.

"So astute, Jackson. Yes, Mr. Shelton participated in our meetings and provided unprecedented feedback from his constituents. He seemed very unstable after our last meeting and he has been avoiding our attempts to reach him this week. We have plans to spin any change of direction on his part. We were more than generous with our offers to that group. Unfortunately, they were unreasonable and unreceptive." Hayman stands to stretch his legs and to attempt to change the direction. "If you notice, the teachers' unions are fully in support of the changes in regard to standardized testing. Jackson, make sure you read Dr. Parker's notes on the subject. They're glowing remarks. We have also worked out a press schedule over the next two weeks to market the highlights of the plan."

Jackson closes the folder and sits back in his chair, placing his napkin on the table. "This is wonderful work. Thank you both for the time you put into the negotiations. I have taken some notes. Let me look over this again tonight and Hayman and I will finalize everything tomorrow if I'm comfortable with it."

Hayman slightly bows his head in frustration.

"Now, if you'll excuse me, I have a date with the most amazing woman in DC." Jackson beams.

~Masterpiece~

With the help of Marcus, Haddie lays out plates, napkins, and forks on the small table in the West Sitting Room. Marcus brings out a pitcher of milk and three glasses as she cuts the brownies into large squares. This time Marcus accepts half a brownie after smelling the chocolatey goodness. "I can't resist. Thank you Miss Haddie."

"Let me know how they taste. I haven't made this in ages. They were my sister's favorite. It didn't feel right to make them after she passed, until now. I just had a strong craving for a taste of home." Haddie sweetly smiles as Marcus bites into the moist dessert.

"Oh my. Yes, this is definitely worth every calorie. Your uncle must be very proud." Marcus winks at Haddie.

Startled, Haddie asks, "How did you know?"

"Malik and I have worked together for quite some time. He is a dear friend. I understand why you wanted to keep it a secret."

"I feel so deceitful. At first, I didn't tell Jackson anything about myself. Then, I didn't want to encourage his feelings by telling him I'm the niece of someone he admires. I didn't plan on it, but it got to a point where I'd waited too long to tell him. Now, I feel as if I'm lying to him, but that wasn't my intent." The words stumble from Haddie's lips. The confession feels good to share with someone else. "I just assumed someone told him or that it was in my bio for him to read."

Marcus walks closer to her and pats her hand. "My dear, I'm sure it was, but Jackson didn't read your bio. He wanted to get to know you the old fashioned way. Yours is the only bio he didn't read." As Marcus's words sank in, Haddie's heart warmed.

"Miss Haddie, he may be surprised at first, but he'll understand. Although I've only worked with him for a short time, it doesn't take long to learn that he is a good man. He just needs good people to surround him to bring that out more." Marcus squeezes her hand before quickly leaving the room when he hears Jackson and Hayman approaching. She quickly rubs the wetness from her eyes and straightens the pan of brownies.

Jackson sees Haddie as soon as he turns the corner and begins walking down the Center Hall of the residence. She is casually dressed in black skinny jeans, tall black riding boots, and a long grey and turquoise flowing sweater. Her long brown hair falling in loose curls down her back and over her shoulders. She is a sight to behold.

Haddie turns to face him as she senses his gaze. Her full face smile reflects his own. They lock eyes as he walks towards her. Jackson picks her up in a bear hug and twirls her around once. He kisses her on the cheek as he puts her on the ground and stares longingly into her eyes. "You are not leaving any time soon! This isn't another eat and run date. We're going to spend quality time together tonight." He demands.

She smiles and nods in agreement. "Your wish is my command."

Hayman clears his throat, reminding them they are not alone. "Miss Robinson, I see you've exceeded the level set last night. These brownies look wonderful."

"Thank you. I hope they taste as good as they look. I was just telling Marcus I haven't made them in a few years, since my sister died. With everything happening so quickly, I guess I just needed a taste from home this week."

Hayman looks surprised, "I didn't know, I'm so sorry for your loss."

"She was very young. Ovarian cancer. She left behind a baby daughter and a husband."

"Chloe. She has her Aunt Haddie's eyes." Jackson proudly shares. He worked hard to get Haddie to share with him, he wants her know that he sucks up everything she says like a sponge.

225

Haddie holds his hand tighter. "That's the main reason I'm attending medical school. My goal now is to focus on oncology or cancer research." Haddie steadily looks Hayman directly in the eyes, trying to read him.

"What a noble cause Miss Robinson. I'm sure your parents are very proud."

"I'm surprised you didn't know this already. I just assumed it was all in my bio and investigation report. You two may want to check into your security screening. I could have been a clingy stalker." Haddie shrugs.

Hayman awkwardly smiles. "I'm sure all of that and more is in your file. I must admit, I left all of that to Miss Lyn and Mr. Miller. I'm embarrassed to say, I only looked at the headshots." He pauses, then adds, "I can tell you that you were the prettiest." He bashfully looks at Haddie.

"I can vouch for that!" Jackson makes great effort to drag her chair across the carpet closer to his. "Now, let's eat these brownies."

Haddie serves brownies and pours milk into their glasses. "I hope no one is lactose intolerant, but I was taught you can't eat brownies without milk." She sheepishly smiles.

The three eat their brownies and discuss their favorite childhood desserts. Haddie intentionally stays away from naming family members or delving too deeply into details. She strategically keeps the topic focused on desserts and encourages Hayman to talk about himself, which turns out to be extremely easy.

As they finish and sit back in their chairs, Hayman suggests they discuss the PR plan for their relationship. He explains that he will take their ideas to Madison and Rich downstairs once they have worked out a basic outline.

Haddie breathes deeply and silently prays for discernment.

"We need to strike while the iron is hot, so to speak." Hayman explains. "This will allow us to capitalize on the publicity from the show and reach a larger audience. The more accessible we make you as a couple, the sooner the media frenzy will fade. You will always be a paparazzi prize, but we think this will also help with security."

Jackson cuts a small piece of brownie from the plate and looks at Haddie. "I'll do whatever she says. She bakes like an angel and she's the perfect woman. To steal your line, 'your wish is my command.' Ask me anything and it shall be granted." Jackson pops the brownie in his mouth and waits for Haddie's response.

This is the moment of truth, I guess. Here goes nothing, or everything.

Haddie reaches out and takes Jackson's hand. She smiles at him, remembering every inch of his face in case this doesn't work.

"Well, I hate to throw a damper on your plans, but my life has taken a sudden detour and I may have to transfer medical schools."

A look of panic crosses Jackson's face as he sits on the edge of his seat. "What are you talking about? I don't understand."

She nervously rubs her thumb over his hand. She turns in her chair to face him as she inches closer to the edge. "Jackson, this is part of what I've needed to talk to you about in person. You see, I assumed you had read my bio and knew my background,

227

but I realized quickly that you hadn't based on the questions you asked. I thought it was cute you were being so inquisitive so I played along thinking you were being coy about knowing everything about me. That is, until I realized you didn't. You know that my parents live in South Carolina and that I attended high school in DC, but you don't know that I came to DC to live with my uncle and aunt. My roommate is my cousin, their daughter. I am Malik Lavalier's niece, I was staying at his house last week to avoid the media."

The room is silent. Haddie watches Jackson intently trying to gauge his response. Hayman's face is crestfallen once more today. His blood pressure begins to rise. Jackson processes the information Haddie is sharing. He looks at her questioningly. He needs to know more. "Malik? My Malik? Why didn't he say anything? Why didn't you?"

"Technically, he's my Malik." Haddie nervously shrugs. "Like I said, I assumed you knew, then it felt weird saying something." She waits for a response.

"I have to say I'm shocked and a little relieved. I was starting to believe that you were married." He laughs and leans back in his chair while keeping her hands in his. "That doesn't explain why you have to transfer schools. Is Malik leaving me?" Worry creases his face.

"That is the problem I'm facing now. My uncle, my cousin, and I must move from DC. My options are to move back to South Carolina with my parents or to West Virginia with my grandmother and extended family."

Still confused, Jackson tries to piece everything together. "I was with Malik today, he hasn't said anything about leaving. Why would he leave? Why would you leave? Haddie, help me to understand what is happening."

"You see, Jackson, we must move because we are being persecuted."

"What? That doesn't make any sense. From the media? Is that what this is about?"

She places her hand on his face and rubs her hand on his cheek. "No, Jackson. I would face an army of paparazzi for you."

He shakes his head, completely bewildered. "Then who is persecuting you?"

"You. Your government. You see, I am a Christian. The order you signed last week takes away my freedom to worship."

Jackson stumbles out the words, trying to make her see. "No, no. Hayman tell her. The order is to stop extreme Evangelicals from radicalizing and causing more division. You would never fall into that category. Those are the people behind the assassination attempt. I did it to protect you. This is to protect people from their hate speech and attacks." He pleads with her to understand the difference.

"See, that's where you're wrong. The Bible calls all Christians to be evangelists and spread God's love. It's called the Great Commission. Therefore, I'm an Evangelical. this government has told me that I don't have the right to listen to, preach, and read the Word without government oversight. I must leave the country if I want to worship freely. I've read the order, it's very clearThe true hypocrisy is that no other religion or faith has these restrictions, only Christians. I find it ironic that a country founded by Christians to preserve everyone's right to worship as they want, now protects and celebrates everyone's rights but the Christian's. I'm not sure what prompted the attack, but you obviously feel strongly about it since you crafted an executive order." Haddie feels the hurt and anger seeping out of her words as she speaks.

Jackson stands and pins Hayman with his questioning gaze. "Hayman, what is she talking about? Tell her this is a mistake." Hayman fidgets in his chair attempting to process the massive turn of events.

Jackson is yelling now. "Were there additional stipulations? This can't be right. I need to see the order right now. This has to be a misunderstanding. I thought we were protecting the country from a small group of extremists, not the entire Christian faith. My grandparents are Protestants!"

Jackson paces as he's speaking and processing. He pulls out his cell phone and calls Madison. "Madsi, I need to see the executive order I signed the other day about religious extremists. Yes, the entire document. I'm coming to your office right now." Jackson turns to Haddie and points at her. "Don't leave. I'll be right back." He stops, then turns, "Please. Don't leave."

Jackson sprints down the Center Hall and down the stairs. Madison breathlessly, practically collides with Jackson in the Palm Room. The document in hand. "What's going on, Jackson?" She looks at him with concern and worry.

"Walk with me." He turns around and reads while walking back towards the residence."

Hayman pounces to the chair next to Haddie and grabs the arms of her chair. Haddie recoils and presses as far back as she can into the chair.

"Haddie, you must know, I had no idea. I have been hitting resistance from every angle from Evangelicals with this education bill. I didn't mean to offend you. You can help me fix

230

this. We can go on air together and you can explain that you're a Christian and you support me. We can tweak the order." Hayman rambles, trying to convince her.

"Get away from her!" Jackson roars as he dashes down the hall. "How dare you Hayman! Don't blame her for your audacity. This is not at all what we discussed. You took advantage of my trust in you. I want this order retracted immediately!"

Hayman stands quickly and approaches Jackson and Madison. "Jackson."

Jackson shoves passed Hayman and kneels in front of Haddie. "I promise you I will fix this. Tell me what to do. I can't lose you." He is shaking and has both of her hands in his.

Hayman tries to speak. Jackson holds up a hand to silence him.

"Haddie, please." He wipes the tears from her cheeks. "Say you'll stay. I'll fix it."

Haddie nods. She reaches down and hugs his neck. They hold each other tightly.

Madison tugs slightly on Hayman's arm, "Let's leave them alone for a little while."

He pulls his arm away from her and scowls. "Jackson, we need to talk about this. Don't destroy everything you have built for a woman."

Jackson stills cold as ice. He doesn't turn around to face Hayman, he stares at Haddie's face. "Marcus!" The gentleman quickly enters the room. "Please escort Mr. Barnes back to his office and call Travis. Make sure security watches him clean out his office and vacate the premises. Madison, you are now my Chief of Staff. Call Rich and coordinate your efforts. Your first job is to fix this on every level. I'll meet you in your office after Haddie and I talk."

Jackson stands and pulls Haddie to her feet. He takes her hand and leads her out of the sitting room, through his master bedroom, into his private living room. They hear Hayman protesting in the background. He closes the door behind them. She trails him to sit on his leather couch. A box, beautifully wrapped in metallic purple and silver paper sits on the coffee table in front of them. He picks it up and holds it for a minute, looking into her eyes, deciding what to say next. His thumb glides over her porcelain skin. "Haddie, all I need to know is if you love me. After everything we have been through over the past month, everything you have learned about me, do you love me, Jackson Cashe? Because, that's all that matters to me. Everything else, we can figure out together. I can't do this anymore. I need you with me. You're either in or your out, time to put your cards on the table."

She wipes a straggling tear. "Jackson, I tried so hard not to love you." She laughs. "Heck, I tried hard not to like you at all. Yet here we are, and I'm completely and totally yours. Yes, I'm all-in and I raise you all my chips."

Jackson smiles with his whole face. He hands her the box. She slowly opens it, carefully trying to not damage the lovely wrapping too much. She holds a white box in her lap and opens the lid and smiles. She picks up the stethoscope with purple tubing with an *H* scrolled on the diaphragm. The engraving on the chestpiece says *You are my heartbeat.*

"I hope you like it. I didn't really know what I was doing, but the person I talked to said this was the best. It has soft-sealing eartips, whatever that means. And you can alternate between low and high frequency sounds without turning it over, or something like that. Do you like it?"

"I love it and I love you."

He leans in and softly kisses her.

"I need to go see Madison and fix this mess. I think I also need to call a few people about the education bill too. Something hasn't sat right with me about it and I think I know what it is now. Will you please stay? It might be a late night, but I'll feel better with you here with me. There is a private study right outside of the Oval. I can work in there with Rich and Madsi. Okay?"

Haddie stands and holds out her hand. "Lead the way."

Chapter 10

~Breaking News~

Morning comes early in Washington, DC. Lines are forming in the Metro stations. Street vendors are opening up shop on corners. The streets are filling with people trying to get to work and tourists trying to get a jump on the lines. It is supposed to be unseasonably warm in the city today. The bright sun and clear blue skies confirms the forecast.

The White House is lively with activity. Many staffers were called in last night, others came in before sunrise. Madison sent her assistant to her apartment for a change of clothes. Rich, is already working the rounds in the press room after a quick shower and change. Everything is off the record for now, but the anticipated news briefing is on everyone's mind.

News broke overnight about Hayman's firing. Rich made a few well-placed calls and the story grew. The lead on every news channel shows pictures of Hayman Barnes with the word *fired* somewhere on the screen. Rich leaked key facts to several reporters who managed to piece the entire story together by seven in the morning.

Jackson and Madison spoke with every member of the education committee and patched together what transpired over the past few weeks. In an unprecedented move, he spoke with the leaders of both parties and asked for their education priorities. The two leaders were happy to make a late night visit to the White House. With only the three of them in a room, open and honest communication and negotiations were able to flow.

Jackson reviewed the facts and wishlists from every entity involved then brainstormed with some junior staffers and Madison. After shrewd negotiations and compromises, he crafts a better and stronger education reform package. One that strongly reinforces the public education system's mission to provide a quality education to all children while offering breaks and benefits for private and charter schools as well as homeschoolers. The teacher unions are satisfied with having greater input on national testing, curriculum, and standards. They feel heard, and more importantly, supported. Wording is added to shed light on the importance of individual educational plans so that all children have learning opportunities. The new bill maps out options and opportunities within and beyond the public school system. The focus is on the importance of education not party politics and strategy.

Jackson, Madison, and Rich work on speaking points for every member of the education committee as they do interviews throughout the week, including an appreciative Mr. Shelton. They also create a speech for Jackson explaining the retraction of the executive order. Rich rises to the occasion and manages to make Jackson look like the hero. The final script looks as if it is written for a movie finale. Haddie will stand next to Jackson in the briefing room. The gesture will be the only announcement made of their relationship for now.

As far as Jackson is concerned, Hayman made his own bed. The only official statement from the White House is to confirm that Hayman Barnes is no longer employed. The press is already filling in the blanks on their own. Jackson doesn't want to rub salt in the wound.

Jackson is freshly showered. His walk down the West Colonnade is surreal this morning. Taking it all in, he thinks about the tasks ahead of him today. The first hurdle will be the press conference this morning, but he has one task that is his top priority. He walks through the Oval office and into his private study. Haddie fell asleep around four in the morning on the couch. He didn't have the heart to wake her and he didn't want

235

her to leave. He watches her sleep under a cashmere blanket that was given to him by his secretary last Christmas. Her breathing is steady. He will wake her up after his task is completed. He plans on insisting, after much begging and pleading, that she come to Colorado with him this weekend. They could both use some fresh mountain air and skiing.

He greets people in the hallway as he makes his way to the White House Kitchen. Malik Lavalier is in his office sorting through papers he abandoned yesterday so he could be honored by Jackson. Haddie texted him last night with a very abbreviated version of what transpired. His goal is to get organized this morning then meet with his staff later today. He is grateful that he won't have to deal with Hayman Barnes any longer.

The knock at his door shakes him from his thoughts. He stands as he sees Jackson. "President Cashe, is there something I can do for you?"

Jackson walks in and shakes Malik's hand then sits in the chair across from his desk. Malik sits back at his desk as Jackson starts talking.

"Malik, I owe you an apology. I'm sure Haddie will fill you in on the details, but I want you to hear it from me. Madison told me how Hayman has been treating you. I had no idea. I am sorry. I am also sorry that I failed in my duty and signed an executive order that targeted your family and your faith. Please, accept my heartfelt apologies. I have learned some very valuable lessons over the last twenty-four hours and even more since I've met Haddie. I understand I owe you my gratitude for helping to raise an extraordinary human being. I am deeply honored that she didn't leave me."

"Mr. President, you don't owe me anything, but I appreciate your sincerity and honesty. Haddie is a very wise woman. She must see something of great value in you. For what it's worth, I agree with her assessment."

"Malik, that means more to me than you know. I can't thank you enough for saving my life and now extending me your forgiveness."

"It has been a true joy to work here and get to know you and your staff. I look forward to watching you 'President,' as Haddie would say." Both men snicker at Haddie's humor.

Jackson inches to the edge of his chair and grins. "There is actually one other matter I need to talk about with you. I need your help with something that only you can pull off for me. It involves chili."

~The Speech~

Members of the press cram into the briefing room. Anyone who could score an invite, grabbed it. An excited buzz fills the room with loud talking and speculation. They know President Cashe will be speaking but they don't have the specific talking points. Guesses are made if the announcement is about Hayman Barnes, his late night meeting with the party heads, or the education bill that is supposed to be introduced. Everyone hopes they can get questions in about Haddie Robinson, but the Barnes story has replaced the president's love life.

A hushed rumbling settles over the room as Rich stands in front of the horde of reporters. He makes a few housekeeping announcements and reminds everyone that the president will not be taking questions after his speech. Rich calls on a few reporters and responds with, "No comment" to every Hayman Barnes question and a "They're doing great" after the Haddie questions. He jokes with various people in the room like he's holding court in his fraternity house. Rich is at home in front of the cameras and shines during a crisis.

Jackson hears Rich bantering with the press as he walks down the hallway with Haddie and Madison by his side. The sound of his friend's voice fills his heart with warmth. Jackson has learned so much about people and loyalty as of late and greatly values the familiarity of Rich and Madison. The door to the press briefing room is being held open by staffers overflowing the space. Jackson gently shakes hands and squeezes elbows as he enters the room. A complete silence falls over the crowd as Jackson and Haddie climb the stairs and stand behind the podium. The only sound is the clicking of cameras.

"Thank you all for coming today. Based on the size of this crowd and the numerous breaking stories, I doubt we could have kept you away even if the building was on fire." Jackson flashes his smile and the room bubbles over with a wave of laughter. "As I stand in front of you and the nation, I want to send a clear message that the United States of America is moving forward. I hope you all will see this in my personal and public life. While we're on my personal life, I would like to introduce you to the lovely Haddie Robinson. Let's get this out of the way so we can move on an address the issues that truly matter in the governing of our country. Haddie is a retired ballerina, a medical student, a daughter, granddaughter, niece, aunt, and….a Republican from South Carolina." Low laughs follow Jackson's smirk.

"I'm sure you all will be hounding us for years to come, but for now, this is the official announcement you have been asking for since the show's finale. We are dating. We are happy. We are "Two peas in a pod" as my grandmother would say. Thank you for the well wishes and please be respectful of Haddie's privacy as this is new for her." Haddie smiles and offers a shy, mini curtsy to the crowd, trying to embrace her new life. She continues holding Jackson's hand as he winks at her and turns back to the audience.

"I would like to begin by apologizing to Christians under my regulation. I failed in my duty to protect your rights and interests. As the most quoted line in the Declaration of Independence states, 'We hold these truths to be self-evident, that all men are created equal, that they are endowed by their Creator with certain unalienable Rights, that among these are Life, Liberty, and the pursuit of Happiness.' The decree I signed last week, restricted those rights. In an effort to secure the rights of all humans, we have restricted the rights of others. The Christian faith is the perfect example. In our current climate, we seem to fight for the rights of all religions while bilaterally taking away the rights of Christians who have held these rights since the founding of our nation. While other religions are being protected, the Christian faith is being attacked. The decree invalidated my promise to protect every citizen. For that, I am truly sorry. Moving forward, Christians will possess the same rights as every other religion in this nation."

"I have learned more about the art of compromise the past twenty-four hours than I have during my entire political career. I hope that shows in the Education Reform Bill being sent to Congress today. The irony of the Separation is that both sides worked so well to separate. Imagine how effective we would have been as a nation had we worked that hard at staying together. From this point forward, I vow to focus on issues and not political lines and special interests. I vow to represent every citizen and not just those I agree with on policies. I encourage us all to listen to the other side. Listening does not mean agreeing with, it means respecting others and their rights to 'Life, Liberty, and the pursuit of Happiness.' Perhaps if every citizen vowed to listen, our countries would not have had to endure years of violent clashes and protests."

"This great nation was founded on freedom. Freedom of religion and freedom of speech must be honored and upheld, regardless of whether we agree with that religion or speech. Being a nation made up of various races, ages, genders, socio economic backgrounds, and heritage, we are uniquely designed.

Our differences may be strong, but we all strive for freedom. We must offer that same freedom to others."

"I urge every citizen to live with the following four goals: One, live your beliefs in a positive manner for others to see; Two, listen to the other side and respect their right to freedom; Third, always take the time to research information before believing it and spreading it; Finally, and possibly the most important, teach your children to listen and learn from others and the past. Today, our youth are being taught by pop culture and we're doing them a great disservice. We are losing the art of discourse, respect for authority and others, and honor. Those who do not learn from the past, are doomed to repeat it. Our nation has already suffered enough, we need to come together and strengthen our resolve to uphold our freedoms."

"I find inspiration in the words of President Lincoln's second Inaugural Address. 'With malice toward none; with charity for all; with firmness in the right, as God gives us to see the right, let us strive on to finish the work, we are in; to bind up the nation's wounds; to care for him who shall have borne the battle, and for his widow, and his orphan—to do all which may achieve and cherish a just and lasting peace, among ourselves, and with nations'."

"In closing, I think we all can learn a lesson found in the Gospel of Luke, 'Be merciful, just as your Father is merciful. Do not judge, and you will not be judged. Do not condemn, and you will not be condemned, Forgive, and you will be forgiven. Give, and it shall be given to you. A good measure, pressed down, shaken together and running over, will be poured into your lap. For with the measure you use, it will be measured to you.' Thank you for your time today. May God continue to bless the United States of America."

Epilogue

~R & R~

The snow covered mountains are majestic as they glisten under the setting sun. Winding roads lead them back to the resort where they first met. Jackson holds her hand as they both watch the scenery passing by them. Haddie is curled up in her wool sweater. She looks at him questioningly as they pass the resort entrance and begin traveling up a long and winding road. He smiles at her but says nothing.

Haddie looks out the windows as they drive higher up the mountain. She feels more at peace, the farther they drive. The past two days were even more eventful than the past five weeks. After the press conference, Jackson and Madison were busy setting things right. They held meetings and made phone calls all day. Rich was on every channel oozing with confidence and charisma. Jackson handpicked an eclectic group of politicians to serve on a committee whose only task is to bridge the differences on issues facing the country. He personally interviewed each member to see if they were up for the task of complete bipartisanship. Senator Marchio was the first call and subsequently became the chairman after their talk.

Haddie spent the day in the residence working on her laptop. She didn't think twice when Jackson suggested a long weekend in Colorado. She emailed her professors, finished some assignments early, and packed her bags. They would finally have some time away from cameras and the spotlight.

The black cavalcade of SUVs comes to a stop in front of a luxurious brick and stone house. Light emanates from the floor to ceiling windows. The house is huge. There is a four-stall garage on the side of the house with snow mobiles parked in front of the last stall. Haddie looks questioningly at Jackson. He shrugs.

"I thought we could use some privacy. Well, as much privacy as the President is allowed to have." He chuckles. "I hope you like it here, I used to come here with my parents. There are eight bedrooms and a guest house. In the morning, we can walk right out the back door and ski down the mountain."

"Jackson, this is amazing. Thank you." She leans in and kisses his cheek.

Jackson squeezes her hand and gets out of the SUV. He walks to her side and opens the door to help her out. They climb up the stairs to the red front door. The cold air is refreshing and invigorates the senses. Jackson wraps an arm around Haddie's shoulders and pulls her tightly to his side. They walk through the door into the vast expanse. She can smell the fireplace. She turns to him as she hears voices coming from inside the house.

"That's the best part, come." Jackson leads her around the corner of the entrance hall into the large open kitchen. Haddie freezes in shock as Chloe runs full speed into her arms. "Aunt Haddie's here!"

One by one Haddie's family members walk over to her for hugs. Her parents, brother-in-law, Nunnie Mary, Uncle Malik, and Maryssa are all there in the kitchen. She sees two other people off to the side that she doesn't recognize. Jackson walks over to them and offers hugs.

"I can't believe you are all here, how did this happen?" Haddie wipes her eyes as she stays curled up in her father's arms.

Maryssa laughs, "Umm, you're dating the President. I can't imagine there's much he can't pull off if he wants something."

Jackson walks over, "Haddie, we've had such an unconventional relationship from the start, I thought I'd add to the crazy by having our families do a speed dating sort of meeting too. This is my Dad Jack and his wife Sophia."

Jack extends his hand towards Haddie, but she goes in for a hug instead. "I'm Italian, we hug everyone." Jack smiles at Jackson.

"I already like her, Jackson." Jack pats Jackson on the back.

"I can't take all the credit. Malik helped Travis organize everyone on such short notice. Then, I had a surprise phone call from Nunnie Mary to ask me some questions before she would accept my invitation. I'm actually thinking of hiring her as the CIA director. She has some intense interrogation techniques." Everyone laughs.

"That was just over the phone, wait until I get you alone in person!" Nunnie Mary winks.

Haddie walks over to Jackson and places a big kiss right on his lips. "Thank you so much! I'm so glad you didn't let me hate you." More laughter erupts from the group as Malik announces that dinner will be ready in five minutes and everyone should fill their glasses.

Everyone gathers around the long table, choosing chairs and filling the table with laughter and smiles. As the table settles, Malik asks, "Nunnie Mary, will you offer the blessing for us?" Heads bow. "Oh, Dear and Heavenly Father, we come to you this evening in thanksgiving. Thanksgiving for a special time of fellowship, new family, and an abundance of blessings. I am so amazed by your storytelling. You are the author of life and you gave us a front row seat as you scripted a beautiful love story. Like the delicious meal before us, You prepared a feast of epic proportions for Haddie and Jackson. You are the Master Chef who gathered the ingredients, added a pinch of this and a pinch of that. You cooked it in the fire and out came a feast of love and redemption for your children. As always, you were in every single detail from the beginning. Every conversation, event, and new friend was planned by You. All the while, You were measuring, stirring, mixing, and plating. Thank you for protecting our right to worship you. Thank you for Jackson and his family, for now, I'm still reserving judgement on that one." A trickle of soft laughter passes around the table. "Sweet and loving Father, we thank you and praise your name. We ask for your wisdom and guidance in our lives and your strength during the trials. We love you and we know you love us, because you offered the life of your Son for us. Please grow long, deep, and intimate relationships between us and You. Bless this food to nourish our bodies and Malik for using his gifts to serve You. We pray this, in the name of Your Awesome and Powerful and Wonderful Son, Jesus Christ. Amen."

A chorus of "Amen" is followed by spoons being lifted to serve and plates being passed. Haddie spends the entire dinner listening to Chloe talk about her stuffed animal collection. Her favorite is the purple bear that sings *Twinkle Twinkle* that Haddie gave her for Christmas. Jack and Sophia talk with Maryssa about their favorite restaurants in Paris. Nunnie Mary practically gives Jackson a physical with all the personal questions she asks. He graciously answers each one while holding Haddie's hand under the table.

After dinner, Esther and Beau take Chloe upstairs for a bath and bedtime. Haddie promises to come up for a story after Chloe's bath. Jackson is outside on the deck with Haddie's father John while Jack and Sophia retire to the guest house for the evening. Haddie helps Maryssa and Malik clean the kitchen, their seamless routine transposes in a new space. The familiarity of working together gives her a sense of calmness.

244

Maryssa walks over and places an arm around Haddie. "You know, I'm still waiting."

"For what?" Haddie looks at her cousin with curiosity.

"For an apology and some major gratitude." Her face is serious and anticipating.

Haddie laughs, "How dare I forget? I'm so very sorry for being angry at you for signing me up for a reality television show, without my consent, even though you knew it was the last thing I wanted to do."

Maryssa looks at her Dad, "Did that sound like an apology or a thank you?"

Malik folds the dish towel he is holding and places it on the granite counter. He smiles at his two favorite girls. "Coffee?" He laughs.

"Seriously, thank you Maryssa. To paraphrase one of my favorite Bible stories, 'What I thought was meant for harm, was actually part of a greater plan.' However, I'm not apologizing to you for anything until you admit that you stole Billy Blane from me in fifth grade."

Maryssa swats Haddie on the shoulder and both women laugh. Malik walks over and wraps them both in a giant hug. "My heart overflows."

~Future FLOTUS?~

Snow covers every inch of the ground. The fireplace is roaring. Esther and her mother are playing *Go Fish* at the large family style table with Chloe. Everyone else walks around the house gathering snow gear and finishing mugs of coffee. Haddie sits on the floor wrapping her ankle tightly in the elastic bandage. She covers it with two layers of socks. Jackson walks over and offers both hands to her. He pulls her up from the ground and wraps both arms around her as he places a kiss on the tip of her nose.

The others make their way to the garage doors. Haddie and Jackson trail behind them holding hands. Everyone laughs and spurs each other on as they don their ski boots, goggles, and poles. Maryssa and Beau grab snow boards while everyone else grabs skis. They make their way to edge of the property which opens to a ski trail for the resort. Maryssa pushes Beau off kilter before getting a quick jump on him down the slope.

Jackson helps Haddie with the ski on her weak ankle. "Take it easy out here today. Travis heard there are patches of slush towards the bottom. I don't want you reinjuring that ankle."

Haddie laughs. "You take it easy. I'll be just fine. You're just scared I'll beat you down the hill, even with a bad ankle."

"Oh, Miss Robinson, you're on. Last one down, buys hot chocolate."

"Perfect, I like mine with extra whipped cream." Haddie pushes off down the hill leaving Jackson racing to put on his skis.

"Cheater!" He screams at her back.

"Sucker!" She turns her head to yell back at him.

The two of them create wide figure eights as they attempt to best each other down the slope. Haddie spots an ego bump and straightens course for full speed. She narrowly pulls off a quick Indie grab. If Jackson wasn't watching her intently, he would have missed it, it was so quick. He chuckles at her stubbornness.

Haddie reaches the base first. She cuts and turns waiting for Jackson acting as if she's been there for minutes instead of seconds.

Malik turns towards Haddie and Jackson as the others skate to the chair lifts. "We're going to grab a quad lift. Maryssa and Beau are heading to the black diamond at the very top. We'll either see you two at the top of the mountain or back at the house. He smiles then turns.

"Double or nothing, Miss cheater?"

"Your money, cowboy." She heads towards the lifts. She spots the secret service agents from a mile away standing by the ski lift and all along the base. The Resort opens late this morning, giving the President and his guests exclusive access to the slopes and lifts this morning. Haddie and Jackson bend as the seat hits their knees knocking them back into the chair. They take in the scenery as they start back up the mountain.

Jackson nudges her arm. "Last time we were here, you weren't very nice to me."

"Last time we were here, I still thought you were a player and a jerk." She smirks.

"Yes, but that was before I won you over with my impeccable charm and wit."

"I think it was the altitude and the scenery affecting my senses."

Jackson mutters quietly, "I'm counting on it."

She turns, "What?"

"Nothing."

Suddenly, the lift stops moving. Jackson and Haddie are left hanging in midair halfway up the mountain. She looks at him concerned. Travis and another agent are two chairs up from theirs. Travis turns and yells back to Jackson. "Sir, the liftie is working on the problem. We should be moving in a few minutes."

Jackson nods. Haddie looks around and holds onto the chair a little tighter. Jackson fidgets with his gloves and pulls his goggles to the top of his head. He puts his hands in his pockets.

"I love being up high on a mountain skiing. It seems so simple up here. You get to the top and use your body and equipment to achieve your goal and get down the hill. The cold, fresh air clears my senses and invigorates my mind. The quiet. The Beauty. I think better in the mountains."

Haddie watches Jackson as he philosophizes. "You seem awfully calm for someone dangling fifty feet above the ground."

"I'm not calm. I'm actually terrified."

Haddie turns towards him as much as she can without scaring herself. "Oh Jackson, I'm so sorry. Are you afraid of heights?" Her concern for him, outweighs her concern for falling to her death.

"I'm not afraid of heights. I'm afraid of rejection."

Confused, Haddie's eyes close slightly as she looks at him warily.

"I can't believe this is happening. I give speeches in front of millions, but I can't remember anything I was going to say to you." Jackson squirms in his seat.

"Hey, look at me." She tries to focus his attention.

He stares deeply into Haddie's eyes and takes a deep breath. "Please don't think I'm being pompous by talking in third person, but I need to make a point." He pulls his hands from his pockets. He holds a box in one hand and places the other on Haddie's gloved hands. "Haddie Robinson, Jackson Cashe wants to spend every day of the rest of his life with you. You'll have to share him with the rest of the country for three, maybe seven, years but after that, he's completely and totally yours."

Haddie stares open mouthed at him. She is in shock.

"I know this seems way too fast, but I've never been so sure of anything in my life. I asked both your dad and your uncle for their blessing. I know that's important to you."

"What did they say?"

He grinned like a Chesire cat. "They said I should have asked Nunnie Mary, which I did. She said yes, since you're already mine. The more important question is, what do you say?"

"Maryssa is going to be insufferable now." Haddie pauses and smiles back at him. "Nunnie Mary is right. I have been yours since you brought me peanut butter cookies. Yes, Jackson, I'll marry you."

Haddie pulls off her glove so Jackson can place the three carrot, heart shaped ring on her finger. The stone is flanked by two round amethysts on either side.

"Just so you know, I reserve the right to not vote for you in three years." She grins.

"I would expect nothing less." Jackson leans in to kiss her just as the chair begins moving. They hear hoots and hollers from Travis and the other agent. Travis shouts into his microphone. "She said yes!"

"I designed it myself. Madison helped a little, but I knew you would want simple. The purple shows your personality, and of course, you have my heart."

Haddie warms at the thoughtfulness Jackson put into the design. "It's perfect, thank you. Thank you for everything."

"Haddie, everything I have is yours. Ask for anything and I'll give it to you."

She leans into his side as they ride to the top of the mountain. She sees her family in the distance waiting for their chair to reach the top. The sun is glistening off the snow covered caps surrounding her. She breathes in the cold air and strong pine from the trees. Her life is not how she had imagined. The twists and turns that once seemed overwhelming and confusing, led her to a place of beauty and blessing that is far beyond what she ever dreamt.

Dedication

Jeremiah 15:16 "When Your words came, I ate them; they were my joy and my heart's delight, for I bear Your name, Lord God Almighty." Thank you Jesus. You are my everything.

This book is dedicated to my amazing husband, crazy kids, patient parents, and my niece who thinks I'm still the cool aunt. Your unwavering support, unconditional love, and unending words of encouragement mean more to me than you'll ever know. I love you all....more (It's in print now). I have to thank my partner in crime, Janel, for her keen eyes and always appreciated advice. Great big shout outs for my "when the bottom falls out" forever friends, Gena, Lee, and Kelli; I love you bunches and bunches and bunches. To my dear sister in Christ Jessica, who is constantly carrying me in prayer. To Pastor Sam for steadfastly shepherding his flock and for helping me to see the book of Esther with new eyes. Finally, to the brave readers who took a chance on an unknown author. I hope I didn't let you down.

Thank you to my sweet daughter and father for helping me with the cover.

~Inspiration~

The story of Esther is tucked neatly into the Old Testament. It is an historical account of the time during which the Israelites are living in a foreign land under the reign of King Xerxes. Only ten chapters long, this book has it all; romance, murder, a divided people, attempted genocide, betrayal, political upheaval, and ambition. God's name is never mentioned once in the entire book, yet His fingerprints are entwined throughout every word. This is my take on the story of Esther if it were to happen today. In these pages, you'll find all the drama and intrigue as the original in a modern day setting. Instead of a powerful king, a president. The White House in lieu of a palace. Instead of a harem of beautiful maidens, a reality television cast. Just as with our lives today, God is in every detail, whether we choose to see Him or not. This is the story of Haddie, who was created *for just a time as this*.

Prologue Based on the Book of Esther

This is what happened during the time of President Jackson Cashe, the President of the new United States of America who led after the Separation of States. At this time, President Cashe leads twenty-four states from the White House in Washington, DC. While the Allied States of America took possession of one third of land, the United States held the majority of the population.

For a full six months, in the first year of his presidency, he hosted state leaders as well as foreign leaders and dignitaries to display the vast wealth and innovations of the country. He showcased advances in technology, science, music, arts, and humanities. The showcase culminated in a seven day celebration and banquet in Washington, DC. Each state was encouraged to host their own celebrations. The White House banquet boasted of every opulence available. Several Grammy winning artists performed throughout the evening. World renowned chefs worked together to create the feast of all feasts. Celebrities not in attendance, hosted their own extravagant parties in every city. The country's finest vineyards and distilleries shipped in crates and barrels for the banquet. Wine was served to guests in goblets of gold, each one different from the other. Liquor was served in heavy crystal old-fashionends. Every VIP guest left with an enviable gift bag.

President Cashe's strategy to preserve the country's reputation and establish a strong presence, is successful.

United States of America

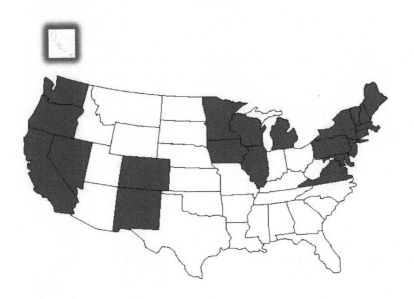

The Allied States of America

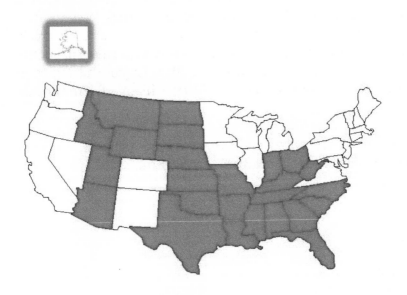

CPSIA information can be obtained
at www.ICGtesting.com
Printed in the USA
BVHW01s0235201217
503303BV00001B/369/P